MAR 1 5 2024   W9-CRE-971

MURDER
AT LA
VILLETTE

MURDER
AT LA
VILLETTE

CARA
BLACK

Again, for the ghosts.

Published by
Soho Press, Inc.
227 W 17th Street
New York, NY 10011

Library of Congress Cataloging-in-Publication Data
Names: Black, Cara, author.
Title: Murder at la Villette / Cara Black.
Description: New York : Soho Crime, 2024.
Identifiers: LCCN 2023037990

ISBN 978-1-64129-447-8
eISBN 978-1-64129-448-5

Subjects: LCGFT: Detective and mystery fiction. | Novels.
Classification: LCC PS3552.L297 M77 2024 | DDC 813/.54—dc23/eng/20230919
LC record available at https://lccn.loc.gov/2023037990

Printed in the United States of America

10 9 8 7 6 5 4 3 2 1

The April moon doesn't pass without frost
—French proverb

*Nothing fixes a thing so intensely in the memory
as the wish to forget it.*
—Michel de Montaigne

He who pees in the wind wets his teeth.
—French saying

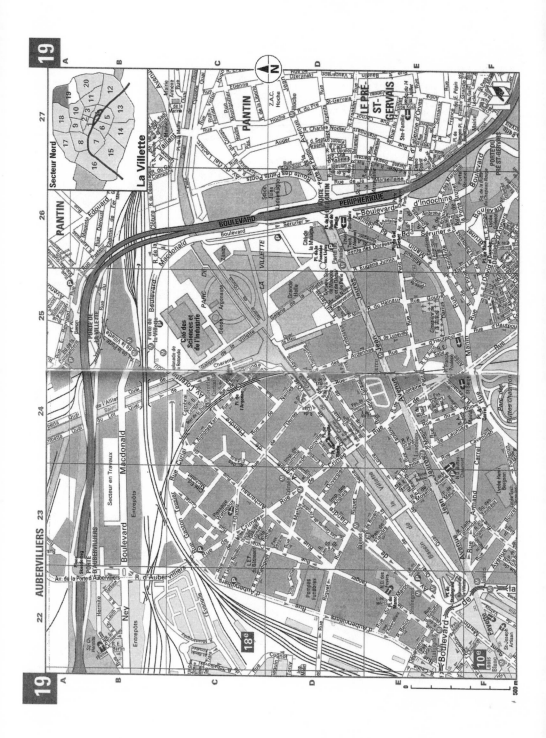

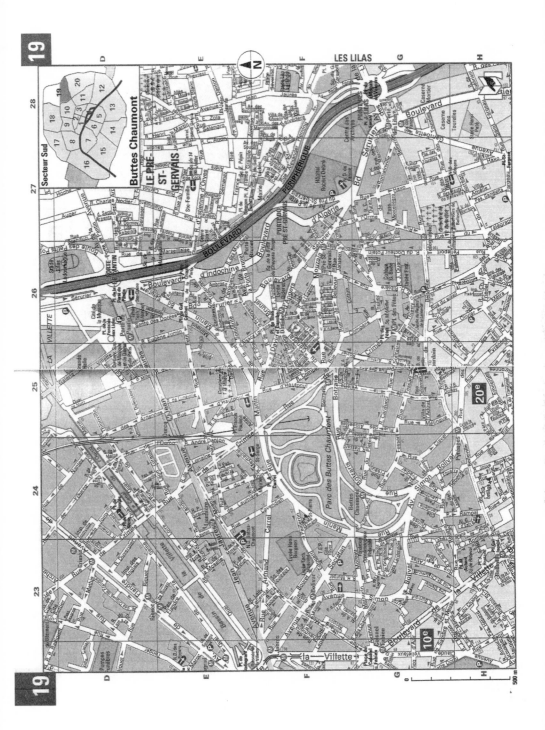

19

LES LILAS

Secteur Sud

Buttes Chaumont

LE PRÉ-ST-GERVAIS

Parc des Buttes Chaumont

20e

10e

la — Villette

500 m

April 2002 • 11:00 P.M.
Monday, Avenue Secrétan, Paris

APRIL IN PARIS rarely feels like the song, thought Aimée Leduc, shivering as she buttoned her leather jacket. Glocron's cold, cavernous office, in a threadbare 1930s movie theater that had been chopped into workspaces, was embellished with faux rococo swirls and chipped plaster ceilings. It felt as aesthetically pleasing as an aircraft hangar.

Last time Aimée would take a job like this. Too much working overtime. It didn't help that this whole consulting gig was fake—she was really here at this tech start-up on an under-cover contract for the Ministry, trying to nail down evidence of a saboteur in the IT department in between her humdrum security work. Plus the added strain of constantly battling with her ex, Melac, the biological father of her daughter, over cus-tody was taking its toll.

She hit save on her computer terminal and logged out of her security program.

To Aimée, this odd open office plan had only one redeeming feature—a view of the Marché Secrétan, a covered market where she used to go shopping with her grandfather, her hand in his, to buy rabbit from his favorite butcher. Now the dilapidated art nouveau covered market looked in need of some love. Just like her.

She packed up, rubbed her chilly hands. Thank God her work-space had an outlet for a portable heater. The other employees wore their coats indoors and huddled by the espresso machine for any kind of camaraderie.

Shouts and the scrape of chairs came from a terminal nearby. "Who cares about your disabled brother!" Pépe, the wiry Basque programmer, was yelling at Isabelle, the cleaner. He twitched in anger. "Clumsy *salope*, you spilled my coffee over my printouts!"

Isabelle, her long dark braid clipped up, paused mopping the floor. Her silver nose ring glinted under the harsh fluorescent light.

Before Aimée could stand up, Pépe'd taken a swing at Isabelle.

Isabelle ducked. Not soon enough. His blow knocked the mop she'd held in her tattooed arm clattering to the floor.

Was the fool jacked up on caffeine or wired on something else—like speed?

Aimée rushed over, catching Isabelle before she hit back, and shoved the programmer back into his chair.

"Are you all right, Isabelle?" Aimée asked, concerned. "Let me see your arm."

"He barely grazed me," said Isabelle, her eyes like daggers.

L'idiote—the programmer didn't know who he'd bullied.

Isabelle, a biker *fille* from up the canal, had gone to school with Aimée's cousin, Sébastien. Both had been junkies who'd cleaned up, gotten straight. Staying clean was hard, but Aimée's cousin had done it. Aimée sometimes wondered if Isabelle had gone back to her old ways.

Once a junkie . . . No—think positive.

Isabelle looked healthier than Aimée had ever seen her.

Aimée turned to Pépe and summoned authority in her voice. "Since when do you hit women?"

She pulled her digital camera out of her purse and started snapping photos of the mark on Isabelle's arm.

He sputtered, "Hey, you can't do that."

"Too late. I have."

"They'll fire you when I report this, *salope*," Pépe said to Isabelle. He had spotty skin, potato ears, and a temper.

"Report what? You're a lying weasel. I didn't spill your coffee."

"*Et alors*, aren't you aware of the firm's policies against violence?" said Aimée.

"This isn't over," Pépe said, grabbing his backpack and storming out. "You'll never get that recommendation!"

Isabelle picked up her mop. Her hands were shaking. "*Merde!*"

"Isabelle, take a second. Calm down," Aimée said. "Tell me about your brother. Is this about him? Is he okay?"

Isabelle took a deep breath. "Muscular dystrophy. It's getting worse. He's going downhill."

Aimée vaguely remembered hearing Sébastien mention it.

"I need a recommendation from my employer to qualify for adapted housing. Pépe knows it, too."

"I'm sorry," said Aimée.

"Pépe pretends he cares, then attacks me. Just because I won't go out with him."

Mean to the bone.

Aimée couldn't believe the toxic work culture fermenting here.

After Sébastien had gotten clean, Aimée had guaranteed Sébastien's business. He'd branched out as a building contractor and now owned several framing shops. Sébastien had been the one to steer Isabelle toward the program that matched her with this job—the tech start-up got tax incentives for hiring locals. The locals benefited from jobs and access to fast-track housing. It was a win-win.

Too bad the boss, Robért, a preening narcissist, had no management skills to speak of. Just last week he'd reduced the intern program and frozen the promotions of five programmers, who'd then quit. Isabelle would not be able to count on him to be sympathetic.

"I'll report Pépe and back you up," said Aimée.

"You shouldn't," Isabelle said. "The boss is a *salaud*, I don't want you in trouble."

Defending Isabelle would be thorny—Aimée couldn't afford to rankle Robért if she wanted to keep her undercover Ministry job. But she had to help Isabelle with this second chance.

"*Excusez-moi.*" Robért was striding toward them. The hanging fluorescent lights reflected off his rimless glasses. He wore a tight bargain Monoprix suit and clearly thought it looked good on him. "Pépe's filing a report against you," he said to Isabelle. He probably didn't even know her name. "Look, we can't tolerate harassment from contract workers."

Isabelle's eyes welled. Aimée wondered if she'd break out in tears or slug him. Before either could happen, Aimée wedged herself between Isabelle and Robért.

"Harassment by whom?" She held up her camera for him to see. "I've recorded Pépe's demeaning insults here and documented his physically assaulting Isabelle. She will be filing a complaint and charges against him. This will go all the way up to the board of Glocron."

No company board relished dealing with a problem like this. Robért knew that could impact their funding. He looked deflated.

Isabelle's eyes widened. She was scared but defiant. She needed this job.

"But," Aimée added, thinking on the fly, "Isabelle might consent to continue working here *if* Pépe took anger management classes *and* she was transferred to a different floor and office."

Too harsh? Would this get her fired? Working undercover, Aimée needed to stay under the radar.

Her handler in the Ministry was on her case every day.

But right now she couldn't care less.

Robért steepled his fingers. "If we do that, she wouldn't press charges or file a complaint?"

Isabelle's jaw clenched but she nodded.

"I'll get that in writing and have you sign it."

With that, Robért hurried to his office.

"*Merci*, Aimée," said Isabelle. "I owe you."

"*Pas du tout*," Aimée said. "The creep can't get away with what he did. And he won't. What's your number?"

She wanted to follow up and make sure Isabelle didn't suffer a fallout.

"Can you remember *nobodylu?*" she said, then spelled it out: "N-o-b-o-d-y-l-u?"

Aimée nodded. "Why?"

"Easiest way to remember my phone number. 06 26 39 58." She mimed typing it on a phone keyboard, which would spell the phrase. "Contact me any time."

Aimée went back to her desk, logged back on, downloaded the photos from her digital camera—just in case—trashed her junk mail and powered off her computer. As she was reaching for her bag, she found an envelope with AIMÉE LEDUC DÉTEC-TIVE PRIVÉ typed on the outside—and *URGENT* written underneath in familiar hard-to-read scrawl. Looking over her shoulder to make sure no one was watching, she opened the envelope.

We have to talk. There's something you need to know. It's important. Last time, Aimée, and I won't take no for an answer.

Melac, hounding her again. Chloé's biological father wanted to move Chloé to Brittany. Melac also wanted to get back together, but that train had left the station long ago. Aimée'd let nothing jeopardize her new relationship—which was already tricky—with Bellan, a divorcé who cared part-time for his three children.

They'd already talked about this ad nauseam, including yesterday—a long conversation that had gone nowhere. She'd had enough.

Why had he left her a note at the office? Why not at home? The only thing she could think of was he was working nearby. *Great.*

Her phone rang. Melac. Again.

She hit the red button and sent him straight to voice mail where he belonged.

Monday Late Evening • Quai de la Loire

MELAC CLICKED OFF his phone. Why wouldn't Aimée answer? The tarnished spring moon filtered through a wispy web of clouds. Pale pewter lights reflected on the choppy canal's surface farther down the lamplit quai.

He ground out his cigarette on the stone bank with his toe. The place felt dark as a witch's *derrière*, as they said in Brittany.

He needed to stay alert.

Brrr. He rubbed his hands and paced in front of a weather-warped shed bearing a plaque with the Paris city motto, *Fluctuat nec mergitur*, Latin for *It rocks but does not sink*.

He didn't like doing surveillance here—he was exposed. An open target.

He climbed over a fence to get better reception and finally found it by the old bridge crossing the canal. The pulleys that controlled the lift deck, opening and closing the bridge twenty-five times a day, cast rippled shadows on the quai.

He called his liaison on the surveillance job but only got voice mail. Irritating. He hated working with amateurs. As soon as he'd put his phone back down, it rang. Fuming, he looked at the tiny screen.

It wasn't Aimée. It was the liaison whose line crackled and kept breaking up. This latest security contract was a pain, too. He hated surveillance and wished he were back working with

his colleagues in counterterrorism. But surveillance work was
the only way he'd get the steady paycheck he needed to guar-
antee shared custody of Chloé.

"*Allô?*"

"Abort . . ."

He couldn't hear the rest and stepped out of the wind to
shelter by the ancient hydraulic lift bridge's toll house.

"Abort why?" he said. The job was still an hour off. Tense, he
looked around, alert to what had gone wrong.

The bridge railings were cast iron and finished in light blue.
On either side the two old warehouses stood like hulking senti-
nels, narrowing the Bassin de la Villette.

The call broke up. Static.

Abort? That meant no paycheck. Couldn't these people
follow security protocol? He needed more confirmation and a
reason before he'd abort a mission. Meanwhile he'd stay in the
quartier and catch Aimée.

He legged it down the canal, past the anchored *péniches*.
Wavelets lapped the quai. The lanterns were dark and broken,
and he stepped on broken glass. He hadn't noticed this last
night—the streetlights had been working then. He paused
where the canal narrowed into the lock—Napoleon's design
for sending barges to the Seine—and inhaled the mossy, wet
smells. Water gushed over the lock's rim. He'd waited for Aimée
here every night this week, watching her going to the Metro or
whizzing past on her scooter.

A long aluminum barricade paralleled the canal and hid the
walkway on the quai. He stepped through the gap he always
used, summoning his courage.

He had a new plan—he would admit his selfishness in
insisting on moving to Brittany. If he gave her the moral high
ground, maybe she'd agree. Then he'd forget taking her to court.

He would raise his daughter however Aimée wanted—as long as it was in Brittany.

He rang Aimée yet again. As usual she was late leaving work. Late, always late.

A noise caught his attention: the fluttering of wings, a soft splash. Then the rushing sound of the water draining from the lock filled the air. The fishy algae smell had gotten much better since they'd cleaned up the canal.

He passed a homeless man, *sans domicile fixe*, or SDF—to use the politically correct term. The man had camped out under the *passerelle*, the art nouveau arched metal bridge. Melac had noticed him before—once a *flic*, always a *flic*. He'd never lost his roaming eye and awareness of his surroundings. If you let down your guard, you won't last—that's what Jean-Claude Leduc, Aimée's father and one of Melac's teachers at the police academy, had taught him.

The SDF stood at the old metal doors under the *passerelle*. He flicked a match, trying unsuccessfully to light a cigarette. Then another.

Melac hit Aimée's number again.

"Monsieur, got a light?" The SDF gestured with his unlit cigarette.

Was there something familiar about his voice? Melac had been a *flic* in this quartier on his first assignment. Could the man be an old "client," the jargon beat *flics* used for serial offenders?

Melac never forgot a face, which had served him well in the counterterrorism unit.

"*Mais oui.*" He scrounged in his pocket for a lighter, then handed it to the man as the call went to Aimée's voice mail. Again.

The man sparked the lighter. The flame wavered in the wind. He cupped his hands to shield the flame. For a moment the man's face was illuminated.

That face. So familiar.

But it belonged to a dead man. Someone Melac had seen buried—he'd attended the funeral himself.

His breath caught. Without thinking, he spoke into Aimée's voice mail: "Aimée . . . I've just seen a ghost."

A smile painted that familiar face. The man hissed. Batted the phone away. "Naughty boy. You shouldn't have said that."

A flash of silver arced through the air.

Monday Evening • The Square at Marché Secrétan

AIMÉE CHECKED HER phone and saw Melac had called. Multiple times. She was fed up with his demands, his threats, his protestations about how much he cared. He hounded her day and night.

She'd fight a court battle to keep Chloé with her. The girl had grown up in Paris—it was all she knew. It would be cruel to uproot her so abruptly, and besides, Aimée's work, her whole life, was in Paris. Brittany was the countryside. Not enough cafés for her. As the biological father, Melac had claimed paternity and could, in theory, have a legal shot at part-time custody.

He'd never win. Would he?

The first message was static, buzzing like the alarm on his watch, then a muttered curse and what sounded like the word *morgue*. Was he late for an appointment at the morgue?

Not her business.

She wanted to hit delete all. Instead she clicked to the next message.

He panted as if he'd been running.

"Aimée . . ." A pause. "I've just seen a ghost."

A clattering as the phone fell. Then silence. The voice mail was cryptic and unlike Melac. What did he mean?

Guilt assailed her. What had happened? But then, it could be a ploy. Would he be waiting outside her work to hound her again, like the other night? Or would he stalk her on her way to the Metro?

She stepped outside the theater side door and scanned the empty square, the dark hulk of the covered market, the doorway of the butcher next door.

No Melac.

She needed to go home. But how? Her scooter, temperamental and Italian to the core, was in the shop, where it lived most of the time.

There were no taxis in sight.

It would be faster if she took the direct Metro line 5 from Jaurès.

Every night after work, she traveled through this sketchy quartier. The nineteenth arrondissement, once a manufacturing hub, had boasted three sugar refineries, biscuit-making companies, the abattoir at la Villette, and everything in between. Warehouses still lined the canal, and sprinkled among that bygone commercial age were high seventies housing blocks, blights on the old skyline. Since the nineteenth century, émigrés—from the French countryside or other countries—had worked and lived here with their families. It was cheap. Still the cheapest in Paris for what you got, more space being the big attraction for families.

If she knew Melac, he'd be waiting under the arched bridge over the canal. Just beyond the Jaurès Metro entrance. Better get him off her back once and for all.

She'd assumed Melac's incessant calling had been about Chloé, but what about that strange last message? What had he meant?

I've just seen a ghost.

Monday Late Evening • Quai de la Loire

A SEAGULL SKIMMED the canal surface, its wings silhou-etted against the distant Rotonde de la Villette. Aimée hurried. Melac's words bothered her more than she cared to admit. They were so unlike him.

The flash of blue light from the drawbridge over the dark canal caught her eye. She shivered, a strange feeling coming over her out of nowhere. The rumpled silken surface of the canal churned in the dim mist. Aimée pulled her leather jacket tighter against the wind and struggled to knot her wool scarf.

She wished that there were other people around, that the quai, with its scuffed barricade, didn't feel desolate and deserted. Then she remembered the championship games were playing and everyone was glued to the *télé*. Only the just-blossoming chestnut trees kept her company.

Encroaching fog wrapped vague shapes resembling charcoal clumps of silhouettes. The tall aluminum barricade covered most of the walkway, except for one section, which had been pushed aside. She rang Melac. His phone trilled behind the bar-ricade.

Instantly her concern turned to annoyance. Melac was waiting for her again. But hadn't she decided to end his nagging for good?

"Melac?"

"Aim . . ."

It sounded like Melac calling her name. Fear leapt into her heart. Had he been attacked?

She saw no one. Heard no bus or car. She put her keys between her fingers and made a fist as she slid through the opening in the barricade, glad she didn't have her bulky Hermès bag with her—just her Metro pass, ID, camera, keys, work phone, and cash in her pockets. She stuck her cheap personal phone in her boot and, work phone in hand, ran up the cobbled quai toward where she now heard splashing. More aluminum fences had been pushed aside. Her footsteps crunched over glass. No streetlights shone. Had someone smashed the lights?

She heard a cry and stiffened.

Good God, had there been a fight? Was Melac involved?

"Melac?"

No answer. Gurgling. Splashing.

She could make out the rushing water, the stream of the overflow from the full lock and the narrow waterway bordering the lip of the stone-paved quai.

Only a dim glow from the small screen of her work phone helped guide her. She kept flicking the buttons of this new device, trying to make it brighter, but the light dimmed after only seconds.

Impatient, she shook it. Then shook it again.

Merde. The battery was almost dead.

Her phone's light wobbled on the cobblestones to a barely visible metal-grill footbridge flush over the lock. The grill almost touched the black water's surface.

In the dark mist, she followed the splashing sounds, feeling her way and climbing down a few steps to the thin walkway alongside the water. Below the lock lay walls lined with moss and a sheer drop to the next empty basin.

The moon flitted between the clouds, and it was all gray, even the reflections from down the canal.

A figure, moving.

"Melac? Are you all right?"

Was that a moan? She heard a sickening crunch, like bones breaking. Oh God, was Melac getting slammed into the canal's grill? Sucked in and pummeled by the rushing water?

She stepped on something and tripped.

She caught her balance on the railing before she lost her footing. What had she stepped on? Had she kicked it away?

She'd dropped her keys on the stone. *Great.*

She knelt, patting at the cobbles, hoping her fingers wouldn't close on broken glass. Here was something—but she dropped it when . . . she saw him. There was Melac, all but his head and one arm under water, his body caught against the raised walkway. His face was shrouded in shadow. She knelt, stretched out and tried to grab Melac's arm but couldn't reach him.

Panicked, she reached out again and almost lost her balance.

How in God's name had he gotten in here? This couldn't be happening. But it was.

The rushing water echoed off the damp, mossy stone walls. Gurgling sounds, as if he were trying to speak. He was drifting away. *Merde.*

"Melac?"

Her heart pumped like a jackhammer.

She crawled closer, across the narrow footbridge wide enough for only one person. The rushing water was so close it splashed her. What was he doing here? Why hadn't she come earlier? Why hadn't she just agreed to meet him? No time for that. She had to use every bit of her reach. Somehow, she caught his wet elbow.

"Melac . . ."

No answer.

He was too slippery; she was losing her grip. She grappled for his cold hand. Pulled as hard as she could, gasping with the effort of keeping him above water.

Then she saw it—the gaping bloody gash serrating his neck. Aimée's throat caught. Melac's frigid, wet hand slipped from her grasp. The water sucked at him, the pull too strong.

The next thing she knew, a whack sent her staggering against the bridge rail. Reeling, she felt a crushing blow to her windpipe. Then another whack to her head and everything went black.

Monday • Close to Midnight • Quai de la Loire

RUSHING SOUNDS FILLED Aimée's ears. Pain seared her side. A harsh light glared everywhere.

The snick of a pistol sounded by her ear. "Don't move."

A metallic clanking came from near her feet.

All of a sudden, her arms were pulled behind her. Handcuffs enclosed her wrists, the metal biting into her skin.

White flashes and sparks danced and swirled in her vision. Everything blurred.

With the throbbing ache in her head, all she could think was that she would never see again. She was reliving the attack in the Bastille years ago that had blinded her temporarily. How dumb she'd been to take her recovery for granted.

Another blow like the one she'd just taken and her ocular nerve would be damaged beyond repair. This time she wouldn't see again.

The scents of dirty water and wet stone assailed her. Blinking blindly, she tried to reach out, but she couldn't. Her hands were bound. All she could feel was the slippery moss catching under her fingernails. She concentrated on the feel of the air current, trying to orient herself.

She heard a sucking in of breath, caught a whiff of garlic and cigarette smoke mixed with the metallic smell of blood as she felt mist hit her cheekbones.

She fought the urge to scream—what the hell was going on here? Was this a *flic*?

"Help me, I can't see. It's all white and blurry."

Only rushing water.

"Who are you? Listen, call an ambulance. That man needs help."

Sirens blared in the distance, growing closer all the time.

"Melac? Melac?" she shouted, but got no answer.

She felt someone picking her jacket pockets, removing her wallet and work phone.

A thief?

She heard a low whistle, a man's throaty whisper. "Aimée Leduc of the high heels, red lips. *Enchanté.*"

Her blood curdled.

"Wait . . . do I know you?"

Any minute he'd be saying "I'm placing you under arrest on charges of . . ."

But blaring sirens filled the air.

"Lucky me. Two birds with one stone."

Or that's what she thought the man had said. The sirens grew louder. She couldn't distinguish a damn thing between the flashes in her head and the jagged light shining in her face.

A jiggle of the handcuffs, a metallic clank, then her hands were free.

"Just open your fingers. Slow and easy. All right, on three . . . *un, deux* . . . Do as I say . . . Now just open . . . *trois.*"

A low laugh.

She felt something sticky, sharp: the blade of a knife being folded into her hand, cutting into her palm.

Good God. Had this been placed in her hand to implicate her?

Shouts came from over the water. A hard kick connected with her chest. She felt a white-hot burst of pain in her ribs and doubled over, clutching her side. Slipping . . . her feet were slipping. He was going to push her into the water.

But he didn't. Abruptly, footsteps pounded away from her. The man was running. Why?

Breathless, she yelled, "Who are you?"

She toppled onto her side, writhing on slick wet stone. Her leg was halfway in the water of the canal's lock.

Arctic cold water.

"Freeze, don't move."

She was sliding—she couldn't stop herself. By instinct her arms reached out, scrabbling at anything to grasp and hold tight. Her elbow caught on the quai lip. She could only see a gray haze, only feel her ice-cold, soaking wet leather pants, their damp weight pulling her down.

Arms lifted and swung her out of the water.

Voices reached her ears. "*Mon Dieu.*" Then the sound of someone being sick.

What was going on?

"Bag the knife for evidence. Her hands, too. Then get her in the *pompiers* response vehicle," a voice barked. "Now."

Tuesday • 1 A.M. on the way to Hôtel Dieu Hospital

AIMÉE'S VISION CLEARED by degrees. The darkness settled into a deep grayish blur, then gradually morphed into a light haze. She felt a huge cold rock on her temple until she realized it was an ice pack for the swelling. The interior of the firemen's first-response vehicle came into view. She grew aware of beeping noises and the cold metal of a stethoscope on her chest. Her vitals were being taken. Her vision focused on a screen—reddish dots and a blue background.

Thank God. She was seeing again. Her pulse thudded. Was this all a bad dream?

Her throat hurt like hell. And her ribs. Why? Until it all came rushing back: the bloody gash on Melac's neck, his cold, wet hand, the rushing, swirling water and the stinging whack, then the thunder in her head.

Tears welled up.

All of a sudden the doors were yanked open and her stretcher was slid out, the wheels clanking on the ground.

"Emergency bay two," someone was saying.

Harsh lights and searing brightness. Painful. She squinted and shut her eyes. Then another voice said, "What's your name?"

"Aimée Leduc," she said, rasping. "Where's Melac?"

"Melac?"

Her throat burned, but she made herself speak. "He was in

the water . . . the canal. I tried to pull him out." She wanted to pull the baggies off her hand. "What happened to him?"

"We're examining you before the *flics* start your interrogation."

Her stomach churned.

Interrogation.

ON AND OFF her vision blurred. But it was better than before. She could make out figures. After the CT scan and X-ray, she could distinguish faces and features. Fear ate her. The last time she'd had a head injury and lost her vision, she regained it. Luckily. But the eye doctor, Guy Lambert, had said next time she wouldn't be so lucky.

She hadn't been lucky with him. Their affair had gotten off to such a good start, and for a while it looked like she'd be a doctor's wife—until she realized that would mean moving to Neuilly and hosting luncheons for the other doctors' wives, giving up her career in Paris for a lifetime of hostessing and wifely duties.

A messy breakup. The last she'd heard, he'd joined Médecins Sans Frontières in Afrique.

She wished he were here now. She couldn't trust new doctors who didn't know her previous condition and would take too long to get her files.

But that was the least of her worries.

"Mademoiselle Leduc?" The man who belonged to that voice came into focus. "I need to ask some questions. The doctors deem your condition stable enough for you to be moved to the sixth floor, the secure unit. We'll follow you up there."

She smelled antiseptic. Hell, she was on a gurney in a corridor. Everything was shrouded in whitish fog.

"Where am I?"

"Emergency at Hôtel Dieu. Didn't anyone inform you? You're in custody."

The sixth floor in Hôtel Dieu, the public hospital, was the medical unit for injured suspects and the convicted.

"W-why?"

"You're a suspect in the murder of Jérome Melac."

Aimée exhaled sharply. Murder. Melac was dead. She'd hoped there was a chance he'd survived.

"But I heard Melac . . . He was calling me . . . from the quai under the bridge, but . . ." she rasped, her throat raw.

"He was alive?"

"I think so," she said, making herself talk despite the pain. "I didn't kill him. I tried to save him."

"We found more than enough evidence to get you convicted."

Liar. They'd say this in hopes of getting a quick confession.

Her heart jumped. It came back to her now: the sticky knife in her hand, the man who'd been there, who'd seemed to have known her.

"There's been a mistake. There was a man who handcuffed me."

"You were discovered with a knife and bloody hands. No restraints."

"That's right. The siren sounded and he took them off."

"Sounds convenient. But the lab work will tell us."

Typical *flic* talk to scare her.

"Make it easy on yourself," he said. "Get this over with and you'll feel better."

"Are you insane?"

Her throat felt like sandpaper.

"Was it a crime of passion? Was he jealous? We know he wanted to get back together with you."

Who was this officer? He had a mustache and thick hair, but it was hard to see him distinctly. He hadn't even arrested her yet.

"Show me your credentials."

That was stupid. She couldn't see. But maybe she could gain a little time to think.

"And get Commissaire Morbier," she said. "He's the only one I'm talking to."

Tuesday • Hôtel Dieu Reception • Ground Floor

WHAT IN GOD'S name has Aimée done now?

Dragged out of bed, catching a taxi, and still only half-awake, retired Commissaire Morbier rocked on his worn brown heels in the lobby of Hôtel Dieu. He'd looked at many police reports in his time. This time, however, his goddaughter Aimée had gotten into more trouble than ever before. The little clout he maintained working part-time in the Special Branch had gotten him a peek at the report and a visit. No more.

According to this report, she'd be charged with killing the biological father of her child, a former *flic,* who had been threatening to fight Aimée for custody. She'd been discovered with the murder weapon in hand. Damning evidence and a motive.

Not to mention she'd talk only to him—and only if he contacted her babysitter first. As if he were an errand boy.

He pulled out a match and flicked it against the matchbox until it caught with a *thupt* and lit his cigarette. He took a deep drag and inhaled his Gauloise. Oh, Melac. Poor *mec,* a good *flic* and an even better counterterrorism operative. Relationship-wise with Aimée, not so great.

Merde.

He coughed and looked around for an ashtray in the green-tiled hallway. On the left, the view of Notre Dame filtered through the old colored-glass window, spilling blue on the tiles.

To his right, the busy wing resounded with the pad of rubber soles.

Morbier didn't know any of this new crew of *flics*. He'd aged, and as a former *commissaire*, his connections were with old-timers of his generation. All the strings he could pull were short ones.

He knew Aimée. He thought of her anguish and bitterness at Melac. If she'd killed him . . . but *non*, how could she?

A doctor wearing a white coat and a haggard face passed by, clutching a file.

It had *new admit Leduc, A* written on the tab.

"What's going on here?" Morbier asked.

"Going on?" a doctor said. "You're family?"

"I'm her godfather," he said. *Practically raised her*, he almost added. Instead he flashed his police ID. "We need to talk," he said.

"Not here."

The doctor indicated the adjoining door to the hospital gardens. Once outside and on a bench, Morbier puffed and exhaled a spiral of smoke in the night air.

"Aren't people retired at your age?" said the doctor.

"Retired and not retired, doctor," said Morbier. "If you get my meaning."

The doctor, probably around Morbier's age, with graying sideburns and temples, smiled. "I hear that a lot."

"Please answer my question, doctor. Tell me the scope of her injuries. You should know she's got preexisting conditions."

"Her CAT scan revealed previous damage on her ocular nerve. Is that what you're referring to?"

"She went blind temporarily."

The doctor took a deep breath. "She's not out of the woods. Too early to say. But no severe damage has been done. So far, her eyesight's clearing. Still could be touch and go."

Morbier realized he'd been holding his breath.

"Where is she?"

"After triage, we sent her up to the sixth floor."

The wing for criminals and suspects in custody.

The doctor checked his watch and stood. "I have to get to a surgery. Don't jump the gun, monsieur. There's still so much we don't know."

Morbier wondered where Aimée's business partner, René, was. Had anyone reached him? He'd tried and René's phone rang and rang. No voice mail.

At least Chloé was safe. He'd gotten through to Madame Cachou, the concierge of Aimée's building, who would keep the girl until . . .

Well, either until he could think of something else or until Aimée was out of this mess.

Who knew when that would be.

Morbier noticed the surly looks from the *flics* on duty on the sixth floor. He had to talk to Aimée, find out what had happened.

He showed his ID and was let through. Once past the doors, he was relieved to see Daudet, an old colleague, at the ward night desk.

"Didn't you retire, Morbier? Enjoying the fruits of your pension?"

"You're the second one tonight, Daudet. And you're no spring chicken yourself."

Daudet nodded. "No argument there. I'm on a half-time scheme to bolster the new recruits' training."

Whenever that happened, it meant the budgets got tightened.

"What do you know about what happened in the nineteenth with Leduc?"

"That one? Looks odd to me. But she's your old colleague's girl, right?"

"Good memory."

Daudet lowered his voice and leaned in. "They set up her father. But I never said that."

What if they were doing the same thing to Aimée?

Tuesday • Hôtel Dieu Criminal Detention Wing,
Sixth Floor

AIMÉE HEARD THE door ping open, then registered the slant of light and smelled the cigarette smoke clinging to the figure in a damp wool coat.

Her godfather, Commissaire Morbier.

About time.

"Took you long enough, Morbier," she said hoarsely, wishing they'd given her something for her throat. "Can you confirm that *flic's* credentials?"

"What *flic*?" said Morbier. "I just got here, Leduc. You're on drugs."

"They said I stabbed Melac." Each word felt like a razor in her throat.

The hospital bed sagged. She heard springs moan. He'd sat at the end.

"Did you?"

"Stab Melac? Of course I didn't," she said. The rasp in her voice made her sound less trustworthy. "There was someone else there. He knew my name and said he was getting 'two birds with one stone.' He handcuffed me."

"Did you see him?"

"The streetlights were out or broken. I only saw Melac in the light from my phone screen." Her breath caught.

"Go back to the beginning," said Morbier. "You've got motive. So start at what happened on the canal."

She leaned back against the cold, stiff sheets. "My head's splitting. You've got to get me out of here. I've got to get home to Chloé."

"Tell me what happened from the beginning."

Could she convince him to get her out on bail?

"Look, Morbier, I was working late, tying up my project." She sighed. "René'd gone to Amboise for his mother's birthday." She left out that it was an undercover Ministry job. "And Melac was haranguing me," she said. "Hounding me with texts, calls . . . He must have even snuck into the start-up where I'm working and left a letter in my things."

It struck her how irritated she still was with him. How insensitive it sounded. How his death didn't feel real.

"Was that usual for him?"

"*Mais non.* His last phone message unnerved me. He said he thought he'd seen a ghost."

"*Quoi?*"

She repeated it.

I've just seen a ghost.

"I was going to the Metro but first I walked toward the bridge . . ."

Her memory faded. What next?

"*Oui*, now I remember. I was wondering why it was all dark. Why no streetlights shone."

Tears pooled. She blinked, but they ran hot down her cheeks.

Now it was hitting her.

"Is he really dead?"

Quiet, except for a phone ringing and staccato clips from a nurse's clogs in the corridor.

"Unfortunately, yes. He was stabbed, then his throat slit."

There'd been so much blood.

She knew Melac had trained in counterterrorist tactics even after leaving the squad. He'd kept in shape, used his skills during surveillance, yet had gotten killed in a dark place. While waiting for her.

She remembered that blue light on the canal, the sound of crunching and his moans. How he'd called out. A shudder passed through her.

"Anything to say, Leduc?"

A scream roared from the pit of her stomach.

SHE SCREAMED AND thrashed in the bed for she didn't know how long. Until she was restrained and felt a prick under her shoulder.

A nurse said, "You'll feel calmer now, it's just a short-acting sedative."

How could she feel calmer? He'd waited for her. Melac.

But the sedative dulled her panic like a heavy blanket. She must have nodded off.

Morbier was talking to her. A blindfold was over her eyes.

"No way you're going anywhere without diagnosis or treatment," said Morbier. "Besides everything else, you got a nasty gash. The bandage is still bloody."

She heard the sound of tearing paper, then felt something being stuck in her mouth. A straw.

"Drink this. It's good for shock."

Aimée sipped sweet orange juice. She hadn't realized how parched she was. She was dehydrated and her electrolytes were out of whack.

"Who arrested me, Morbier?"

The juice trickled, sweet and full of pulp that stuck in her molars.

"Far as I know, you're under observation. Same thing, really."

"What? Then whoever that was is out of line. Why haven't I been questioned yet?"

"Forget that for now, Leduc. I've contacted Martine to step in and help with Chloé."

Martine was Chloé's godmother and had been Aimée's friend since *lycée*.

My baby girl. Why hadn't that hit her right away? Her dog, Miles Davis, would be waiting for her. Her business, the ongoing contracts needed her attention. She'd be out of commission, blind and in jail.

Then she remembered. "He took my phone and wallet."

Fear vibrated through her. He'd know everything about her.

"Your keys?" asked Morbier, alert now.

"Those, too. *Zut*, Chloé's at home and she's not safe."

DESPITE IT BEING way past midnight, within ten minutes Morbier had scheduled a locksmith. He'd also notified Madame Cachou and tipped off a colleague to watch her building. He stepped out to make more calls.

Aimée's unease was taking over.

If she let stress overtake her, her condition would only get worse. She might never get her full sight back.

She forced herself to breathe. To fill her lungs and exhale. To concentrate until her mind cleared.

She'd have to compartmentalize and let go of things she couldn't control.

She'd have to focus on each step and complete it, pull her emotions out and let rational thinking guide her.

Your life's falling apart, a little voice screamed inside her.

Her phone had been stolen. Her wallet. *Breathe.*

She knew the drill. Cancel the cards and alert her office building.

Her panic didn't recede. Yes, she'd done this before. But never with a baby to protect.

And not being able to see made it three times harder.

One step at a time. Breathe.

The father of her child murdered because she hadn't gotten there in time.

Breathe again.

The cloud of fog in her vision seemed granular now. Charcoal shapes emerged then receded. The back and forth scared her.

All she knew was that she had to get out of there.

Listen to your gut, her father would say.

Her eyes rested on the small gash in her palm, treated and pulled together with butterfly strips. Her vision shifted, getting worse, then cleared, a fringe of light haloing when she turned her head.

This had happened last time. It was a sign of getting better. Wasn't it?

She'd come up with a plan by the time Morbier returned. She made out a white lab coat beside him. A doctor, a nurse?

"The doctor's here for your next checkup," he said.

She had to speak up. Get their help. Get out of here.

"My diagnosis and treatment records are at Centre Hospitalier National d'Ophtalmologie des Quinze-Vingts. Get me over there." She spoke with authority to the doctor and nurse. "The specialist said to come to him immediately if this happened again."

All that was true. Although that specialist, Guy, had left that practice years ago.

She heard muttering as the doctor and nurse consulted.

"It's a question of rapid treatment or losing my eyesight," she said. "Morbier can vouch this is true. If I go blind because you haven't allowed me the prescribed treatment, the Préfecture will have a huge lawsuit on its hands. I'll sue."

The odors of alcohol and disinfectant were getting to her. She felt weak again.

Morbier tutted. "This isn't Amerique."

"That's all you can say? I'm telling you what I'll do. Send me for treatment of my preexisting condition exacerbated by a criminal attack or . . ."

"Hold your horses, Leduc. They'll contact your doctor at the eye hospital for your records."

She knew how the system worked. Slow. It would be too late.

"I can't wait for the wheels of bureaucracy to grind to a halt. I need an eye specialist's diagnosis and treatment."

Which was not something offered in a public hospital. Did she need to spell it out for Morbier?

A visiting surgeon, attracted by the brouhaha she made, concurred after a brief examination.

"She's correct. We have a duty of care and the eye hospital will provide it."

Finally.

ONCE IN MOTION, the early morning transfer to the Centre Hospitalier Quinze-Vingts happened quickly. The central eye hospital had been founded by King Louis IX for soldiers blinded in the Crusades. Quinze-Vingts, meaning *three hundred*, the number of beds in the medieval way of counting, was a premier ophthalmological hospital for eye surgery and rehabilitation.

Aimée's hearing had amped into high gear. The hairs on her arm quivered as the air moved when a person walked past. All her senses were heightened; she noticed every sound, smell, texture. All the tools to navigate the world or a corridor the sighted took for granted.

Who would take care of Chloé? Martine couldn't keep her forever. Aimée didn't want to ask her mother for help. Ever. But it crossed her mind.

Her American mother, a former radical turned CIA agent, was excellent at disappearing. Aimée had been eight years old when she'd returned home from school and found that Sydney was gone and had left only a note. Aimée had been raised by her father; grandfather Claude; and godfather, Morbier. Her father had refused to talk about her mother, whose name soon afterward appeared on the world terrorist watch list. A few years ago, Sydney had reappeared in Aimée's life. But she was always on the run or undercover—depending on which story she was telling that time.

Aimée had promised herself she'd never treat her daughter like that. Or let Chloé experience the gaping wound of abandonment. She'd be there for her.

Yet right now she had no choice. She needed her family, such as it was, to keep Chloé safe while she got herself out of this mess and somehow dealt with the numbing loss of Melac.

In whose murder case she was the chief suspect.

Morning light cast a faded glow over the Formica bed tray. Breakfast.

Wait.

Her breath caught.

Her right temple ached and her hand throbbed. But she saw colors, the vivid yellow from the bowl of flowers, the shiny green ivy spilling out of it. Everything had come into focus.

Morbier snored in the corner. His body sprawled atop a chair, pillows behind him, and his scuffed brown loafers rested on another chair. A hospital blanket covered most of him.

A warm feeling filled her. He'd slept there, had guarded her, despite his creaking joints and arthritis.

The door pinged open. A white uniform came into view with a thermometer.

"Naughty. You need to keep the blindfold on to avoid straining your eyes."

"But . . ."

The nurse applied the blindfold, took Aimée's temperature and said, "Your fever's down, good news. I'll feed you."

Like hell she'd let her.

And then it struck her. The minute her vision returned, she'd be sent back to the prison ward at the public hospital. Or with a doctor's note, sent for questioning while being held in a cell.

She'd keep her mouth shut until she got the lay of the land.

Her vision returning might be only temporary. Still, she'd get out of here. She remembered this hospital's layout well. She knew she was in the modern wing where vision-trauma patients were seen on an emergency basis. The outpatient clinic was across the street, near the Bastille.

Unless everything had changed in the ongoing renovation. The story of Paris these days.

"Open," said the nurse.

The smell of cantaloupe made her gag.

"Coffee, please. I don't eat breakfast."

"Nor I," said Morbier with a groan.

Poor man.

"Would you get us coffee, nurse? It would help me wake up and question her."

"*Bien sûr, commissaire.*" The nurse's tone was fawning. "We've got an espresso machine in the staff lounge. A real one."

"Music to my ears, nurse," he said. "You're always so kind. I won't forget."

Mon Dieu, another of Morbier's contacts. After so many years on the force, he had them everywhere. He nourished his web of contacts, granting a favor here, making a friend there—insiders from an old case, people who owed him. It was how a good *flic* worked.

And Morbier was good. The best, after her father.

He was also a godfather who wouldn't let her get away with anything.

Morbier sat on the hospital bed. She smelled a whiff of butter and heard the crunch of a crisp baguette as she felt crumbs on her wrist.

"What happened to your diet, Morbier?"

"What kind of diet makes sense without butter?" he said, crunching away.

Her blindfold had slipped. She saw Morbier's thick fingers, nails yellowed with nicotine, his bloodshot eyes with bags underneath like a basset hound, his pilled sweater-vest under his corduroy jacket and wool scarf. His gray hair curled over his collar.

A ping as the door opened and the room filled with the tantalizing aroma of coffee. She pulled her blindfold up.

"Ready? I'm going to hand you the cup," Morbier said.

The aroma made her want to snatch it from his hands. But she didn't.

"Merci!"

The hot demitasse, the steam moistening her upper lip, the dark, rich taste . . . For a moment she was in heaven.

"Go slow, Leduc."

He always called her *Leduc.* Not *Aimée.* The times he didn't were few—the odd moment of *tendresse* over the years.

"I'll need another," she said. "To get my brain moving."

And then he was leaning toward her, his wiry mustache tickling her cheek, the odor of a recent cigarette clinging to him. He kissed her forehead.

"You had me worried," he said. "Now you sound like the Leduc I know."

She hugged him with her good arm, the one free of the bandage, and inhaled his signature scent of old cologne and nicotine. She felt like a little girl again. Remembered how he'd hand her his big, thick handkerchief to dry her tears and wash off her dirty knee after she fell from her bike. How he'd tell her to get back on. Her godfather, who'd pick her up from school if her father was on stakeout, take her to piano if her *grand-père* was visiting his mistress—although she'd found that detail out later.

Now he treated Chloé like his granddaughter. In essence, she was. Aimée knew he'd do anything for Chloé.

She hated what she was going to do to him.

He'd hate it even more.

"What's happening? What have you found out?"

"Slow down, Leduc. That's the caffeine talking. We need to know how your vision's doing."

She let that go.

"Who'd want Melac dead? Who could get away with murder?"

"We'll talk about that later."

"Right now. It's ridiculous. I'm a suspect."

"Like I said . . ."

"The murderer got away. He could be a *flic*. He definitely spoke like law enforcement."

Aimée had grown up with *flics* at the kitchen table every Friday night for card games. She knew how *flics* acted and talked.

"He handcuffed me, acted like he knew me."

"Convenient."

"Said he'd hit two birds with one stone. But I didn't recognize his voice. He must have stuck the knife in my hand. When the sirens got close, I heard him run off."

"A phantom killer, eh, Leduc?"

Was this really her godfather talking? It almost sounded as though he suspected her. "You can't believe I'd kill my daughter's father," she said, shocked.

"Melac had issues in the force. He wasn't easy, I know," said Morbier. "But it looks bad. The murder weapon was found clutched in your hand, and Melac's blood on your sleeve."

"I was set up," she said, "and since when does the lab work this quick?"

"Leduc, let's make it easy. I know *la proc*. She's pragmatic.

Understands how a fight between a couple can get out of hand. How tempers can heat up and boil over in one second. If Melac had gotten rough with you and you had tried to defend yourself, knowing he had his knife strapped to his ankle, as a last resort, you'd grab it, just to threaten him and make him stop."

Morbier paused. Sipped.

She couldn't believe he was saying this.

"A volatile situation. Melac got jealous that you were seeing someone. He was fighting dirty in your custody battle for Chloé. He stalked and harassed you, and then . . . an accident happened. You'll get off on diminished capacity, crime of passion, self-defense . . . take your pick."

Her jaw dropped. Did Morbier really believe that?

Traitor.

"Do you think I'm lying? Don't answer that," she snapped. "However things were between us, I'd never kill my daughter's father. I couldn't look Chloé in the eyes if I did."

That was true.

"Easy to say."

She paused.

"If you're interrogating me, Morbier, it's illegal this way. As you well know."

"I'm doing my job."

Cold. It stung.

"You're retired from the *brigade criminelle.* The other work you do is usually undercover, *non?*"

Morbier expelled a long sigh, then coughed.

"Back to fighting form, Leduc. But we're going off topic here. Let's get back to *your* situation," he said. "You've been heard arguing with Melac, then complaining that he was hounding you. You said you were going to deal with it once and for all."

"Who said that?"

It could be only someone at work.

"Like I said, the facts speak for themselves. You were covered in blood, the knife was in your hand."

She thought again how the killer had put the knife in her hand. But it had been dark. Was it Melac's knife?

Morbier played both sides. No surprise there. He acted true to form.

But if she'd killed Melac, she'd have done the exact thing he'd suggested. Make nice with *la proc.*

Or maybe not.

Moot point.

"What progress has been made on the investigation?"

"Nobody's been interviewed yet. The autopsy's later, but we know he never would have survived his throat cut."

Sickened, her stomach clenched.

If only she'd gotten there in time.

Morbier sighed. "Closed casket."

Was it that bad?

How could this have happened—who would do such a thing? She tried not to visualize it, but she'd never be able to erase this from her mind.

She'd cared for Melac. And now . . .

It tore her apart. For all his faults, he hadn't deserved this. No one did. Especially not the father of her child.

Once a *flic,* always a *flic.* If they thought she was a cop killer, the whole police force would be against her.

So that's why Morbier was here. To warn her. To offer her a way to negotiate a lighter sentence?

Her own godfather?

She caught a whiff of wet wool, felt the rush of air. Morbier had gone. Not even *au revoir.*

The door pinged open.

"Mademoiselle Leduc? You've been a patient with us before, I see. Dr. Guy Lambert attended to you at the time."

The paper rustled as he paged through her chart.

"I'll examine your eyes," he said. "Have you noticed any blurring of vision, sunspots, dark dots, or headaches?"

"You mean before I was assaulted and suffered a concussion?"

"Excuse me?"

"Don't you see that on the intake report from Hôtel Dieu?"

More rustling papers.

"Nurse? There's information missing from the patient's chart."

Good. This would buy her some time.

"Meanwhile, apart from what you've just told me, have you had any of the symptoms I've mentioned?"

Aimée shook her head.

Mistake. A throbbing dizziness.

"Not before yesterday. I use techniques to reduce stress . . ."

Blah, blah, blah. She gave him the usual. Because of the missing intake report—which Aimée had stuck under her pillow—she'd gained time.

She half listened as the doctor scheduled tests and a thorough exam, which he said were predicated on finding her report.

Mentally, she ran through what she knew: the man at the bridge had sounded like a *flic.* Of that she was sure. The streetlights had been broken. But had Melac been lured there because he'd seen a ghost?

She needed to find a witness.

Would Isabelle have seen something on her way home?

It was a place to start. Aimée came up with a quick and dirty plan to escape. She'd picked up that a uniformed *flic* guarded the door. She could hear his one-way conversation with command on his walkie-talkie.

Unstable, she clutched the bed rail, swung her legs around

and stood. Dizziness washed over her. She kept her breathing steady, remembering what the eye-clinic therapist had drummed into her: breathe and count . . . one, two . . . exhale. Slow and measured. She held the hospital gown around her and realized she had nothing on underneath.

Little by little, her equilibrium returned. She felt around and found a plastic bag holding her underwear, an Agent Provocateur black lace bra and panties, and her boots.

Everything else had been taken for evidence.

No shirt, her leather pants or jacket. And it was a cold, biting April.

Merde.

When the police guard took a pee break, she slipped out of the room, her hospital gown covering her underwear. Her vision had cleared. The depth of field wavered. She took a minute, keeping her gaze on the exit sign.

She hadn't wasted time thinking this through. She needed to play it as it came, improvise. She kept moving, then ducked into the next room down the corridor. Good thing it was by the exit.

Aimée looked around. No nurses or staff—but for how long? The bed was surrounded by curtains, from behind which came the sounds of a respirator and the beep of machines. She had to make this fast and use what she could find.

A plastic bag with a woman's belongings sat on a shelf.

She removed a gray wool sweaterdress and a thin leather jacket, big in the shoulders. The dress was large and wafted cheap perfume. She slipped it on. For now, it worked.

Footsteps came from the hallway. Conversations. Hospital gown back over her, she hid her boots inside the leather jacket and tiptoed out to the nearby exit. She pushed the swinging doors open and took a breath. Then another. She smelled fresh laundry and a whiff of lemon polish in the stairwell.

At least she could see, despite the fuzzy glow wafting over her vision every so often. Perspiration broke out on her neck.

She could do this.

Couldn't she?

She wedged her right foot then her left into her Louboutin knee-high boots. Something was jammed inside. Of all times!

Feeling inside, she remembered that she'd stuck her personal phone in her boot. The killer had only her work phone, neither the police nor hospital staff had found it.

Thank God.

But the battery was dead. And the damn thing felt damp.

Worry about that later. Keep moving.

She grasped the railing with one hand and tried to keep steady on her feet as a wave of nausea hit her. Like being seasick on a boat. She forced herself to keep breathing and look straight ahead. To act mindfully. To concentrate on going down each step and keeping her gaze forward and focus on the middle distance.

At the ground floor exit, she recognized the chapel standing to the left within the fourteenth-century hospital complex and found the huge gates. Closed.

Panic flooded her, and her vision started to swim.

Stop. Remember. She'd been blind before and had navigated with her senses. Even if it came to the worst, she could get out of here in one piece.

Staff and visitors mingled at the exit by the concierge loge.

She followed and melded into the stream of visitors. Several orderlies stood on the street for a cigarette break. No one paid her any attention. At the garbage bin, she tossed away the hospital robe.

Ahead of her, an older man used a white-tipped cane, feeling the ground with a *tack, tack, tack.* Would that be her? Using a cane and depending on the traffic lights chirping to indicate green?

Now on the narrow street, she'd gained her sea legs. Her center of gravity righted. She recognized the area: rue de Charenton. If she kept walking, she'd join Place de la Bastille. From there, it was a quick bus ride to her office on rue du Louvre. She'd go to her office, get a backup phone, grab money and a credit card and be out again.

Praying no one would check for her Metro pass, she slipped in through the bus's back door, somehow found a seat and sat as the street swam past the window.

Breathe, breathe. Close your eyes and count the stops. She tried to ignore the waves of nausea, the dull throb in her temple.

Somehow she got off at rue du Louvre and hadn't thrown up. More and more the blurriness receded.

She passed Marcel, the one-armed Algerian vet who ran the news kiosk on the corner. She kept Marcel on retainer and he kept an eye out. Before she could wave, he'd raised a copy of *Le Parisien* with its signature blue banner. MURDER ON THE CANAL . . . was all she could make out.

Her spine jittered.

Marcel touched the side of his nose. Once. Twice.

Merde!

A signal. Her pulse thudded. The *flics* were waiting at her office.

Double merde.

Time for plan B.

She couldn't remember when she'd last refreshed the emergency kit in her go bag. *Dumb.* It was one of the things she should have kept updated. Her father had drilled this into her. But a three-year-old, a business to run, consulting gigs and a sort-of relationship got in the way.

Excuses, her papa would say, paved the way to problems. When you need something, you need it now. Preparation remains the ace in the hand.

Her go bag, no matter what state it was in, would have to work.

Don't stress. Remember the tips to keep your eyes from fatigue and overuse in fragile times.

The shrill whine of a siren from rue de Rivoli jolted her. Too dangerous to stay on the street.

She caught Marcel's eye and tapped her head. After the woman ahead of her at the kiosk bought a magazine—*Madame Figaro*—Marcel gave her a wink and a quick handoff. Seconds later, she donned his navy beret. Head down, wearing the long sweaterdress and big-shouldered leather jacket, she could only hope to enter her building unnoticed.

Keep going. Don't stop. Don't look back.

She entered her building and crossed the worn tiled hallway through to the ground floor's back exit. The small back court-yard, once a stable yard, was surrounded by hedges and magnolia trees with white blossoms.

She paused and listened. No footsteps. No shouts of "stop."

To the left, by a boulangerie's back door, stood a brick-and-wood-roofed shed, part of the old stable, where the baker stored his flour.

Warm baking smells drifted. *Heaven.*

Years ago her father had found the baker's long-lost sister. Instead of the minimum fee, Jean-Claude Leduc had made another arrangement.

Inside the shed she found the Leduc locker, once her father's, spun the combination code and opened it.

Not even mildewed. Or damp. Just had a faint scent of flour and baking.

Her go bag, a custom Longchamp leather backpack, was classic edgy chic.

She hunted through the outfits stuffed in the long locker. She didn't have much time. She emptied several silica gel packets into a baggie, then stuck in her phone—a trick that sucked the damp out. Usually.

She changed from the hospital patient's sweaterdress into overalls, high-tops and an oversize fleece-lined denim bomber jacket, then stuck her spiky hair under a wool cap and donned dark round glasses.

Finally, she found an outlet by the door and plugged her phone in. Would it come to life?

Not a flicker. Should she take out the SIM?

She waited one more minute. How much longer could she risk?

The small screen flickered on. *Thank God.* She'd charge it more later.

She tried Martine.

No answer.

Not a good sign.

No answer from René, her business partner, either.

A really bad sign.

Their phones must be tapped. Her calls could be traced. She clicked off before her number would register in triangulation from a cell tower. Her collar, damp from perspiration, stuck to her neck.

She tried her cousin, Sébastien.

Voice mail.

Hadn't she seen Melac's murder on the front page of *Le Parisien*? The *flics* were waiting at her office. She couldn't go home. And now the people closest to her were being monitored. She could thank Morbier and the grapevine for that.

Another day at the office.

She felt an echoing throb in her temples.

Also in the locker was Chloé's emergency go kit. Half the clothes wouldn't even fit Chloé now. She stuffed it into her go bag, even though Chloé was safe.

Wasn't she?

Her stash of cash was two hundred euros, the debit card held five hundred. She wouldn't get far.

Think.

Who owed her? Who wouldn't give her away? Whom could she trust?

Where could she go? Hide?

She checked the address book she'd remembered to throw in. She hadn't updated it since last year, but it was pen on paper. Real. No digital trace.

Then it clicked. There was one person no one knew she was in contact with. Her number wasn't in any phone or file on her computer. It was on the card clipped to the back of the much-thumbed address book under "possibly useful."

Disconnected.

The throbbing in her head intensified. Thank God she'd put Doliprane, bandages, water and antibiotics in the bag. She popped a pain reliever and antibiotic, rebandaged her hand, closed her eyes and rested, hoping the medicine would take effect soon. The warm oven scents wafted, and she concentrated on listening for unknown voices, a phone conversation, walkie-talkie static.

From the third floor open window, she heard the voice of Enzo, the travel agent, conversing in Italian. Heard the rumble of the pipes that snaked down the back of the building. Her fingers ran over the knots in the ancient wood door, each burl and raised whorl imprinting itself on her mind.

Visualize, the therapist in the eye clinic had urged, use your senses to lock into the landscape and visualize where you are, what's ahead, and remember. Build a sense memory.

She ran the logistics in her head.

This shed led to the back of the bakery, which led out onto rue Saint-Honoré and beyond to the rue du Louvre where, in her disguise, she could lose herself among the pedestrians. She visualized the pavement busy with shoppers; mailmen from Hôtel des Postes, the main post office open twenty-four hours; the slice of the twelfth-century wall. From there, it was a quick dart over to the giant Châtelet station.

Her father had drilled into her the importance of details—even innocuous-looking ones. They were all small pieces of a larger puzzle. She had to put them together to see the full picture.

She relistened to Melac's message.

She wrote it down. Rested her eyes. Reopened them and knew she'd forgotten something.

What was it?

She listened again.

In the message before Melac's last, she'd heard him saying "morgue." At least it sounded like that. The morgue.

With the little juice her phone had, she called Serge, her old classmate from premed, now a forensic pathologist at Institut Médico-Légal, the city morgue.

He answered after a few rings.

"Who's this?"

"Aimée. Please listen and answer my questions, okay?"

A ruffling and crackling as he put his hand over the receiver. She imagined his tiled, antiseptic office overlooking the Seine. He cleared his throat. "Um . . ."

"Did Melac have an appointment with you?"

Pause. "*Non.*"

"Did you see him recently?"

"Negative."

Merde.

"Did he call you for information?"

"Why?"

Someone was in his lab.

"He said something about the morgue."

"You know everyone refers to us as *the Institut Médico-Légal*—especially *flics*."

Melac had been a *flic*.

"I have to go," he said.

"I'm in trouble, Serge."

"I know."

Merde again.

"Does everyone know?"

"Does wildfire spread?"

"I didn't kill Melac."

A low whisper. "So prove it, Aimée."

Everything was stacked against her.

She heard footsteps in the background. Voices. She had to push her feelings away—deal with them later.

"I'm being framed, Serge."

"If someone were doing that to me," he said, above a whisper, "I'd prove them wrong."

Click. Serge had hung up.

She stuck the phone back in the charger. Then thought.

The only other morgue Melac could have been referring to was the newspaper archives.

Aimée had to push through the bad memories to get to the good. She remembered Melac telling her over *pain au chocolat* one morning about loving research—about where answers could be found and where no one looked.

It was like he was telling her a great secret, and she let him think that. But she went there frequently. So had her father.

After news articles died, they were cataloged in the archives. Or digitized if a researcher got lucky. Sometimes, journalists called those archives *the morgue*.

Why hadn't she thought of that?

But first she needed to get out of here.

She ran through the Metro lines and connections like a road map in her head, visualizing the entire route in case her eyesight wavered. As a native Parisienne, she could recite them by heart. She planned on teaching Chloé when she was old enough.

The next part would depend on whether the person she called would answer.

Tuesday Morning • Courtyard Behind Leduc Detective

AIMÉE RECALLED *NOBODYLU* and punched the corresponding numbers on her barely charged burner phone.

"It's Aimée," she said. "You said if I ever need help to call."

A pause. "Where are you?"

"I'll take the Metro to—"

"Give me a street corner," interrupted Isabelle, the cleaner and former junkie she'd stood up for last night. Last night—it seemed a thousand years ago.

Aimée told her.

"I'm sending someone. You'll get picked up."

Fifteen minutes later, Aimée stood at the corner of rue Étienne Marcel and rue du Louvre in front of the central Hôtel des Postes. The teeming corner was full of activity as people came and went by the bustling post office, shops and back alleys of the Banque de France.

She heard the distinctive honk of a motorcycle and saw the flash of headlights. This must have been her ride.

A helmet was thrust at her by a gloved hand. She strapped on the helmet, then hopped on the bike behind a rider wearing black motorcycle leathers, chunky boots and a helmet and visor that covered their face. The swift and smooth pick up took fifteen seconds.

She reached her arm around the rider's torso, and they were

off. The driver rode, winding through back streets, below the aerial Metro line which clattered on the tracks above them. They zipped along the canal and past Stalingrad Metro, riding parallel to Bassin de la Villette, which glistened with a smooth gel surface. She felt a chill remembering how it had looked last night—such a contrast to today's peace. The driver zoomed through the old quartier around rue de l'Ourcq. High-rises dotted what had once been the rundown industrial district and pockets of remaining two-story workers' housing.

The streaming air rejuvenated her, and she felt light. All she had was a simple go bag and a journey into the unknown.

She missed Chloé and felt a deep sadness Melac wouldn't be around for her childhood. Warts and all, he'd done his best.

Hadn't he?

It felt like she was stuck in a snowstorm, fighting against gales. There was no way forward except to set her shoulders and go headlong through the storm to the other side. She'd never leave Chloé; in her bones she knew finding Melac's killer was the only way to be able to return.

Otherwise she could lose everything: her daughter, her business, her freedom.

Did she have a choice?

The motorcycle braked, then stopped at the corner of rue Curial and rue de l'Ourcq. The rider jerked a thumb.

Aimée got off the bike, removed her helmet. For the life of her, she couldn't tell if the driver was male or female. Without another moment lost, the rider revved the engine and was off.

Across the cobbled street was a Moroccan couscous *resto*, behind her a rundown café with locals spilling out to the *terrasse* and the crowded pavement. On the other side was a printing press, and across from it on rue de l'Ourcq was her goal.

A biker bar and tattoo shop.

AIMÉE CHECKED THE address: 94 rue de l'Ourcq. Chez Angels.

Chez Angels was lodged in a nineteenth-century storefront on the ground floor of a pale brick building with balconies and rusted metal shutters. A leather-clad man lounged in the doorway.

Did Isabelle live in a biker bar?

Or was this a front?

She walked past him and through the dull purple storefront.

"What do you want?"

Aimée gulped. Her mind raced for a way to word her question.

"One color, two colors or more?" said a man, his arms and neck covered with ink. He stood at what looked like a barber's chair in front of a mirror and wore a leather cap and an earring. "That costs extra."

Tattoo. He meant getting a tattoo. She already had one. A Marquesan lizard on her back.

"*Non*, I'm here to meet Isabelle."

The place was bright and it hurt her eyes.

"Who?"

"She gave me this address. We're supposed to talk."

"Talk?" He took her arm. "Why didn't you say so?"

Inside the tattoo parlor, he patted her down professionally: under her arms, between her thighs, over her ankles.

"Quit enjoying that," said a voice from someone in a barber's chair. The rotary tattoo machine's whirring sounds and the muted heavy metal music gave the shop, which looked like a former *épicerie*—an everything corner store—a feeling of being lost in time.

A worse for wear generator labeled EMERGENCY USE ONLY sat under the mirrored counter, a loose wire hanging from it. Two eras competed—eighties posters of iconic rocker Johnny Hallyday on his motorcycle alongside 1920s zinc countertops and old signs for rat traps and Persil soap.

The place felt like a front. Drugs, stolen goods? Did this place launder money?

Five or so bikers appeared as if on cue.

Like rats, they encircled her.

Mon Dieu. She'd come here for help, not to be the main course. *Think.*

"Leave her alone. Get to work. *Et alors*, the shipment's due any minute."

The men turned and were gone. Isabelle strode in with a grin, accompanied by a young leather-clad *mec* who limped and used a cane. LUCA was embroidered on his belt.

"They listen," said Isabelle. "They're trained."

At the start-up, Isabelle performed menial work and cleaned, whereas here, she was *la patronne*. This was a whole other side of her.

Aimée was impressed.

"Aren't you going to introduce me?"

"I'm Luca, Isabelle's brother." The trunk of his body twisted in a way to make him look hunchbacked. "Later."

Before she could tell him her name, he'd gone.

"This way," Isabelle said.

Aimée followed Isabelle through the bar and past the tat-tooing tools, barbers' chairs and garish sheets of colorful tattoo designs on the walls. She'd gotten her tattoo while escaping from the *flics*. It had hurt—a lot. And now it was happening again. Almost like going from the frying pan into the fire.

They ended up going outside through a damp backyard fringed by greenery to a glass-paned atrium adjoining a rear tim-bered house. It was quiet, apart from birdsong, and had a faded nineteenth-century charm. Inside were mismatched furniture, odds and ends and antique plates filling a salon opening into a kitchen. An old-fashioned oil heater warmed with a sputter.

What kind of place was this?

Isabelle sat down on a rattan recamier and indicated for Aimée to do the same. "You came to the right place, Aimée."

She almost blurted out *A biker squat?* but bit her tongue. Beggars couldn't be choosers, as the old cliché went. No one would look for her here.

Guaranteed.

"How are you . . . involved with all this?" Aimée asked care-fully.

"I'm clean. No drugs anymore." Isabelle rubbed her hands together and flicked out her palms. "*C'est fini.* Here we whole-sale cigarettes. A lucrative business." Isabelle eyed her. "But you never heard that."

"*Bien sûr*, it's not my business, Isabelle," she said.

Aimée knew dealing illegal cigarettes was a huge money-maker. It raked in thousands.

"Why do you work the cleaning job?"

"Benefits, like I told you," Isabelle said with a dismissive shrug. "It's my fallback plan. You saw my little brother, Luca.

He'll never get better, his disease is degenerative. He needs more than I can do alone."

Aimée nodded, wishing she didn't want to smoke one of those cigarettes from the open pack on the side table.

"My job puts us top of the list for special housing, if I don't blow it. That stupid Pépe. Luca and I have only each other and *les Anges*," Isabelle said. "Our father was a member until . . ." She paused. "He's gone. They're our family now."

"So you take care of your own?" said Aimée. "Fine. But I'm not one of yours, and I feel bad you're taking a risk."

"I owe you, Aimée. That's enough for me." Isabelle regarded her with a smile. "You're safe here. We're the police in the quartier."

Startled, Aimée leaned forward. Bikers were *les flics*? She'd had no idea.

"Since when?"

"Long as I can remember." Isabelle reached for a cigarette. Flicked a lighter and inhaled.

Aimée could taste it.

Isabelle let out a puff. "Someone had to step up and protect the neighborhood after what happened."

"What do you mean?"

"After that sixteen-year-old girl died at the hands of the serial killer, the one who struck all over the nineteenth. She was on her way to a party."

Familiar.

"Fifteen years ago, he claimed his first victim on rue Petit," Isabelle said, her tone hollow and sad. She exhaled a plume of smoke. "Her name was Carine. My father's friend lived in the same building as her family. No one talked of anything else. Nothing like this had ever happened here before. He claimed eight victims in the nineteenth arrondissement over several years."

Now Aimée remembered. She'd been studying for the bacca-laureate. Had been a carefree teen who'd snuck out of the *prépa* study course to smoke with her best friend, Martine. Although halfway across the city, she'd still worried for her own safety. Everyone had worried.

Even her father had warned her to never go to a party alone.

"The *flics* were useless back then, just like now," Isabelle said. "So . . . we took our safety into our own hands. Of course, I was young then."

"I understand people protecting their own and appreciate you helping me." She tapped yesterday's freshly lacquered nails, already chipped, on the table. "*Alors*, Isabelle, I'm being framed."

Isabelle nodded. "No judgment, Aimée. Last night's murder on the canal sparked rumors."

"How's that?"

Isabelle flicked ashes into the cracked porcelain ashtray.

"That the *flics* got it wrong again. Rumors going around how the killer's back."

Startled, Aimée leaned forward and grabbed the recamier arms.

"Back after all these years? Do you know if it's true?"

"Rumors are rumors. But on Sunday a young woman was attacked from behind. A man tried to strangle her by the canal. She couldn't see who it was. The attacker was interrupted and fled, but he left a wire."

"How's the wire significant?"

"This was *le Balafré*'s signature. He strangled his victims with a wire—the thick heavy-duty kind. He wired their limbs so it looked like they were praying."

"*Le Balafré?*"

Didn't that mean *pockmarked* or *scarface*?

"The nickname for this serial killer."

"Look, Isabelle, I don't know about the serial killer, but I'm a suspect in that murder on the canal. The victim—he was my ex. My daughter's father."

Isabelle exhaled a stream of smoke.

"Well, did you kill him?"

"No!"

"Good enough for me," she said. "*Zut*, if I ever see my ex again, it'll be too soon. My ex caused me big problems."

"Mine, too," Aimée said.

"Look to the family, they say. What about your ex's ex?"

"She was a problem." Melac's ex-wife, Donatine, had caused plenty of drama trying to get full custody of Chloé. "She was obsessed over having children. She practically kidnapped Chloé once." An ugly time. "But Melac said all that was over. After their divorce, she found God and emigrated."

Isabelle blew a smoke ring. "Could she have hired a hit man to whack you both and take Chloé?"

"Doubt it. She left for some commune in Australia to spin wool and live with nature."

Other than Donatine, who had been out of their lives for a long time now, who could have wanted to hurt Melac and Aimée? Troubled, Aimée fell silent.

"Look," Isabelle said, ashing her cigarette, "you're here under my protection. My word's good here. But is it good enough for you?"

Isabelle was offering her help—help Aimée was desperate for—on her terms. Aimée nodded. "I don't know what to say . . . I'm so sorry to bring this on you."

"You helped me when you didn't have to, Aimée. When nobody would. Call us even."

Phew, thank God. Safe—for now.

"*Merci*, Isabelle," she said. "There's so much to face."

"You don't have to tell me. I don't care what you did."

Aimée sucked in her breath. For the first time someone wasn't judging her. "But you might be a witness," she said. "You were not far away when it happened."

So, while Isabelle listened without expression, her cigarette smoke trailing to the ceiling in a blue spiral, Aimée told her what had happened, keeping it simple.

"Last night, did you see anyone when you finished your shift?" asked Aimée at the conclusion of her account. "Or hear anything?"

Isabelle thought, twisting the tip of the long black braid hanging over her shoulder. "My shift ended an hour later, and I don't pass that way."

That would have been too good to be true.

"What about security cameras?" Aimée tried. "Do you know of any around there? If the *flics* haven't looked for the footage."

"Security cameras by the canal? Fat chance. The dealers usually destroy them. But like I said, we're the local enforcement around here. So who are you looking for?"

Direct. Aimée liked that.

"Like I told you, he sounded like a *flic*. I can't get rid of the feeling that . . . maybe he was in law enforcement."

Isabelle took a pack of cigarettes from an open carton. Offered Aimée one. Tempted, she was about to accept. Then declined.

Hell, she could be dead tomorrow. Why not enjoy a smoke?

She accepted. Lit up and coughed. "I have to prove my innocence or leave the country."

Isabelle blew a smoke ring. A perfect circle. "Understood," she said.

Tuesday Morning • Chez Angels • Rue de l'Ourcq

AIMÉE ACCEPTED THE burner phone Isabelle offered. Hiding with outlaws had its advantages.

After Isabelle left to handle a shipment of stolen cigarettes, Aimée practiced her breathing. She wished her hands didn't shake so much. She closed her eyes, trying to concentrate on the warmth from a patch of sun on her arm.

Following her father's murder in the bomb explosion in Place Vendôme, Aimée took over Leduc Detective. She'd refocused the agency from spousal surveillance and lost persons to IT and computer security. This often entailed going undercover: embedding herself as a mole in a company to investigate corporate espionage, being the new hire, masquerading in IT in a law firm, assuming a new persona and staying under the radar—like at the start-up near the canal. She'd blown the under-the-radar part. Would put that on hold—worry about it later—and get René on it.

Her fingers trembled. She was wanted, on the run. This was the only way.

Wasn't it?

Good thing she remembered Bellan's number at work.

She rang and was put through to his office.

"Who's calling?" said a receptionist.

"His wife's sister," she said. "It's urgent."

"Concerning?"

"Family issues. Please put me through."

She hoped that would work.

"Can you be more specific? He's in a meeting and I don't want to . . ."

"His son."

A moment later, she was patched through.

"Bellan. Who's this?"

His familiar voice filled the line, that breathy catch to some of his words. She missed him.

"Where are you?"

She heard a chair scrape, a mumbled excuse. A door closing. Footsteps.

"Aimée? More importantly, where the hell are you?"

"You don't want to know."

"You didn't come last night. I waited. And then this morning they say you murdered Melac."

"I didn't," she said, tearing up.

Upset, she paced back and forth in the squat's atrium. Did he suspect her?

"*Zut*, you know me, Bellan. He's . . . was Chloé's father. Right now I need you to check on something."

He lowered his voice. "I can't get involved."

How could he say that after all they'd been through together? He'd practically lived at her place since Melac had stormed out.

"You're involved whether you want to be or not."

"We're renegotiating custody of our kids. My ex is finally coming around." His voice sounded frosty. Distant. "We worked out the child support, and she's letting go of alimony. It's crucial. Nothing can get in the way of that."

She heard an intake of breath. A deep sigh.

"*C'est simple.* I'm not breaking the law and losing my children."

Now she heard a rush of emotion. There it was—what mattered most to him. She hated him. She also understood him.

She'd probably do the same.

"Understood. But you don't have to break the law. Or lose custody."

"You're a fugitive and I can't talk to you. What you've done is wrong."

"The only wrong thing I've done is save my skin. I've been set up."

"Everyone says that."

"It's true. And no one's going after Melac's murderer."

A pause.

"Maybe. But it can't be my problem, Aimée."

This from the man who slept with her almost every night? Called her several times a day? Adored Chloé?

He was the first man she'd felt in sync with for a long time. It was a shock.

"Why? Because Melac was a colleague? You had each other's back? I hate how you all stand up for each other. Look what it did to my father."

Her father's brothers in blue hadn't supported him when he was framed for corruption. It had taken her years to clear his name.

Bellan took a breath. "I have to go back to the ministry meeting."

"You're a coward," she said. She was spitting mad. "Who's really controlling you, Bellan?"

"Don't go there, Aimée. I'm going to hang up."

Stupid. She shouldn't accuse him. She'd get nowhere that way.

"At least tell me the investigation status."

"Status? The report landed on my desk this morning. It's you. An all-points bulletin, arrest on sight. *Merde.* And you know I can't trace this call from my work phone."

"I didn't kill Melac," she snapped.

"So come in and prove it."

"I will when I *can* prove it." Frustrated, she didn't know what else to say. She was getting away from her point, the reason she'd called. "Just help me with one thing. Look up the file of Carine Joffre, a girl raped and killed in the nineteenth, fifteen years ago. She was the first victim of a serial killer."

Pause. "*Le Balafré?*"

Pockmark.

He knew right away.

"That's right."

Bellan missed nothing and remembered everything—even events before his time.

Yet no one had caught this serial killer—infamous for his pockmarked face.

"Isn't the case still open?"

"Until he's apprehended. No statute of limitations on this. His composite police sketch from a witness, the girl's brother, still hangs in the *brigade criminelle*."

A question rose in her mind.

"Did Morbier work that case?"

"Wasn't he working with your father then? *Non*, too late for that. He wasn't in *le crim*."

Short for *brigade criminelle*.

Another pause. Voices in the background. "But you should know there's been a letter from a witness who saw you," said Bellan, voice lowered. "The lab's processing and testing pieces of your clothing with Melac's blood."

"Of course there's blood on my clothes. I was trying to pull him out of the canal."

"There's unknown DNA on the knife. They suspect it's yours."

How did he know that? It was impossible to test DNA that quick. The liar.

"I need help, Bellan."

"You need a lawyer."

Click. He'd hung up, scared and afraid for his own *derrière*, like the rest of them.

Part of her was searing in hurt. But the other part understood—Bellan had a lot to lose if he got involved: his children, his job . . . Yet he'd lose her, too.

She summoned her courage. But tears came out instead, big hot tears running down her cheeks.

Alone, on the run and worried for Chloé, she had to figure this out. Fix it. Do whatever she could before she got caught.

Focus.

Too much was at stake to sit spinning her wheels.

Her father always said to go with what you find—from this go to the next, always adapting. Always ready to pivot.

Morgue.

Until she could follow another lead, she'd scour the *Le Parisien* archives. What was her contact's number?

It took a while, but she finally found it in her back-up Moleskine. She never threw one away. Thank God she'd stored it in the go bag.

"Long time no hear, Aimée." Emile yawned into the phone. "But then you contact me only when you want something."

"*Bon après-midi* to you, too, Emile. Glad you're on shift."

"*Bonsoir*, technically, and I'm off in an hour."

He hadn't said anything about her being accused of murder. She must not have been named in the press yet. Small blessings.

She thought. "But not if I'm bringing you lunch." What was his favorite? "From Pizza Siciliano, *non*?"

After some back and forth, including which extra toppings, he agreed to cull articles and get her space in the newspaper's reading room.

The newspaper's temporary printing site was close by in a warehouse off the canal. Not near a *commissariat*. A bonus feature. She picked up the pizza and headed to the warehouse, where she eyed the overalls the printers wore. She recognized Emile's bike out front.

Emile, a gangling archives research assistant, who still looked about twelve, shook his head at Aimée's hopeful expression. "Turns out someone booked the reading room for a meeting."

Disappointed, she bit her lip.

"Don't you want this? It's still piping hot."

"Cheer up," he said, taking the pizza box with one hand, clapping her back with the other. "Follow me to Obituaries. I found you space there."

He was a genius in archives research on top of drawing for *bandes desinées*. Comic books for adults, René called them. Emile made more money drawing comics than at his shift at the paper. He insisted he preferred the anonymity and liked this grunt work where he could find ideas for his stories.

Throwing caution to the wind, she said, "Didn't Jérome Melac have an appointment with you last night?"

"Yes, just before . . . Well, we all saw the headline. Wait, were you working with him?"

Emile didn't know about their relationship. Or that she was involved in his death. At least until her name was released as a suspect. It was only a matter of time.

She shook her head.

The horror of it flooded back. Mired her in pain and fear. She breathed in slowly and deeply to quell her emotions, to function—to find who'd murdered him.

She could do this.

Couldn't she?

"Unrelated. But can you tell me what Melac requested?"

Emile expelled air from his mouth. "He wanted crimes in the nineteenth for the years 1986–1994. Homicides specifically related to *le Balafré*."

The serial killer. Again.

"Which makes how many?"

"See for yourself. But eight women were attributed to the serial killer. Very bizarre cases. Local, too."

"What if he's back?"

"*Zut.* Sounds like a headline. 'Serial killer back . . .' Why would you say that?"

She had only a dead man's declaration.

"Humor me. Let's say Melac's murder carries the same signature as *le Balafré*'s first known murder," she fudged. "This girl Carine Joffre from rue Petit."

"Wasn't she raped?" He narrowed his eyes at her. "How do you know those details about how Melac was killed?"

"Because I'm suspected of Melac's murder," she said, desperate. Far-fetched as it sounded, she had nothing else to go on. "I think *le Balafré* committed it."

Emile's mouth gaped open. "That's you?"

He had no idea the headline they'd printed that morning was about her.

He narrowed his eyes at her. "How is *le Balafré* involved? I don't get the connection."

Neither did she. But in every investigation, you had to go with your first leads, tenuous as they were. Percentage-wise, the lead rarely, if ever, panned out, but it led to the next place to investigate.

"I need to start somewhere. I'm tracing Melac's last

movements." Her throat caught. "The cases he was investigating here in the archive—you said he was looking at *le Balafré*."

"Guess you're not on the *flics*' favorites list."

"Nothing new about that," she said. She stared at the old newspaper. "Who's the reporter on the crime beat, the *faits divers*?"

"I could find out."

Relief washed over her. He was going to help. Not call the *flics* on her.

Yet.

After only twenty minutes, Aimée was kicked out by a group needing the space for an editorial meeting. She'd only skimmed the first few articles before the letters blurred. Her head ached.

"Come back tomorrow," said Emile. "My boss is on the prowl."

Great.

"I'll put these aside for you."

SHE KEPT IN the shadows, passing a new bike store. Too expensive.

A few blocks away, she could buy a stolen one from a fence— only cash, and no record.

Some fragment of information wiggled like a worm on the fringe of her consciousness. But every time she tried to grab it, it squirmed away.

What was it?

Her thoughts were scattered. Her head pounded. She usually did better than this under pressure. Usually worked harder, thought faster. Connected things.

Her vision wavered. All of a sudden there were two of everything. Fear filled her. She still hadn't fully recovered from the attack—she didn't need a doctor to spell it out.

Her double vision came from the concussion and damage to her ocular nerve.

Slow down and think smart. She stopped in the shadow of a doorway. Closed her eyes. Drew a mental map of her surroundings so she didn't forget what it looked like in case her vision went out again.

She tried picturing the travel agent's window next door to the bike store. She remembered posters advertising holiday packages: picturesque hiking trips in Brittany and seaside weekends in Vannes.

That word stirred in her mind. *Vannes.* Wasn't that near Melac's farm? She thought she remembered him saying in one of his garbled voice mails how Chloé could go to a good school in Vannes if she and Aimée came to Brittany.

It was all coming back. That night by the fireside at his farm, the best evening the three of them had ever spent together. Chloé had been two. She'd gone to sleep early after a day full of pony riding and collecting shells on the shingle beach. Aimée remembered Chloé's cries of delight when she found part of a sea star. Melac had been watchful since rusted World War II ordnance still resurfaced even now, turning up in the wake of a storm. He'd found a live grenade only that previous weekend. Melac had made homemade soup with vegetables from the garden, and Aimée remembered Chloé's thrill and delight at feeding the chickens with Papa.

It had been a day without arguments. No evening fights. It had ended with a warm cuddle at the fire and a vintage bottle of Château Figeac—Melac's special treat.

That could have been her life: Chloé's childhood spent in the outdoors and learning about nature. But could Aimée have lived overlooking the bleak tin-gray Atlantic? In the isolation from Paris and working from her laptop? She got bored there after a few hours.

Had she been selfish?

Even Miles Davis, a city dog, loved to run on the beach—his happy place. How she missed him. Madame Cachou was probably spoiling him rotten.

But Aimée had no friends in Brittany. And she hated the thought of being reliant on Melac. Morbier and her cousin, Sébastien, were her only family, and they were in Paris. So was her work, all the contacts she depended on for jobs, and the network she needed to stay *au courant* in the rapidly changing tech world. Martine, her best friend and journalist, didn't care for Melac, and no way would René, her business partner and other best friend, travel to Brittany for staff meetings.

Melac had been a good father. But only on his terms.

SOME MINUTES PASSED before she opened her eyes. Her vision had cleared, thank God. She bought a slice of glistening *tarte aux abricots* and a day old baguette at the pâtisserie. She sat cross-legged, feeding the baguette crumbs to ducks and the occasional white swan who glided over.

What was it about the place? Why had the killer chosen to kill Melac here? Her father would always say—despite the fact that it was a cliché—criminals returned to the scene of the crime. He had told her about many cases proving the rule. The crime means a lot to the perpetrator, he'd said. The location is often significant. Remember, murder is about stepping over a line—the ultimate line of life and death. However things appear, the act of murder is imprinted on the killer. The stakes are raised. Nothing is as it was before. Or will ever be again.

Start simple, he'd say. There's a reason the crime happens where it does. Think location. Think convenience, ease of execution, ability to escape.

He'd told her about an old case: a serial killer who had lived one Metro stop away from his crimes. The victims had been discovered on Wednesdays, late at night, behind garbage bins. At the time no one had put together how the attacks occurred on Wednesdays, market days, and centered within a three-block radius. Looking back, it was simple to see all the women shopped at the weekly market. But at the time, the *flics* hadn't paid attention to the produce that fell from the women's bags, the spilled coins from their change purses.

Sloppy policing, he'd said.

The connection had been made only after her father asked the question: What if the perpetrator goes to the market, too, and scouts out his prey? He could be a shopper, another person with a full bag who appears harmless to the women. The serial killer had turned out to be the adult caregiver of an older woman he escorted to the market each Wednesday.

Hiding in plain sight.

The attack on Melac had taken planning. Melac had been watching Aimée every night after work; he'd gotten into a pattern. The murderer must have been counting on his being there that night, too.

The small details were important. Mentally she went back and cataloged what she remembered: a blue light down the canal, the crunch of broken streetlight glass, the sounds of water. She wrote them down in her Moleskine to check later.

The first twenty-four hours of a murder investigation were crucial. After that, the success rate dropped.

She found a bus shelter and clocked the bus routes. She took a sheet of paper from the trash—an advertisement for a local *parfumerie*—and drew a quick diagram, marking the *passerelle* bridge with an *X*. She sketched out the quai and streets on both sides of the canal. Her paper was too small, so she rummaged in the bin for another sheet. Still too small.

So she used her Moleskine. Now she sketched the areas on both sides of the canal that were approximately a five to eight minute walk away from the Metro. She added the bus routes that crossed these streets.

This was a huge area. She'd have to map this out in more detail, fill in the streets, the narrow lanes and the villas, the narrow alleys with workers' houses, often gated, on either side. Grunt work and shoe leather, her father would say. As she walked, most people paid her no mind. After all, the nineteenth was a working-class arrondissement. The residents worked, struggled and paid little attention to things other than laundry, that night's dinner, schoolwork and making ends meet until payday. She liked it because it reminded her of what Paris had been like when she was growing up, before Île Saint-Louis got too chichi. The concierges, the cheese-shop owner, the butcher, the cleaners, the teachers, the everyday people and impoverished aristos who lived in crumbling seventeenth-century *hôtels particuliers*—town houses like hers—without modern plumbing and electricity.

She wanted to study these streets, but it would be too time-consuming. Better to go with a broad-stroke canvassing, then ask herself: Why would a killer use this location? How could they get away and melt into the quartier? What was the best vantage point?

After forty minutes, her legs ached. She felt like she hadn't learned anything relevant.

Then she saw the map of the quartier outside the Metro—a big circle showing a five-minute-walk radius.

Idiot. Why hadn't she looked at this in the first place?

She needed to start where the killer could have watched the quai. Where there was the best view. Somewhere easy to reach.

The bridge.

She hesitated, not wanting to revisit the scene or deal with those recent vivid memories. A stiff drink would help. She walked into the bistro on Avenue Jean Jaurès by the red lacquered wood Chinese restaurant—an old-school homage to the Forbidden City—and up to the bar.

Dubonnet, Pastis, and a score of liqueurs filled the mirrored shelves behind the bartender, their colorful bottles seeming to dance even though her vision was steady.

"Like a rosé *gingembre*? With one of these little umbrellas?"

The older bartender, double jowled and smiling, reached for a glass holding pastel paper umbrellas by the lemon slices.

Tempted, she grinned. "A double espresso, *s'il vous plaît*."

"Ah, you're working?"

Did he think she was a hooker? She nodded and slapped several euros on the zinc counter. "It's not what you think. But maybe you could help me."

"*À votre servis*," he said.

He knocked the grinds into the bin with several loud thwacks, filled coffee grounds into the portafilter and leveled it. Once inserted, he pushed the worn button on the high-end coffee machine, and it thrummed to life.

Getting to the point would cut time.

"Were you working last night?" she said. "When the championship was on?"

"My night off," he said. "Why?"

"Wondered if you remember where you were."

"I do remember. We saw a film at the mk2 cinema—you know, they show old movies—and walked home down the quai. My wife loves Cary Grant."

"Walked home? You live nearby?"

"My uncle owned this bistro. I've worked here since I left school. Now I'm semi-retired and his grandson runs it."

"I don't mean to pry, but . . ."

"You a *flic?*"

Smart.

"Close enough. *Détective privé.*"

She flashed a megawatt smile as he set down the steaming espresso in a turquoise demitasse. Then she sipped and leaned closer.

"This involves a messy divorce case. Remind me never to take one of these on again."

"*Et alors*, divorce? That's no big deal these days."

Didn't miss a trick, this one.

"When it's tied up with money and inheritance, it is," she said. "Sticky and litigious."

"What do you want to know?"

Maybe he'd seen something. Or not. But he could have acute observations.

"My job's canvassing the streets and hotels, and mostly boring surveillance. I wonder if you noticed anything last night around eleven. Or if you heard something. It's about verifying a detail the subject's adamant about."

"What?"

She shrugged. "Afraid I can't say, but . . ."

"I understand. The *flics* said the same thing."

"The *flics?*" she said, alert. Was he onto her?

The waitress shouted out, "*Un* Campari soda, *deux* Limoncellos," and rang up the drinks on the cash register. Aimée waited as the bartender shook ice and mixed drinks, filling the waitress's order, and set them on the zinc counter. The pastel glasses were dusted in the pale vanilla afternoon light.

"I thought you said you were off last night," she said when he put down the last one. "Why were you talking to the *flics?*"

"The *flics* were questioning people on the quai," he said.

Interested, she leaned forward and drained her espresso. "*Vraiment?*" she asked, her tone encouraging.

"We live in the building across the street. I couldn't see from our window, but my neighbor on the fifth floor saw something and told me this morning."

"What did he see? Maybe I should talk to him."

"He was headed to the airport. Majorca, his annual holiday. He won't answer his phone."

A possible lead gone.

"Can you remember what he said?"

"Well, he wondered why the *flics* were milling on the quai, yet on rue Tandou there had been a fight. None of the *flics* responded to it that he saw."

"Rue Tandou?"

Had she scoped that street out? Walked along it? Why couldn't she recall it?

"Just over there. Parallel to the quai. I don't know if that helps, but you're not saying much."

"Sorry to be vague, but I don't want to influence you. Did he say where?"

Tuesday • Midday • Rue Tandou

AIMÉE FOUND THE corner of rue Tandou and rue de Crimée. She stood and looked around: a café, a discount clothing shop and a florist, all closed and shuttered. Two bars across from each other were open, and people sat at tables on the sidewalk, smoking and laughing, a few bundled under tall heat lamps. The bar closest to the canal sent an edgy vibe with a few biker wannabe types.

It gave her an idea. She found the hopefully still-secure burner phone and hit Isabelle's preprogrammed number.

"Oui?"

"Isabelle. I'm at le Provins bar at rue Tandou. Lots of wannabes here . . ."

"You all right, Aimée?"

"Fine. But I could use backup."

"What kind?"

"Like a biker you trust?"

"Give me the specifics and the situation," said Isabelle.

"You sound so businesslike."

Isabelle snorted. "Have to be with these *mecs.* Or it'll be mayhem."

Aimée outlined her idea.

"Make sense?"

"You want to know about a fight that night—who saw what

and when, who got involved and what else they noticed? The same from the café across the street, *non*? If that covers it, I'd suggest you leave."

Good idea.

Down the shadowed street, she rang René. She hated involving him but he'd be back in Paris by now, and she needed all the help she could get.

The rising wind gusted at her ankles. Made her shiver. At least her vision held out.

She let it ring three times—their signal—then hung up.

For now she headed to the bistro near the mk2 movie theater on the water's glass-like surface at Bassin de la Villette before the Metro Stalingrad. The area had cleaned up after the cinema came in, but drug deals still happened. She went to the old pay phone downstairs by the WCs and gave it another minute.

Five minutes later exactly, she called the number of the pay phone in the café across from René's apartment on rue du Renard and prayed the owner would answer.

"Bonsoir, Maxim," she said. "Is my friend around?"

Via this prearranged signal, Maxim, whose name was really Charlot, handed the phone over.

"Where are you?" asked René.

"Is this still secure?"

"So far."

Aimée read him the public pay phone's number.

"Don't you have a burner?"

She gave him that number. "Listen, René . . ."

"Wait, I can't hear. And this is too public. I might be seen. I'll call you from downstairs. Public phone to public phone."

Good thinking. But it worried her. He must sense he was being watched.

Guilt hit her for leaving the business all on René's shoulders. She dumped emergencies on her partner too often. It wasn't fair, as he frequently reminded her.

Thank God Saj, their permanent part-time hacker, was back from his ashram trip in India. He worked the monthly data surveillance, monitored the contracts and took a big load of their work.

As she waited for René, she stared at the diagram she'd made, the streets radiating from the bridge where Melac had been killed. All of this felt useless. She didn't even know what she was looking for.

Would the bikers find out anything? Frustration dogged her.

Who would want to kill Melac?

Could it be fallout from an old case? Revenge? A stalker after him from his counterterrorism days?

It didn't have to harken back to the past. She couldn't discount a current case he'd been working on.

She needed René to hack into Melac's business laptop.

Wait a minute. She'd missed something.

"René, René . . ."

Why hadn't she remembered sooner? Now she'd need to wait for his call back.

But the low, dull headache had burst into a splitting throb. Like a knife. She'd overdone it.

Her burner phone buzzed. Isabelle.

"We need to talk."

Uneasy, Aimée said, "I'm listening."

"There's something you need to see. Now. It's an emergency," said Isabelle.

Great.

Apologizing internally to René for leaving him hanging, Aimée left up the stairs.

AIMÉE HAILED A taxi and gave the address of the tattoo shop.

"You sure about that?" asked the taxi driver. "The quartier's a biker hub. Heavy duty. There're rumors."

A busybody. But maybe she could learn the "lowdown."

"Rumors?"

"Better be careful," he said.

"Careful of what?"

"Gangbangers," he said. "They assault women."

She swallowed hard.

"I thought they maintained order in the quartier. Protected the neighborhood."

"At a price. *Mais oui*, the *flics* don't respond, so it's better than nothing. I live down the street, and one time my apartment building had squatters camping in our courtyard."

"What happened?"

"I had enough. After three weeks of the squatters, you know . . . I did feel bad, but our building got together and called the Angels. They took care of it and we paid them. No more break-ins or squatters. But we keep our daughters and wives out of it and make sure they use the back exit to leave the building."

"I don't get it."

"It's a double-edged sword, *compris*? So I watch out."

She believed him. And she needed something for her head.

"*Merci*," she said, Then tipped him and took his card.

INSIDE THE BIKER tattoo bar, she passed a stocky pale man in a barber's chair. One arm was getting inked, and his other hand held a beer. The electric black-handled tattoo gun whirred. Beside it sat the old generator she figured they kept around for electrical shortages due to the ancient wiring.

The smell of the blood dripping off the man's large shoulder design nauseated her. She couldn't believe how stoic this *mec* was.

She kept going toward the back.

"Blondie," said a voice. "We've got company."

All of a sudden, a blond biker with a thin mean face blocked her way.

"What are you doing back here?"

His attitude needed adjusting.

"Where's Isabelle?"

"Who's asking?"

"Aimée. Isabelle said it's important. That I need to see something."

It was as if she'd stuck a pin in Blondie and all the hot air dispersed—his abrasive aura and aggressive stance were gone.

"Ah, we've been waiting for you." He jerked his head toward a back room. "This way," he said.

She followed and saw Isabelle on the phone. She clicked off. Her usual sarcastic grin was replaced by a frown.

"The *flics* paid a visit, Aimée."

To find her? *Don't panic. Think.*

"What did they say? Did they give a reason?"

"Public safety." Isabelle gave an eye roll. "Whatever that means."

With the *flics* sniffing around, of course the Angels were touchy and paranoid—who wouldn't be with cartons of illegal cigarettes, perfume and who knows what other contraband to the tune of hundreds of thousands of euros hidden in plain sight?

But instead of saying that, Aimée shrugged. "Did you forget to pay a parking meter?"

Stupid. Too flippant.

Several bikers had silently filtered in to this back room.

"We think you know why," said Blondie.

"*Moi?* You think I invited the *flics?* You all know I'm on the run. A fugitive."

Isabelle had told them she was off-limits. Hadn't she?

She took a breath. Wishing she had an aspirin, she spoke slowly.

"How would it make sense for me to bring them here?" She shook her head, wincing. "It was one of you who brought them here," she said. "Or a crime you committed."

They looked at her, then one another. Blondie spoke up. "Of course you'd say that."

She looked over the hostile faces who she'd wished were on her side. Her legs trembled. Things got hazy. She blinked.

She stared at Isabelle until her gaze cleared. She felt sad. "Sorry, Isabelle. You're a friend to me and to my cousin. Friendship goes both ways, eh? I know you've been trying to give back. But it seems it's not working out. I'm leaving."

Before Blondie could push Aimée to the exit, Isabelle grabbed his arm. "Wait. I told you, I owe her. Without her backing, Luca can't get the help he needs. You'll remember this or get out." Isabelle stared around the room at the bikers. "Understand?"

The room spun before Aimée. Nothing remained still. Her brain hurt. She closed her eyes. And then she was falling.

The last thing she heard was "You know what to do with her."

AIMÉE BLINKED. WHERE was she, and was she in danger? Had the hostile bikers revolted against Isabelle?

Her hazy vision cleared, revealing a small studio. She felt a slobbered kiss on her cheeks. Then another.

That sweet smell. That soft skin.

It was Chloé. Joy and relief filled her. How in the world had her daughter gotten here? She was sitting next to Sébastien's son, Gil, and they were laughing.

Aimée grabbed Chloé and smothered her in kisses.

"*Maman*, you make noises when you sleep," Chloé said when Aimée let her come up for air.

"Like this." Sébastien sat on the bed and snorted like a pig. "And this." Suddenly they were all laughing and rocking the bed. The jumping around didn't help the dull ache in her head. But it didn't matter.

"How did I get here?"

"Isabelle called. We're here for you, *ma cousine*."

The danger and the fear fell away. It was like shedding dead skin. Lightness filled her. Her daughter was happy and safe. Aimée's vision had cleared and Sébastien was there to help.

But one glance from him, a side-eye look, brought her back to earth. Sébastien's wife, Regula, was beckoning them from the kitchen.

"*À table, mes enfants*," she said.

"*Tante* Regula's going to feed you animals and then take you to the playground," Sébastien said.

Aimée hugged Chloé, and said, "I missed you, *ma puce*."

"I missed you, too, *Maman*."

Chloé waved a crayoned drawing.

"I drew a picture for Papa."

Aimée's heart tore. Melac was gone. How could she manage?

"Wonderful," she said, battling tears.

Suddenly Sébastien was tickling behind Chloé's knee, then lifting her onto his shoulders.

"Let *Maman* rest, okay?"

A warm feeling enveloped her as she drifted into a light sleep. She did have family, people she could rely on.

But she couldn't put them in danger. Sébastien had his own family and a successful business, people who depended on him for their jobs. She was proud to bits of him.

Nothing could jeopardize any of it.

Once Sébastien had seen the kids off with Regula to the play-ground, he returned to the loft, his smile gone. "Aimée. Regula and I support you, of course, but you can't stay here."

"Did I ask to come here?"

Why was she snapping at him?

"I'm sorry, Sébastien," she said. "You're right."

"Isabelle's worried." His mouth pursed. He was worried, too. "The gang's nervous because of the *flics* . . ."

"That's on them, not me. They break the law, you know."

"Eh, *alors*! I'm working on another place, a job site." Sébastien looked down. She remembered Sébastien did that when he was ashamed. Or guilty. "It's going to be vacant at night, so you could stay there. I don't know for how long." He wrote down the address for her. "But don't get mad."

Now prickles went up her spine.

"What's the matter?" she asked.

"*Zut*, you passed out. Scared everyone. You weren't coming to, so Isabelle brought you here. And . . . I called a doctor." He felt her forehead. "You're warm. The doctor will be here soon."

Aimée batted his hand away, alarmed. "What doctor? No one can know I'm here."

"A specialist."

"That's too dangerous, Sébastien. You know I'm on the run."

"What else is new, Aimée?" he said, severely and dryly at the same time. "After your past trouble, your eyes need care. Get with reality. You need to rest and recuperate like you did last time."

How was she supposed to rest when she had the police and maybe a killer hunting her? When she had a toddler to care for, a toddler who had just lost her father?

Sébastien meant well, but they were in danger. All of them.

Footsteps came from the narrow staircase leading to the loft. A nurse practitioner whom Aimée remembered from the vision clinic at Centre Hospitalier Quinze-Vingts smiled.

"Already you're better, *non*?" said the nurse. "You're seeing me and grinning."

How had Sébastien pulled off a house call this quickly?

"Isn't the doctor coming?" asked Sébastien.

"In surgery. But this stays confidential, as you requested. You're a client, okay? We work in a private practice and consult nearby at Hospital Rothschild."

A renowned eye hospital in the nineteenth.

"Maybe you remember my boss, Guy Lambert," she said to Aimée.

"He's back from Afrique?"

"Several years now. He's married, lives in the sixteenth and has a *bébé* on the way."

That had almost been her life.

"Tell him congratulations! Look, you didn't need to come all this way . . ." Where was she? She hadn't even been to this new place of Sébastien's. He seemed to buy, renovate and move all the time. Or to be doing it for someone else.

"You're still our patient," the nurse said, in that comforting way she had. Her buttermilk complexion and pale blue eyes were offset by the large dark-pink birthmark on her neck. "Always. Even though you ran out of the clinic."

Word got around.

"After I examine you, I'll report back to him and he can diagnose, prescribe. All clients' records are confidential."

The nurse opened her bag, took out her instruments and began the examination.

"My eyes are so much better."

"Any double vision?"

"Some. The haziness and dizziness are gone." Aimée struggled to sit up. "I'm fine."

"Those are signs of your eyes telling you they need rest. Rest, Aimée. The headaches indicate ocular migraines. Effects of your recent concussion. The headaches can come on any time at all, but especially when you have stress or injury. Best to nip them in the bud right away—close your eyes and rest them. A simple ice pack on the temple does wonders."

BUT SHE DIDN'T rest in a dark room. Instead, she went to interview the *Le Parisien* reporter Emile had mentioned, Jacquot Devries. No time to waste. As soon as Sébastien had left for a job site, she headed out.

Jacquot Devries had covered *faits divers*, the crime beat, for more than sixteen years. According to Emile, he'd quit the paper and written a true crime book about crimes he covered in the nineteenth.

After several calls, he'd finally answered and given her his address, beyond the hilly Parc des Buttes-Chaumont and with no Metro nearby. A hike.

His tall pale-brick building, built in the 1920s as social housing, straddled the sloping Parc de la Butte du Chapeau Rouge. A funny name for a quiet enclave on a sloping park with a view of the *périphérique* ring road and the world-renowned Robert Debré children's hospital specializing in neuro-pediatrics. She got a family vibe in this *mixte* quartier with a blend of bougie types, working class and the occasional gray long hair who hadn't left the sixties and was still walking around in sandals and socks.

In the pale sunlight, she crossed the park up a steep path, inhaling the damp grass smells and double knotting her scarf in the brisk air.

Jacquot Devries greeted her at his door. He wore a track suit and stood on crutches, a plaster cast on his leg. He was in his early forties, with thick longish black hair streaked with gray, and large eyes behind his wire-framed glasses. At his side, a growling caramel Rottweiler.

"You're the one who called?"

Aimée handed him her card. The last one left from her go bag. He recognized her name and pocketed the card.

"We talk on the condition you keep my location to yourself. *Compris?*"

Aimée nodded.

"Shhh, Bette."

Instantly the Rottweiler quieted.

"Let's make this quick."

"*Bien sûr,*" she said. But she had no intention of leaving without information. It had taken her ages to get here, and she wouldn't leave "quick."

She followed him on his crutches into a study with floor-to-ceiling bookshelves and an architect's drawing table functioning as a desk. The smell of paper and wet dog clung to the room.

The panoramic view of northeastern Paris, la Villette and beyond bathed the room in sunshine. Sacré-Coeur's pearl dome was incandescent. She could lose herself watching the ever-changing play of light, but she wasn't here for that.

Devries leaned his crutches against the wall and lowered himself to a chair with a grunt, hoisting his leg onto a stained ottoman. Irritated, he checked his phone. The dog found her floor pillow and lay beside him. He indicated Aimée sit on a wicker chair, then pointed to his broken leg.

"Skiing for the first and last time," he said, matter-of-factly.

"I'm sorry," she said, not knowing what else to say.

"Don't be," he said. "Save your sympathy. I get my cast off this week. Eh, Bette, but we still take walks every day."

The Rottweiler looked up, devotion in her eyes. A pang hit Aimée as she thought of Miles Davis, her Bichon Frisé. She missed every bit of his fur-ball self.

Down to business.

"*Bon*," she said. "From your byline, Monsieur Devries, I saw you're the expert on crime in the nineteenth."

"Born and bred here."

She was trying to ease into this. Emile had told her Jacquot was touchy and to go slow if she wanted anything from him.

"Your early article on the tragic school fire impressed me," Aimée said, wanting to get him talking.

"Eh, I was a rookie, a cub reporter. It's where everyone starts. Me, I was just accompanying the assigned reporter who rotated shifts. Our first callout was to cover this fire as possible arson. But it got personal."

"How's that?"

His expressionless face became charged with emotion.

"A little boy who lived in our passage off rue d'Hautpoul burned to death in the fire. My mother often babysat him. I was much older and didn't know him well. They eventually proved it was arson."

He took a pencil and scratched under his cast.

Aimée could imagine the family's pain. "Horrible."

"Tragic," he said. "This reporter I worked with got transferred, and I lobbied to get his job reporting the crime *faits divers*."

"And they hired you," said Aimée. She tried to stifle her impatience. "So this fire inspired you to continue reporting on the crime beat?"

"Got it in one."

A gauzelike veil descended over her vision. A warning she'd overdone it. *Merde.*

She closed her eyes, letting his words drift, and took deep breaths. His voice continued.

"We lived in a two-story workers' house by small warehouses, and at the end was the cemetery de la Villette. The little boy's family lived next door to us."

The sound of a big dog yawn came from Bette.

"They buried him in this cemetery. His parents would say they'd see him every day from the window, and constantly left flowers. People don't forget."

People don't forget.

Jacquot continued telling her painful details about the little boy he'd known while Aimée, guilty, tried not to fall asleep . . .

"Are you listening or sleeping?"

Her eyes snapped open. Everything was clear. Brilliant and shining.

Thank God.

"Every word," she said, ad-libbing. "It helps me concentrate. But there's more to tell me, isn't there?"

"More?" He smiled, warming up. "You mean why I quit my job and write books?"

Time to get to the point. Throw out a theory.

"I mean about *le Balafré.*"

His shoulders stiffened.

"It's rumored this serial killer's back and involved in the *ex-flic's* murder on the canal."

Then Jacquot was standing up. Not easy with his stiff cast, but he seemed determined. His jaw was set, lips in a thin line. He held the chair armrest and pointed with his other hand. Bette stirred. "Out." His mood was like a cold wind. "Your time's up."

Why had he changed all of a sudden?

Bette started barking.

"Wait a minute, monsieur, what happened? What do you know about this?"

"I don't give a damn anymore."

What an about-face.

"According to your articles, you were one of the first on the scene of *le Balafré*'s first murder. Little Carine on rue Petit."

"*Alors*, that was just another chance. Listen, it's late and time for me to take the dog out."

"But you do care. I read your articles." She'd only scanned a few but had read enough to notice his byline and his fixation on *le Balafré*. "You kept pushing the investigation."

"Mademoiselle, I got paid for that. Will you pay me for my time?"

Hesitant, she grew aware of Bette's whining. The dog needed to go out. If he left, she had nothing.

"I could."

"Thousand euros."

"Do you really have information that involves the murder of the man killed on the canal?"

"*Zut*, I won't give you anything until I see the money in my hand. In old francs, it's more than seven thousand."

Like she cared?

"But I don't have that kind of money."

He took her card from his pocket and nodded.

"I've read about you. The *flics* hate you."

"Is that a problem?"

"You're a notorious lawbreaker and you live on Île Saint-Louis. Don't tell me you don't have it."

He rubbed thumb and pointer finger together. Money.

"I work for every *centime*—"

"And your midget partner's been in the paper, too. He's like a little rat climbing out of your shoes."

He was trying to rile her. She wondered why.

"Look, I know you care deep down, even though you're acting like a *salopard*. You pushed for the stories about those local tragedies."

"Like I said, I was paid for that."

"A cynic knows the price of everything and the value of nothing."

"That's a good line. Did you make that up?"

"Oscar Wilde did. But you're not a cynic." She stood and handed him what little money she had left. "That's all I have. Take it. My daughter's father was the man murdered on the canal. I'm being framed for it. I need your help and I'm not leaving until you tell me what you know."

He thought. Then scratched under his cast again with the pencil. "Do you have any association with the Angels, the bikers on the canal?"

Where had that come from?

"Why?"

Maybe she should leave. Maybe he had changed. Maybe he'd sell her out to *les gangs*—or *les flics*.

"I'm a reporter. I need details for an article I'm writing on them, and . . ." He slid her coins and few notes back in her hand. "Maybe we can help each other out."

He sat back down.

Give up Isabelle, who was struggling to support her brother? Ruin her business? Jacquot Devries had something up his sleeve.

"You first."

Tuesday Afternoon • Buttes Bergeyre

"MY FIRST HEADLINE article. Sick, when I think about it,"
said Jacquot Devries. "But I literally was one of the first on the
scene, even before the *flics*."

"How did you manage that?"

"Every day I swam at the Olympic-size pool on rue Edouard
Pailleron, then walked on rue Petit to the newspaper."

"What do you mean? Isn't *Le Parisien* at—"

"My office moved all over," he interrupted. "If you write
about crime, you stand by, hang out at the fire stations, the
commissariat, hospitals, find sources at the café and bars. But
then I'd head to our temporary—they were always temporary—
crime office near the old printing site."

Brilliant.

"You saw him? *Le Balafré?*"

"Just missed him."

"Tell me about it."

Jacquot Devries had heard sirens and had seen a tear-stained
woman, Carine's mother, in front of the apartment building.
Curious, and armed with first aid skills and a reporter's instinct,
he followed several tenants to the cellar and lower laundry room.
That's when he saw Carine on the damp concrete, her wrists
tied by wire as if in prayer. Another wire, noose-like around
her throat, dug into her neck. Since she was tied with wire and

trussed into a kneeling position, for a moment he'd thought she'd committed suicide by strangling herself.

Hideous.

"The killer was never identified, right? There was never a suspect arrested? Then why did the killer get the nickname?"

"*Le Balafré*, pockmark? Carine's brother thought he'd talked to the killer in the elevator the night before."

The hair rippled on the back of her arm. An eyewitness. Yet she'd seen no previous mention of this. "Her brother spoke with the killer? How did he know?"

"He told me there was this *mec* who seemed kind of stiff and odd to him in the elevator. This man didn't seem like a tenant, and he'd never seen him before. Back then you knew the fellow tenants in the building even if only to say bonjour. But he tried to be polite and said, 'Have a *bon soir*, monsieur.' The *mec* replied, 'I will, and *you* have a very good night.'"

Odd.

"So the *flics* knew?"

"At the time? I don't know. He was in shock," Jacquot said. "The kid told me two days later. He said there was a *mec* in the elevator, that's all he remembered. So many people used the elevator. This man had scars like he'd had acne. But the brother had no idea who he could have been or if that was the killer, even. It turns out the girl was going to a party. When her mother called from her night job to check if she'd come home, no answer. This was their routine since the mother left for work at night. But she hadn't turned up at the party, either."

Horrendous, but how did this link, if it did, to Melac? "You wrote that there were eight victims between 1986 and 1994 with the killer's signature."

A nod. "Early on, one girl got away. She remembered how he'd whipped out the wire—like she'd read in my articles—and got a brief glimpse of his face pitted with acne scars. The name *le Balafré* kept popping up."

He took a moment to reflect. "The police confirmed eight, but I always suspected more. And he went against type."

"How do you mean? Didn't he go after teenage girls?"

"You didn't read my book, did you? His next victim was a seventy-five-year-old woman who was found in her apartment building cellar strangled by wire cord, hands bound in prayer. He used the same signature. Raped, posed in prayer and strangled with a common electric wire. For several years his victims alternated: another sixteen-year-old, a woman in her seventies— all in the nineteenth arrondissement."

"So he alternated between attacking young and old women? Did a pattern form?"

Jacquot shrugged. "He was a sicko, all right. But his kills slowed down in 1990, then the last-known victim was in 1994. After that, nothing else."

Done and dusted, then. No connection to Melac's killer. Unless . . .

Her father always said: Ask questions, even ones you think stupid. No question is stupid.

"Do you believe this recent murder was the work of *le Balafré?*"

"Buy my book."

Anything for a euro these days!

"I have," she lied. "But I want it from you. Personally. Not a plea for action, or a crusade like some of your pieces are."

"Straight talker. I like that."

Jacquot Devries heaved himself up again and gripped his crutches. There were no carpets in his apartment, and the parquet floor had visible grooves worn into it from generations of use. He gestured her to the window and handed her a pair of well-worn binoculars with premium-quality Zeiss Ikon lenses.

Aimée held them, remembering. "My grandfather had a pair like these."

"They're the best quality you can find."

Knowing her *grand-père*, he'd probably found them at Drouot auction house. He'd known the auction stewards by name and had decorated the Île Saint-Louis apartment she'd inherited with treasures, albeit dusty and worn.

She lifted the binoculars and focused on the quai de la Loire to see if it was visible from here.

A building stood in the way.

"What should I be looking at?"

"Focus on rue Petit."

She tried to figure out where it would be, scanning the tops of gray slate-tiled roofs, pepper-pot chimneys and trees finally sprouting spring leaves. A few chestnut trees dotted by white flowers.

"Pick out the cemetery de la Villette and veer right until you hit the first tree-lined square—then turn right again before the fat, angled boulevard."

"What am I looking for?"

He described an ugly sixties pinkish housing block on the south side with its back to them. "All you'll see is the decrepit back wall. The staircase in the rear leads to the basement. Where she was raped and murdered in the laundry room. The *flics* think he left by the rear and out the back of the building. That theory's generally accepted."

"But what about the brother's observation of the man in the elevator?"

"The brother saw him leave the elevator and head in that direction instead of going out front. He remembers that."

"Were there ever any sightings of him after that? Other witnesses?"

Devries shook his head, then shrugged. "Like I said, after some years, the murders stopped. When that happens, it's usually due to the perp being in prison or dead."

"What did you think?"

"At the time, I figured his life had gotten complicated and he maybe had a family, but I didn't think he'd stop forever. It was just a feeling."

"And now?"

"Someone asked me this the other day."

Aimée felt a chill up her spine.

"Who?"

"Not part of our agreement." Devries stretched his arms out and then over his head. "Let me show you something."

He gestured to a map on the wall. Aimée hadn't paid much attention to it.

"Stand back and look to see if you recognize a pattern."

She stepped back and closed her eyes for a moment, let a calmness fill her.

She opened her eyes. Thirty seconds later she saw it.

"I'm looking at a star shape, right?"

"That, too. The six points of the star are criminal locations attributed to *le Balafré*."

Kill sites. Eerie. Was this reporter living in la-la land up here in the clouds with his binoculars? Spinning conspiracy theories from his high-top aerie?

But she humored him, looking closer. Then picked up the magnifying glass on the table.

"Was it an *ex-flic* who came around asking you for info?" she tried.

He shook his head. "It was a kid. I won't say any more. I'm a reporter and protect my sources."

"Got a copy of your latest article?"

He grinned. "It's on my website."

Like she could print that out on the run?

"How about you print it for me."

He did.

"You owe me big-time. Let me call you and we'll meet later in Parc des Buttes-Chaumont, and I'll . . ."

"You'll what?"

"Tell you more. And you'll tell me about the Angels."

Ten minutes later, she'd left his apartment and was sitting in the nearby park reading his latest article.

Her burner phone rang. Only two people had this number.

Tuesday Afternoon • Butte Bergeyre

"AIMÉE?"

She would know that voice anywhere.

"René, thank God," she said. "So sorry I left you hanging earlier—I had to move. You're not at the office, are you?"

"Think I'm stupid? Listen, there're more important things to figure out. Where are you?"

"Not on the phone, René." She paused. "I can't wrap my head around what's happened. Melac's gone. We had our disagreements, but he's still Chloé's father."

René exhaled a long breath. Something he did when frustrated.

"Get real, Aimée," said René, over the staticky line. "Did you even know Melac?"

Could you really know anyone?

"What do you mean, René? What are you implying?"

She heard a scraping noise and what sounded like a door closing.

"You'll work it out," said René. "Melac lived several lives. Working undercover, working homicide and counterterrorism . . . Do you even know which of those personas was real?"

Not this again. Not now.

"He's dead, René."

"And you're being framed for it," said René, frustrated. "With him it was always one problem after the other." A pause. "Or did it even matter? As long as he's a *flic*."

That stung. René meant well but it came out harsh.

But he was right. Why did she have to be attracted to this type? Look where it had gotten her.

Why couldn't she have been satisfied with the eye doctor, with throwing luncheons in Neuilly? Was she always looking for her father, searching for a man who would measure up to him?

René was talking.

"We have to figure out if Melac was targeted because of a past case."

"True," Aimée said. "Maybe it was revenge for some case he worked when he was in Homicide. Still, I was set up, René. That takes planning and forethought."

"Or the killer thinks on his feet. He's agile. Took advantage of the situation, and framing you was the bonus."

"Possibly, but he knew who I was."

"Hadn't Melac been hounding you? If he'd trailed Melac, he might have overheard . . ." René sounded unsure. "Maybe it's a stretch. But the *flics* know about your fights, don't they? Whoever the killer is, why wouldn't he know about you if Melac was his target?"

Made sense. "Good point, René. Melac said he'd seen a ghost." Aimée lowered her voice, feeling a little silly even for bringing it up, but she'd come too far to give up on this theory now. "I'm wondering if it might be a serial killer who's been on the loose since the eighties."

"A serial killer? Now I'm intrigued."

"You're the crime junkie. Ever hear of *le Balafré*? Every person I've talked to in the quartier has brought up *le Balafré*, that serial killer who was targeting girls and grandmothers in the nineteenth back when we were teenagers."

"*Alors*, unless *le Balafré* targets male *ex-flics*, that's not a realistic theory. Serial killers have signatures. Rituals. Aimée, Melac would have been young when *le Balafré* was at work, years away from being on the force." A long sigh. "*Quel méli-mélo*, what a mess, Aimée."

"Like I don't know that."

All this talk got her nowhere closer to finding the killer and proving her innocence. Nowhere closer to Chloé, whom she missed so much.

"Remember your own advice. You need to get into the mind of the criminal."

"My father always said that."

She rubbed her pounding temples—kept a circular motion with her fingers, as the clinician had taught her. Still, she needed to pop another Doliprane—her headache was killing her.

"Use what you know," said René. "That's what you always tell me. Melac thought he'd seen a ghost. What does that mean? A man dead to him. The ghost doesn't want to be discovered, so Melac had to be eliminated."

Made sense.

"I need to filter through all his past cases."

She heard the unbuckling of René's briefcase and the rustling of papers. "Halfway done."

"*Mon Dieu!*"

"It's a quick recap from his computer files. You remember that time we hacked him."

A twinge of shame. They'd hacked into his files and installed a tracer a couple of years ago when Melac had gotten married. Aimée'd never dumped the files René had copied for her. Or removed the tracer.

Why hadn't she thought of that before? Her temples throbbed.

"You're a genius, René."

"The case files I saw all seem pretty mundane—at least the ones he entered into his computer. That's the bad news. But sift through and you might see a clue. Or ask his former colleagues and keep it on the down-low."

The shifting barge rubbed the embankment, buffeted by a passing boat's rippling current. A dim light shone on the quai. What was she missing?

"It's a ghost come back to life," she said. "I need to find whoever that is."

AIMÉE SLUNG THE bag with her newly purchased burner phones over her shoulder. They presented a new set of problems. Few people answered their phone these days if they didn't recognize the number. And texting left a record.

Thank God the Doliprane had numbed her headache to a low murmur. Bone-tired, she was running on adrenaline. Not like she had the choice to rest, what with a killer out there and her a fugitive.

After catching a bus to the Left Bank, she'd located the Saint-Germain apartment of Suzanne Lessage, Melac's former colleague on the counterterrorism squad. Her husband, Paul, was Melac's sailing partner. Or had been.

Aimée had seen them at dinner in Brittany several months ago. She and Suzanne weren't close. Never had been. But they shared favors.

And she needed one now.

She stood in the doorway across from their building on rue Visconti, a narrow fifteenth-century street on the Left Bank where they'd moved early last year. Melac crashed there from time to time.

Her heart slowed. She was thinking of Melac in the present. In the now.

No lights shone in the windows of the street-facing apartment on the third floor. She punched Suzanne's number into one of her burners. It rang several times before it cut to voice mail.

"It's Aimée. I need to talk. Please answer."

She clicked off.

Waited.

Three minutes turned to five, then to ten and fifteen. She pulled her leather jacket tighter against the damp evening chill. Her outfit came courtesy of Regula's armoire: silk tank under a cropped cashmere sweater and chic *maman* jeans blended in with the quartier. Just as she was about to call again, a taxi pulled up in front of the building.

Aimée waited. She watched the woman pay the taxi driver and then get out of the car. Blond, tall, slim and wearing a long cream cardigan. Suzanne. She had her arm around a sleepy adolescent whom Aimée recognized as her daughter.

She had to act now. It was a terrible time to intrude, but if Suzanne didn't answer her calls, Aimée didn't know what else to try.

Suzanne was punching in the door code with one hand and supporting her daughter with her other.

Now.

"Let me get that."

Aimée pushed one side of the large green double door open.

The *merci* died on Suzanne's lips.

"Don't call me," she said, under her breath. "You need to leave."

The teenager, Mado, squealed. "Aimée, where've you been?"

"It's late, Mado," said her mother, her voice calm. She shot daggers from her eyes and jerked her head for Aimée to leave. "Aimée's just . . ."

"Having a quick word with your mom. It's an emergency, like always." She grinned, hoping it looked sheepish.

Mado threw her arms around Aimée. "*Fantastique!* I love that lipstick and want to show you my new one."

Suzanne's lips pursed.

"Another time, Mado. It's a school night. You'll march right to bed."

As they climbed the stairs, Aimée stewed in guilt. She was ashamed to have intruded.

But again, if she didn't talk to Suzanne, she wouldn't know anything. Any chance Aimée had to narrow in on Melac's killer, she had to take.

Suzanne indicated for Aimée to wait in the foyer while she saw Mado to bed.

From the foyer, a large white entryway with black and white diagonal tiles, Aimée could see practically the whole apartment. The foyer led to an open-plan living area lined with full book-shelves, plants in pots, rattan furniture, white couches littered with magazines and soft pillows and plush mohair throws. From there, the room spilled into a dining area and a kitchen, full of state-of-the-art steel appliances.

Like a spread out of *ELLE DECOR*.

Aimée wondered how they could afford this—Suzanne now worked part-time in Ministry admin, a desk job—a demotion, yet still a *fonctionnaire*. Together with Paul, an attorney, they somehow bankrolled the designer flat in Saint-Germain. Or maybe they'd come into family money.

She must have an army of cleaners and au pairs.

Aimée recognized the framed photo on a side table, matching the one Melac had at his farm: Suzanne, Paul and Melac on the bow of their boat in Brittany. Their wind-tossed hair, wide grins and blue windbreakers amid rolling waves spoke of a happy time.

By the photo, Aimée saw a pill bottle, a carafe and a glass.

Suzanne returned to the foyer, looking wary.

"I'll give you one minute. Then you get out."

"You owe me, Suzanne. Remember?"

Suzanne's shoulders stiffened.

"I've moved on," she said, "and so should you."

Aimée wasn't sure what that meant. But Suzanne was right to be angry. Aimée had barged her way in, had used Suzanne's daughter's innocence—*oui*, she'd feel the same.

"Melac's murder has gutted me. I don't know how to tell Chloé, or what to do except prove my innocence. That means finding his killer."

"Your minute's up."

Suzanne picked up her bag and took out her phone.

Serious. She was serious.

"Suzanne, you know me. You can't think that I did this."

"Aimée, *you* know *me*." Suzanne's voice rose. "Can't think I'd be friends with someone who'd leave her child's father for his colleague and throw it in his face."

"What?"

"Melac came here every night. We saw what you did to him. He would drink, cry. In the end, Paul, his best friend, had to kick him out. He was frightening the girls."

Aimée, shocked, tried to picture the Melac she knew falling apart. "I had no idea."

"Liar."

"First I've heard of this, Suzanne. But I don't want to argue."

"As parents, you had a responsibility to make things work. Every family does, or it ruins the children's lives."

Aimée bristled. *Family counseling now?*

"You're forgetting that Melac left before Chloé was born. Fine, he wasn't ready to parent. I raised her."

"Are you going to tell me something new?" Suzanne's brittle tone could have refrozen a melting icicle.

"Melac was a good father," Aimée said quickly. "The best. On his terms: on his farm, on his timeline and within his work life. And then when it wasn't on his terms, he was terrible. When I didn't move to Brittany with him, he kidnapped Chloé."

She bit her tongue and took a breath, catching the scent of potpourri.

"That's not why I'm here. I'm here because he tried to tell me something right before he was killed."

"If only you'd listened," Suzanne said. "He was trying to open communications to work on your relationship."

The relationship had been long past saving.

"That, too. But you have to hear the last thing he said."

"You better leave. I shouldn't even have let you in. Melac had his faults, but we made a team. We always had each other's back."

The old brotherhood.

"Then have his back now." Exasperated, she tried to keep her impatience in check. Suzanne wouldn't listen unless Aimée appealed to their bond. "You knew him, Suzanne. Really knew him. I have to know what you think." The front door opened. Footsteps trailed to the back of the house. Paul?

Suzanne hesitated.

"If this will make you leave faster, tell me and then get the hell out."

Aimée looked longingly at that white sofa, wishing she could lie down and sleep until morning, wake up to a *café au lait* with Mado before school like they had when she . . .

"Hurry, I'm tired. I got stuck in court all day."

Aimée found Melac's voice mail, then increased the volume with the side button and hit play.

"Aimée . . . I've just seen a ghost."

Aimée tried to read Suzanne's eyes. Was that a flicker of a change of expression?

"*Et alors?*" said Suzanne.

"Who does he mean by *ghost*?"

"No idea." Suzanne shrugged. "You've overstayed your welcome."

Those counterterrorist teams took their secrets to the grave. Or boasted they did.

"Out."

With that, she pushed Aimée out the door. No doubt she wanted to kick her down the stairs, but Aimée got out of striking distance.

Hadn't Suzanne come to Aimée having seen her own ghost not that long ago? Hadn't Aimée helped her? And this was all the thanks she got for it? No compassion or payback.

She'd learned nothing. Had gotten nowhere.

And she was still wanted.

Disappointed and frustrated, she wanted to kick something. She kept to the shadows and planned her next move, or tried to. Part of her wanted to duck into the nearby *école de médicine*, where she'd often slept during her first and last year of premed, and close her eyes. Everyone used to nap there back then, and she doubted things had changed. Medical students lived in a continual state of sleep deprivation and curled up where they could.

"Aimée." A low hiss. She recognized that voice.

"Paul?"

"*Shhh.*" Melac's best friend was on the street, walking a motorbike. "Get on."

She couldn't get over Suzanne's hostility.

"Only if you talk to me, Paul. Be honest."

He keyed the ignition, revved the engine and handed her a helmet.

"I want to hear Melac's message," said Paul.

"Why the cloak and dagger?"

"Let's go."

"Where are we going?"

"Somewhere we can talk."

Aimée swung her leg over the seat and grabbed on to Paul's shoulders as they bumped over the cobbled street. The frigid night wind sliced her cheeks like ice, waking her up.

They whizzed over the Seine amid the horns of a late-night traffic jam. Jewel-like reflections of blue and dull gold shimmered on the river's surface. The lit Notre Dame loomed on the right. She gritted her teeth as Paul shifted gears, slowing down. The bike's echoing reverberated around the square where he'd pulled over. Hedges of blossoming white camellia bushes left Aimée feeling exposed.

"It's too open here. Look, I need to pick something up. Then we talk where I feel safe," she said.

"Hold on . . ."

"Turn right. Then right. It's important."

A sigh.

She made a quick call to René as Paul rolled down the street. Within four minutes, he'd pulled into the garage around the block from Leduc Detective. The café on the corner run by Zazie's parents was still open.

They were the only people she trusted besides René.

"Do you have a backpack?"

"Not on me. Why?"

"What about in your carry case?"

After a Monoprix canvas shopping bag was found, she gave Paul instructions.

"I'll explain later, but for now, please just go along with it."

A minute later, Paul entered the café. Meanwhile, from her vantage point in the garage, she watched the street and a portion of rue du Louvre. The surveillance was good. Professional. She couldn't pick anyone out but knew they were there.

René was crossing the street, his briefcase in one hand and a bag in the other. He entered the café.

Perspiration beaded her lip. She prayed that Louis, the garage attendant, wouldn't wake up before they left.

Five minutes. Six. Seven.

Paul came out of the café, Monoprix bag in hand. She watched to see if someone trailed him.

No one.

"Did you do what I asked? Were they there?"

"I gave a burner phone to René. Be careful with the bag. It's heavy."

In it were her makeup, a wig and two disguises.

"I told him to expect a call in thirty minutes."

"*Merci*, Paul."

"He asked what your back-up plan is."

"Funny. I'd like to know that, too."

She scanned the street again.

"Keep your motor off until rue Saint-Honoré and then head up Boulevard de Sébastopol."

Seventeen minutes later, they were in the nineteenth arrondissement by the eastern entrance of Parc des Buttes-Chaumont. Aimée had Paul pull over down from the Botzaris Metro. She often brought Chloé here so she could run down the grassy hills, laugh at the spray from the waterfall and feed the ducks by the grotto.

The park, once a gypsum quarry, had been used in the nineteenth century as a dump for the abattoir at la Villette. Once the area had been famous for the gang wars at rue Burnouf's bordellos, immortalized in Brassai's photos. But now the quartier and park were some of the most scenic, child-friendly places in Paris.

People snuck into the park at night through *la petite ceinture*, the abandoned rail track that ran around it. Tracks and underground tunnels abounded.

Aimée needed to check that they hadn't been followed.

She surveyed the connecting streets for any newly arrived car and checked the bus stops for watchers. The only people out were a couple embracing by the Metro before breaking apart so one could run down the steps to catch the last Metro.

She'd done that once. She remembered how she'd run for the last train with Melac's kisses still burning on her neck.

Paul dismounted the bike after her, pulled it up on its kickstand and stuck their helmets in his carrier.

"There's a point to coming here, *non*? A reason?"

Besides her cousin, Sébastien, coming through with a bolt hole a minute and a half away from here, and the fact that she'd clocked three escape routes from it? But Paul didn't need to know that.

Cloud wisps floated in the night sky like cotton puffs. Shadows lengthened on the narrow street. She felt a chill in this fickle spring weather.

"You knew him the best of anyone," she said, measuring her words. If she didn't, she'd explode. "If anyone would know something about the days leading up to his death, it's you."

A flustered look filled Paul's eyes. "Why do you keep pushing this, Aimée?"

If she didn't, she wouldn't learn anything.

Might not anyway.

"Was he worried? Afraid or nervous?"

"None of what happened makes sense. There was a gendarme he mentioned. That's the only thing out of the ordinary recently."

"A gendarme?"

"The one in the village where he grew up. That's all I remember."

Paul had made an effort to follow her. He'd had an agenda.

Was he a suspect? Never rule out anyone, her father would say. An undercurrent emanated from him—of what, she didn't know. Or was he just protecting Suzanne?

Could Melac's best friend have hired a hit man? Why?

He'd offered her little. She knew he was holding back.

"What's on your mind, Paul?"

Paul pushed his motorcycle ahead, then abruptly stopped and turned to her.

"Suzanne's on heavy medication to avoid another breakdown."

Aimée remembered the pill bottle.

"We're trying to keep our family together. Leave her alone," he said. "She knows nothing."

Aimée doubted that last part. "Do you suspect anyone who might be behind this? When did you last see him?"

His brow creased. He smoothed back his hair, something he did when pensive.

"You'll leave us alone?"

She nodded, intending no such thing.

A horn blared. Paul reached out for her and pulled her onto the curb. A delivery truck roared past, clumping over the cobbles and taking a sharp turn into the uphill curve.

"Crazy and off the track, I'm sure."

She'd judge that.

"My neck's on the line here. Anything helps."

"It didn't make any sense to me until I remembered one of those old Breton sailing yarns. You know, like the phantoms of old ships at sea, the mermaids and sirens beckoning sailors to the rocks."

Aimée rubbed her arms. The damp cold seeped through her boots. "Go on."

"It was something his uncle told him. The retired gendarme. But he'd been assigned to Paris fifteen, twenty years ago. He was here."

"Here as in the nineteenth arrondissement?"

"Think so. But Melac mentioned his uncle's colleague who'd impressed him. Seems he was a real hero in Brittany. Inspired him to join the force. *C'est tout.*"

Not much to go on. But now she knew she had to reach Melac's uncle. The lights of Paris shot a hard glitter through the sprouting leaves on tree branches. Moonglow blurred on the slanting slate roofs dipping downhill to the canal. Frustrated, she held up her phone in the dark shadows along the park's grill fence.

"Listen to Melac's message, Paul."

Head down, he listened.

"Play it again."

She did.

"Don't you have any idea of who he meant by the ghost?" she asked.

Paul's brow creased.

"You let Suzanne hear that?" he said. "How could you be so insensitive?"

"I took care of her ghost, Paul. She owes me."

"You've brought it all up again for her. She's been in therapy and all her progress will go down the drain."

Why hadn't she realized how precarious Suzanne's progress

had been? But Melac's ghost had nothing to do with what had happened to Suzanne.

Right?

"I know you're concerned about Suzanne, and I'm sorry. I had no idea about what she's going through. I'm trying to find who killed Melac and is framing me. I'm in hiding, Paul, do you understand?"

Paul rubbed his forehead. Even in the shadowed light she noticed the deep line bracketing his mouth, how he'd aged.

"Suzanne doesn't want to revisit her memories, that hell she went through."

Aimée still didn't see how this connected. She looked around and saw only darkened balconies over the treetops.

Paul blew out a puff of air. "Melac could be a drama queen— at least with us. I've known him for twenty years. Even in Brittany he was like that. Wait, why didn't the *flics* take your phone as evidence? Aren't you the main suspect?"

Worried, she stepped back on the damp leaves, sliding and catching her balance on a tree trunk. Was he working with the *flics*? Had this been a ruse to capture her?

Didn't matter. Before she'd disabled her phone and destroyed the chip, she'd copied and recorded the message on a new burner and had sent the message to a secret account.

Before she could answer, Paul's phone drilled. He turned away to take the call.

She looked around. The dim streetlight glinted on the spikes of the park's fence.

"Suzanne's having a meltdown," he said, shoving his phone in his pocket. "Thanks to you."

"Me?"

Paul pulled on a helmet, straddled the bike and started the ignition.

He pulled out onto rue de Crimée. "Leave us alone."

With that, he popped into gear and roared off.

The gendarme uncle—was there something in that? She found his number in her addresses. Thank God she'd noted it down.

His phone rang and rang. She was about to give up when a breathless voice answered.

"*Allô?*"

"Monsieur Alphonse Melac?" she asked. "I'm sorry to call so late."

The voice turned gruff. "I ran downstairs to get this. Don't tell me you're selling life insurance or a tractor."

"*Excusez-moi,*" she said. "You worked in the gendarmerie, didn't you?"

"Who's this?" he asked, suspicious.

Should she tell him? Or lie? She hesitated.

"You sound familiar," he said. "Who are you?"

"I don't want to get you in trouble."

"Trouble?" He snorted. "I know how to take care of myself."

"Then we never had this conversation and I never called you, *comprenez?*"

"You're the baby's mother," he said. "Little Chloé's Parisian *maman. Non?*"

Smart. They'd never been friendly. She'd met him only twice.

"If I am, will you answer some questions?"

"First, you answer mine. Are you responsible for my nephew's—"

"Murder?" Her voice cracked. "Never. He's . . . he was the father of my child. But he said something odd right before he died. Left me a strange message about a ghost."

"Mind your cockles, mademoiselle."

Clank. He'd hung up.

Rude.

Or . . .

Someone had tapped his line, was listening to his calls.

Melac had used that phrase before, she remembered. He'd used it once when he was going on surveillance and got a call. He'd been standing in her hallway at the coat rack, reaching for his wool jacket.

"Do you always tell your operatives to mind their cockles when they work on assignment?" she had asked. "Kind of old fashioned. Or is this the new caring, sensitive side of police work these days?"

Melac had taken his scarf and wrapped it around his neck, grinning.

"We call them agents, not operatives," he'd said. "That's a fishermen's saying in Brittany. I'm signaling their line's monitored and probably being recorded."

Aimée's skin tingled in the fresh chill of the evening. If Melac's uncle's line was bugged, everything around her was compromised.

Disappointed, she headed to the address Sébastien had given her. Sleep, she needed sleep. But her mind kept spinning.

She replayed Melac's first voice mail yet again, the short one undecipherable except for the word *morgue* trailing off. She heard a slight hum of traffic. He sounded like he was outside.

It had to be there. She just wasn't seeing it.

She remembered Melac's incessant calling while she and Isabelle had been tussling with the IT jerk. Ten minutes later—fifteen tops—Aimée had watched him die on the canal.

The killer would have heard him leaving her these messages and knifed him quick before she got there. As her father would say, make it an equation: why + how = who.

She'd been trying to think along those same lines, but her brain blurred. She'd be no good if she didn't get some sleep.

Like she had time for that.

Maybe the bikers had information.

Aimée tried Isabelle.

"Apologies," she said. "I know it's late and you probably don't want to talk to me, but—"

"Aimée, please know you're welcome here," interrupted Isabelle. "I got to the root of the police visit. Not your problem."

Relief flooded her.

"What I really need to know is what the word on the street is about Melac's murder. What are people saying?"

"None of my guys has learned anything so far."

"People must know something, suspect someone. After all, they don't forget in the nineteenth, from what you said."

"You're right about that." Music drifted in the background with the faint whine of a slide guitar. Isabelle said, "Sometimes getting a no doesn't mean it's a *no*."

True. And Isabelle was older than her years.

"Got to go. Talk to you when I know more."

She clicked off.

Aimée played Melac's message again.

No water sounds, she realized. So he hadn't been along the canal when he recorded his first message.

She'd already asked Isabelle to get her bikers on the bar scene and the fight on rue Tandou. She'd have to wait until the bartender's neighbor returned.

Exhausted, she was walking down rue de Crimée where it sloped along the park. She made herself think. What would it take, fifteen minutes to reach the bridge from here? Less with no traffic at night.

Say twelve.

She wanted to go over the geography. Nail something down. It wouldn't bring him back. But that's how she worked. That was the way her papa had taught her to investigate. And to navigate life.

She kicked at a cluster of damp leaves. Then checked her Tintin watch as she timed her walk. She noticed the plaque where the *résistants* had blown up the retreating Germans on *la petite ceinture*. On a hunch, she stopped.

A whiff of dry chalk caught at the back of her throat. The smell was out of place on a damp night. Where had that come from?

She couldn't let her mind wander.

She carried on: to the left, wreathed in fingers of fog; the almost-hidden entrance of the Russian church; the tall apartment with an underground synagogue on rue Manin.

He could have been in any of these places. Or not. The possibilities were overwhelming. But her father always said hitting the cobbles paid off. Crime didn't happen in a vacuum.

Some trace always remained, whether evidence or a memory.

When daunted or overwhelmed, Jean-Claude Leduc had just kept looking, kept walking.

Nine minutes.

Would Melac have been around here? Why? Cafés and bars were closed. And the last train would be about to depart.

It was an ordinary area. An ordinary night. Another April in Paris.

These streets were a mostly Orthodox Jewish area. A large community with synagogues, kosher markets and a school for girls. Her grandfather had insisted she take piano lessons up here from a renowned pianist.

It hadn't helped Aimée's technique.

Aimée caught the smoky scent of the wood-burning oven in the small bakery that she and Chloé sometimes visited after a day at the park. The rotund baker, in a cloth bib flecked with flour and with his ponytail under a hairnet, was smoking on the pavement.

He spoke into a phone, puffing away and gesticulating with his free flour-dusted arm.

Aimée recognized expletives in Russian.

He jammed the phone in his apron, then tossed the cigarette and ground it out on the pavement.

Aimée had an idea.

"Monsieur, *excusez-moi*."

He looked up and she proceeded to ad-lib a story, showing him a photo of Melac on her phone.

Wasn't he a baker, up all night?

A chance in a thousand. She could hear her father say, "Tie every string or they'll dangle and knot up."

"Who's he to you?" the Russian said.

"He's my ex."

"What happened?"

"That's what I'm trying to find out. He disappeared around here at about midnight last night."

"What's it to me?"

Hostile and uninterested, he turned around.

"Really, I don't mean to impose or bother you, but he's . . ."

"For real? For all I know, you're like . . . What you say here . . . GRU in Paris."

"What's GRU?"

"Soviet military intelligence."

She almost laughed. *Stupid.* Melac had been deployed on an operation against them once, he'd told her.

"Forget Big Brother," she said. "I'm trying to figure out what happened to my daughter's father. I'm worried. I can't find his phone. And the *flics*—you know they're unhelpful."

The baker took in a chest-lifting breath—only an undershirt beneath his apron in the chill night.

"Where I come from, it pays to keep quiet."

"We're in Paris, monsieur."

"Life's unsure, that's universal. Goes in circles. This was a German bakery until the end of the war. Can you believe it? We still bake pumpernickel. Call me paranoid if you want, I don't care. You understand?"

No help here.

Aimée shrugged. "Worth a try." She gave a small smile. "My three-year-old loves your *pain au chocolat*."

"I know."

Aimée blinked. He did remember her and Chloé.

"But *nyet*, I don't see him, this man, when I go for smoke," said the baker. "*Désolé.* Only I hear commotion when I walk home toward the canal."

Aimée pulled out her beaten-up map.

"Please show me where."

His flour-encrusted finger pointed to rue Tandou.

"What time was that?"

He scratched his neck. "Monday, yes? I bake early double shift. We have big order for wedding. Many hundred guests who want wood-oven-fired baguettes. It's a blessing and curse, I tell you, being one of the last bakeries doing this."

"So what time did you finish the shift?"

"Double shift, yes. So tired. Maybe close to midnight."

"What do you mean by commotion?"

"Bar fight. A place I go sometimes after work."

Yuri—she finally learned his name—laid out his evening for her. The upshot of his long night was getting punched in the stomach after a double shift.

"Anything else?"

"A technician was working the drawbridge. You know, going up and down."

"Wait a minute, how do you know it was a tech?"

"Who else does this?"

"I thought it was automated? Most of the bridges and locks on the canal are automated."

He shrugged.

"No *flics*?"

"Later, I heard sirens. But I go home. Throw up."

"You're saying you thought you saw a tech manually lowering and raising the bridge. Or playing with the mechanism?"

Yuri glanced back at the boulangerie. "Bread ready."

"Please tell me what this man looked like."

"Got to go or they burn."

As he hurried to the bakery's rear door, she followed.

"Tell me what he looked like," she persisted as he paused to put on a new hairnet and don thick oven mitts.

He sighed and finally gave her a brief description: dark jacket or windbreaker, woolly hat. Medium height. His hand darted out and thrust her a warm *pain au chocolat* before he shut the bakery door.

AIMÉE WOKE UP under a warm duvet on a soft mattress. Her eyes adjusted to the bright light. No blurriness or double vision, thank God. Handy, this pull-down bed that fit into the wall.

Sébastien's architect client, in the midst of an acrimonious divorce, had hired him to renovate and make his office as sleek and comfortable as could be. Instead of sleeping on friends' couches, the architect had designed this full studio conversion. She loved the battery-powered espresso maker. She needed one of these.

Caffeinated, she showered in the galley-like *salle de bains*. Her legs were sore after all the walking last night. She knew she'd need to change her disguise and check in with Chloé. She missed her smile, the way she pulled Aimée's hand when she wanted to sit on her lap.

Soon, ma chère.

She checked the bag of burners. Found the same model that she'd given René—keeping it simple—and hit his number.

She let it ring twice. Clicked off, then rang again.

He answered as she shut the architect's door behind her. She'd left the place immaculate. Workers were arriving in the courtyard. She stashed her bag in a side vent behind shrubbery.

She waved at the workers. They'd remember a tallish woman in a leopard-print skirt and Doc Martens, with a black ponytail and stylish big black-framed glasses. Not Aimée's style at all. That was the point.

Aimée hooked the clasps of her faux fur coat, took her phone from the pocket and strode off toward Parc des Buttes-Chaumont.

"Talk to me, René," she said, her gaze scanning the street where tree-lined alleys of old workers' houses, many gentrified and pretty in pastel, mounted steeply up to Place des Fêtes—now an eyesore of looming seventies concrete high-rises. There were lots of pedestrians, construction workers and electricians, and they all made her nervous. Too many people. She turned on her chunky heel and went down villa Paul-Verlaine, where the rock-hewed foundations of the maisonettes perched on outcrops. A trio of men in hard hats were taking measurements of the street. Any of these men could have been planted as watchers. Of the vans she'd noted on the street, at least one could be concealing listening equipment.

How could she know? She couldn't.

"Don't tell me where you are," René said.

As if she would.

She walked at what she hoped was an even pace and followed an alley that went under buildings—a real engineering feat, she realized—nestled into the rock. No wonder these little houses hadn't changed or been too gentrified—the whole area was hewed out of gypsum. It was named the villa Amerique since so much gypsum was exported to America.

Footsteps clattered behind her.

Followed already?

Emerging from the tunnel, she turned to see a narrow stairway, as steep as those climbing into her grandmother's attic, leading to another row of houses.

"You're huffing and puffing, Aimée," said René.

"You would be, too." She wanted to stop and catch her breath, but she had to lose this tail. "Tell me what you've found."

"It's complicated."

Her lungs burned. *Damn cigarette.* And her calves protested.

"Condense it," she said, impatient.

She heard René clicking over the keyboard. "I spent the most time on Melac's contracts. The bank deposits noted in his online accounts don't cause alarm."

"No red flags?"

"For contracted work, no. The only thing remotely interesting are his notes. Seems like a three-day surveillance of W. There are no names, and then it ends abruptly. In the last entry, he's in Paris and still surveilling W."

"Nothing else?"

"I'm working on it," he said, irritation in his tone. "You know I need to keep the office running, Aimée. Handle our paying clients."

"I'm sorry," she said, contrite. "Hate dumping this all on you."

A pause. "His last entry was at 21:00 on the night he died."

"How can you know that?"

"It's the new thing for surveillance. I read about it."

"Explain, René."

"A new protocol where the contractee, i.e., Melac, connects his phone so his voice mails are transcribed in real time by their employer. Gets uploaded, *tout de suite*."

Handy.

"Seems he used connectivity at cafés."

Aimée looked around and strode down the rue to the Place de Rhin et Danube.

"I think I've found where he was when he made it. Meet you at the café with the old dog Chloé likes." She heard René sigh. The café at Place de Rhin et Danube was once the countryside where horses foraged before descending to market or slaughter at la Villette. Darker tales spoke of the Communards, the short-lived revolutionary radical government in 1871 who'd disposed of their opponents. Supposedly here in the circular plot with the quaint statue of a dairy maid picking flowers belied its use as a quarry pit holding bodies buried in quicklime.

Melac had loved this place.

Aimée questioned the waiter about Melac, whom he remembered only vaguely. At least it validated Melac making his report. But little else.

She waited for René inside this café on the roundabout, a tarnished remnant of art nouveau with a curlicue-decorated counter and liquor bottles on spotless shelves lining the mirror. Amber and dark green hues reflected from Cointreau and Ricard onto the old cash register. A lived-in relic of better days. Like time travel without the anxiety, she imagined.

The café's caramel-colored fluffy old dog stirred, licked his paw, then yawned, uninterested.

A moment later, René strode into the café, all four feet of him, handmade Lobb brogues and Burberry trench tailored to his height.

She was so happy to see René. She almost hugged him.

But affection flustered him. Or so he'd said. Businesslike was best.

And she had little time.

René's place in her heart wouldn't ever change. But she'd asked him to go above and beyond, yet again.

"I printed out the log." He handed her a Monoprix shopping bag with a folder inside. Then took off his Burberry trench and sat down. "A few emails, too."

"Did you discover other locations in the nineteenth?"

He ordered tea from the waiter. "Look, Aimée, you can read that later. It's all inside."

She picked up on his unease. A pushback. "What's bothering you, René?"

"What's not bothering me?" he said. "Please talk to Morbier. Work it out. He'll pave the way with the *flics*."

"Are you crazy? It's not just them. It's whoever killed Melac that will find me."

René adjusted his silk tie and the cuffs of his handmade Charvet shirt, then cleared his throat and looked around.

"I don't know if I can keep this up," he said. "The business is suffering."

Her thumb and forefinger tightened on the demitasse of espresso as she held it to her mouth. The curl of steam moistened the tip of her nose. *Think.*

"You've got Saj. He said he'd take over the IT job at Marché Secrétan remotely."

She'd have him pass info on to the Ministry, too.

The waiter set down René's tea.

"Why am I the last to know?"

Irritation rippled in his voice. He sipped the scalding jasmine tea and winced.

Stupid. She should have let René know but had completely forgotten.

"Something else bothering you, René?"

"Did you . . ." He hesitated. "Did you . . . fight with Melac, and then an accident happened?"

Startled, she spilled her espresso on her skirt. The spill blended into the leopard print.

Breathe. How could René even ask that?

But Aimée and Melac had fought all the time, after all.

For a long moment, she wondered if René would jump ship. Leave. He'd done it once before.

Her stomach tensed.

She had to breathe. *Inhale. Slowly exhale.*

She had to not stress or she'd aggravate her eyes. Would make things worse. If that was even possible.

"You don't trust me, René?"

"It's what a lawyer will ask. What Morbier wants to know. Tell him the truth. He'll help you either way."

So René was Morbier's messenger.

"I've often wanted to do Melac in," she admitted. "Make him disappear. Kick him off the planet. But he's Chloé's father. If I really wanted him out, I would have banned him at the christening."

She stared at René.

"I know, I was there," he said.

She paused, looking at the floor, the old mosaic with chipped tiles. How many had walked here?

"I wish we'd found a way to work things out, but . . ."

"Spilled milk and all, Aimée."

"Don't they realize if I killed him, I'd never stick around with the murder weapon?"

"Self-defense, that's what a high-powered attorney would argue."

René's phone beeped, then stopped. Five seconds later, her burner rang. René nodded at Aimée, and she answered the call.

"*Oui,*" she said.

"There will be a secure laptop at the pool café," said Saj. "On it you'll find Melac's last coordinates."

It was a code they'd worked out. And it *was* the café by the pool—sort of. Of the thirty-nine public pools in Paris, most had a café nearby, often several.

Aimée hung up, stood and left some euros on the marble-topped table.

"I'm sorry to put so much on you, René. If you need to take a break, I'll ask Saj to do what he can."

"That's not what I meant. It's about facing the problem. This won't go away, Aimée. You can't ignore it."

She skittered her chipped blood-orange lacquered nails over the sticky table, then grabbed a napkin to wipe her fingers.

Relax.

Like she could?

"I didn't kill Melac. I'm being followed, and I'm fighting for my life."

"Right now you should take all the help you can get. Getting in touch with Morbier would be a good idea."

Fat chance.

"I miss Chloé so much, but I want her safe."

René tugged his goatee, like he did when he was nervous.

"She misses you."

Aimée looked out the door. Clear. Or she thought so.

"Here's a burner with Morbier's number in it." He palmed her a phone under the table.

"*Merci*, René."

She took off toward the Parc des Buttes-Chaumont, tossed the burner with Morbier's number in the trash.

Wednesday Morning • Parc des Buttes-Chaumont

AIMÉE FOUND A secluded bench under a weeping willow. First she'd read Melac's notes that René had printed out, then get the laptop Saj had left. Crisp sunshine took the edge off the chill. Her grandfather always intoned, "*En Avril, ne te découvre pas d'un fil,*" the old countryside proverb to never remove a thread of clothing in April, since the warm weather never lasted. She blew on her fingers, wishing she had her wool gloves.

René had copied and printed Melac's notes of about ten pages chronicling a surveillance of W. He'd prefaced it with a few lines of explanation.

Missing persons case, pro bono for uncle's neighbor, three-day commitment extended to fourth day in Paris.

Interesting.

Seems X., his client, wanted to know if a teenager in the next village was her grandchild.

Aimée read the next log note. Melac had been surveilling W., the teenager. This promised to be boring.

But she scanned Melac's notes.

6:00 W. walked dog, bus #37 to school, stayed at school until 16:30 for drama practice, bus #37 back to village, stopped at café and met friends . . .

Tuesday, Wednesday . . . Every day was the same. Complete with notations under the photos Melac had taken with a telescopic lens. He'd developed them and labeled the photos with names and precise locations. René had printed these out with his new state-of-the-art printer—which she'd paid for; the quality was worth it. The photos in black and white showed recognizable faces, and René had done a good job increasing the pixels.

But most of this seemed de rigueur. Flat, boring and nothing personal. Nothing that would seem to initiate repercussions or result in consequences.

Rote and routine surveillance work was beneath his skills. Melac had been in the elite counterterrorism squad with Suzanne—he was highly trained and skilled. This was more like a rookie training exercise.

It must have been a favor for his uncle. She wondered if Melac had just reported back to his uncle or if this had been a more formal job contracted by the client, X.

On a final reread, a note caught her eye. Under the photo of a crowd scene he'd added: *middle-aged male, average height, cap and sparse beard, only profile, unable to identify.*

This man stood by a line of boats on a wooden-planked walkway by a motorcycle. In the foreground were the girl and her friends. He seemed like a random person caught in the shot.

However, Melac had noted it.

The next page showed a sketchily drawn map of a stretch of the canal in Paris, the quartier and several streets marked by wavy and broken lines without names. Melac had also included bridges and monuments. She could recognize Parc de la Villette, the forking canal and the office where she'd been working. A circle had been drawn where Melac had been staked out watching her every night.

Stalking her.

A shiver went up the inside of her arm. If the *flics* saw this, it would point to a stronger motive for her.

But why would Melac have noted his surveillance of Aimée down in the same place as this case work of the girl in Brittany and the unidentified motorcycle man? He wouldn't. Knowing Melac—linear and logical in his movements, at least most of the time—she would bet that he'd been working this case or another one before meeting her.

Somehow it had to tie in.

Didn't it?

She had to quit spinning her wheels. She needed to get the laptop.

Consulting her map, she plotted out where Saj had left her the laptop. She crisscrossed the park on a high path that gave her a panoramic view of Paris below. Even as far as the Tour Eiffel. The damp grass still sparkled with dew in the sunlight. Joggers, people walking their dogs and a line of preschoolers close to Chloé's age walked with their teachers in matching blue T-shirts. Her heart thumped. She missed Chloé. She pulled out her phone and started to punch in a number, just to hear Chloé's voice, but stopped. She couldn't be selfish and risk her baby girl's safety.

The sooner she got evidence pointing to the real murderer, the sooner she'd see her baby. The waterfall and infamous "suicide" bridge on her left gave way to the carpet of jade green grass by the jagged rocky ravine. Not an area she cared for. She hurried up rue Edouard Pailleron where the Olympic-size pool—a favorite of hers—was closed for cleaning. Also on this street was the site of the terrible school fire that Devries, the journo, had obsessed over.

Turning right downhill, she passed the Bolivar Metro, hurried by the entrance of the start-up where she'd worked IT and passed the covered market. The glass-and-wire nineteenth-century roof needed a cleaning and, as ever, some love. She ducked into the local café, which was usually full of parents who'd dropped off their children for swimming lessons at the pool and lap swimmers like she used to be before Chloé. Nobody from work would come here, she knew that. They favored the café two doors down from the theater and congregated in front for a smoke.

Not to mention the shifts wouldn't change for a few more hours. No one, not even the mucky-mucks, left the building since all meetings and appointments were conducted on site per the board mandate. A local restaurateur furnished the meals. All in the spirit of keeping it local.

While she appreciated this, it felt like prison.

Along Avenue Secrétan were small shops: optometrists, a butcher, a fishmonger, a *supermarché* and apartments.

Still, she was taking a risk—balancing the off chance that someone from her job came walking out of the Metro, hurried to a dentist appointment or ducked in here for a napkin after stepping in dog poo. She kept her head down, grateful for the disguise.

Thank God the café was open—only just. Now she'd consult the laptop Saj had left.

Aimée popped inside and found Zia—short for Patrizia, "part Italian but all French," she'd said—stocking wine. Zia's pride and joy, her collection of refrigerator magnets from many of the eighty French departments, plastered the back mirror. Cartons of wine bottles had come up from the cellar on the old dumbwaiter, the *monte-charge*.

Most important, she trusted Zia.

Aimée leaned over the counter and gave her *bises* on both cheeks.

Zia gulped. "*Mon Dieu*, I didn't recognize you."

"Let's keep it that way," said Aimée in a voice just above a whisper. "You have something for me, *non*?"

"*Alors*, I have to finish this . . ." She looked around. The only patrons were sitting on the terrace. "Go down and use it. Right wall on the top shelf."

Aimée followed the curved zinc counter to the side spiral stairs that went downstairs to the WC, telephones and staff door.

She checked. No one. She darted through the staff door, then flicked the old porcelain light switch to illuminate the cellar crammed with cases of beer, wine, paper goods and stacked towels.

She found the laptop in a cloth tote bag that read *you haven't meditated until you've meditated at Vinay Ashram*. Classic Saj. The cellar was cold, illuminated only by light coming from the ancient coal grate flush with the pavement, and she sat against the old boiler as she booted up the laptop to find new information Saj had loaded inside.

Saj had included an old *brigade criminelle* case where Melac had testified. The defendant, a young woman, was convicted and sentenced and served time. Drug related. Melac's next to last appointment showed him being at 6 rue Bellot, the young woman's last-known address, a squat.

Aimée stuffed the laptop in her bag, then turned her faux-fur reversible coat inside out to reveal a nubby wool charcoal coat. She pulled up her skirt so the black leggings below covered her legs. Shoes were always the giveaway, so she added dark leg warmers to cover the ankle laces of her Doc Martens. She tucked her wig under a matching wool cap and added tortoise-shell sunglasses.

A new look.

"Ciao, Zia," said Aimée.

Zia winked. "Ciao, *bella*."

SHE KNEW THIS northeast quartier, la Villette, a sprawling crime-ridden swath up from Stalingrad. The streets that ran parallel to the Gare du Nord rail tracks and switching yards held grimy gray-façade two- and three-story buildings between sixties and seventies tower blocks. Several people slept on the grills in the street where the Metro's hot air vented, a few others slept in doorways. Criminals hid here since no one asked questions.

Aimée wondered why Melac had visited one Madame Olivera here on the day he died.

She passed an old municipal pawnbrokers, officially called *le mont de piété*, but commonly known as *visiting my aunt*—deserted by the look of the dusty filigreed rosette grillwork. Farther on she found the address on rue Bellot—a crumbling building behind a tarnished black metal fence. One side of the double gate sagged open, like a tired arm beckoning her to a weed-choked courtyard with garbage bins labeled PROPRÉTÉ DE PARIS. One of the upper windows had cardboard for curtains.

A motorcycle was chained to an old-fashioned rusted water spigot in the wall. The building formed a two-story *U* of apartments, ringed by a narrow, open wraparound walkway on the upper floor. It was an old workshop with remnants of past workers' housing—the workers had not only lived above the shop but also couldn't get away from it.

A tall man with ebony skin sat down on a stool. He wore blue plastic shoes, a red embroidered cap and an African tribal robe that hit above his ankles. He took out papers and a tobacco pouch to begin rolling a cigarette.

She searched for Madame Olivera's mailbox. Nothing. She tramped up an interior spiral staircase to the second floor and the door on the left.

She knocked. Knocked again.

"Madame Olivera?"

The door opened. A man wearing a stained undershirt fiddled with a hearing aid in his ear.

"*Quoi?*"

"Madame Olivera, please."

He frowned. Shook his head.

"When does she return, monsieur?"

"Next door."

He slammed the door.

Friendly.

Aimée was about to knock on the next door but before she could use her knuckles, the door flew open. She caught a draft of spicy aromas and cooking oil.

"What do you want?" asked a woman partially behind the door.

Aimée pulled out her father's police ID, updated and retouched with her own photo. Always handy in these situations.

The woman, who had black curly, crinkly hair shot with gray and eyebrows that met like Frida Kahlo's, stared at her ID.

"*Et alors?* What else do you want now?"

What else?

"May I come inside, Madame Olivera?"

The woman peered closer.

"Not the best photo you've ever taken," she said, mimicking Aimée's puckering mouth. "You look like you just sucked a lemon."

"This won't take long."

She shrugged and looked around. "Make it quick."

Aimée slid past the woman into a cramped room—a studio with a galley kitchen and sleeping alcove all draped in warm orange-and-yellow wall hangings, rugs and draperies. Cozy and colorful. It must hide a multitude of flaws—fissures and cracks in the ceiling.

"I'll get to the point."

"Good, because I'm not giving you more than a minute of my time."

Aimée hated pretending she was with the *flics*. "I appreciate . . ."

"No, you don't," said Madame Olivera. "My daughter Maria died in prison the day before a stinking parole hearing her lawyer had worked for since last year."

Is that why Melac had come here? The case he'd worked on in the *brigade criminelle*?

"I'm sorry," she said. "My colleague . . ."

"The one who put her there came here the other day." Madame Olivera's voice rose. "I'll tell you what I told him. Get your stinking ass out of here. Prison killed my Maria. And you put her there."

"The system did, madame," Aimée said. "I'm a mother, too, and if I were you . . . *alors*, I'd want justice."

"Easy talk. Like you care."

"I'm not familiar with your daughter's case." Aimée looked around and saw the photos of a young woman smiling, wearing cutoff jeans, swimming. "Is that her?"

A hesitant nod.

"Why don't you tell me about her? What happened? How did she end up in prison?"

A wail of anguish erupted from Madame Olivera. Tears coursed down her cheeks. Her shoulders trembled, and Aimée helped her into a chair.

"She grew up here, that's why." Madame Olivera wiped her tears with the back of her sleeve. "This rotten place."

"What do you mean?" said Aimée. "I'm here to listen."

Madame Olivera deflated, her anger and frustration gone. "Why? Doesn't matter now. She's gone. Dead at twenty-two. Can you imagine that a girl with a degree in hospitality management and with a five-star-hotel job in Lisbon, waiting . . ."

Aimée sat and listened as a river of pain tumbled out. Madame Olivera and her husband had come here from Portugal and found jobs as the concierges of this building and another. Her husband had worked a second job at *la poste*. Her daughter had loved to study. But *les Modous* had gotten claws into her.

"*Les Modous* are the Senegalese dealers around the corner on Place du Maroc, and all over here. Six months and she was stealing from us, lost her internship, got caught in some robbery. Later I found out they'd promised to burn our building down if she testified against them."

"I'm so sorry."

"That's what I tried to tell the *flics*, the therapist, the lawyer, all of them. But it was too late."

Aimée tried to put it together. "So why did Melac, the officer, come here?"

Madame Olivera stood, a haggard slump to her shoulders, to go stir the pot simmering on her stove. Garlic, onions—something wonderful.

"He'd promised to put in a good word for her at the parole hearing. Yet it was too little, too late. She was dead. He came to apologize and offer help—he said he felt guilty that the real culprits didn't pay."

Deep sadness filled Aimée. He'd tried to do right by her.

A church bell chimed.

"Madame, Melac was murdered after he came here. That night."

A pause.

"So you think I'm involved," Madame Olivera said. Her face was instantly harsh again.

"*Non*, but—"

"Get out."

"I need to ask you questions."

"That's what this is about, eh?"

"It's about piecing together his movements. What time did he come here? Did anyone from the area have it in for him?"

"Ask me if I care."

Hostility radiated in waves from this woman. And Aimée understood. Still, she needed her help.

"Please talk to me," she said. "I'll put in word that you assisted the investigation."

She didn't know how, but she could try.

"Like that changes anything?"

"You owe me nothing, I understand, but he's the father of my child, madame," Aimée said. All of sudden it welled up inside her—the shame and guilt. Her last words to him had been so angry. She could never take them back. "We had a fight and then . . . he was murdered."

Madame Olivera sighed. "*Et alors*, he came in the evening. Ten or eleven, I don't know. He could have walked into trouble outside."

Why hadn't she thought of that?

Alert, Aimée stood, parted the shade and looked out.

"You mean with *les Modous* who'd set your daughter up?"

She shrugged. "Who knows? He's a *flic, non*? This quartier's infested with drifters on the run or lying low. The dealers like it that way. It keeps everyone quiet. He said he'd noticed some of his 'former' clients. It goes both ways, if you know what I mean."

Surprised, Aimée joined the woman at her stove.

"Are you saying what I think you're saying? He'd seen someone he'd been investigating?"

"Maybe. I don't know." She stirred the pot. "I've got to get this to my stall in the Portuguese market. Look, my husband dropped dead of a heart attack when my girl went to prison. To get by I clean apartments and sell my soup, *caldo verde*, green broth."

"Is there anything you can remember? Anything he said about noticing someone from his past? A ghost?"

Madame Olivera looked away.

"There's nothing here for me anymore. *Nada.* I'm going back to Portugal to build a house on the land we bought."

Why didn't she answer Aimée's question? Or did she need to read between the lines?

"Madame, it's only us talking. Just you and me. You're leaving, you'll be out of harm's way, so you can level with me. Point out who he meant."

She shook her head. "I don't know. He just said if *he* were hiding, *he'd* hide here."

Was this connected? Revenge from a gangster who'd spotted Melac visiting Madame Olivera?

"I get a criminal hiding here from the law, but wouldn't the locals demand bribes? Payback to keep incognito?"

That cliché of honor among thieves rarely rang true, according to her father. A thug turning on a thug—it happened all the time.

"*Oui et non.*" Madame Olivera shrugged. "There're ways to do it. The *flics* won't set foot around here." She tasted a spoonful. Reached for the salt. "*Les Modous* like it that way. You trade, share, pay in some way, keep your head down and go to ground. Justice takes place here in different ways. But it happens."

Madame Olivera, widow and distraught mother, wanted vengeance for her daughter.

"Tell me his name," said Aimée.

She snorted. "And you'll do what your colleague wouldn't?"

So she'd asked Melac for help.

"No promises."

"His name? Never knew his gang name, he's just *un Modou*."

"Is he here? Around?"

"Not for a while."

"Help me and I'll help you."

"If I do?"

"Sit down."

She did, and Aimée outlined her idea.

"You mean keep my eyes and ears open and keep in touch, *c'est ça?*"

Aimée took one of the burner phones from her bag. Thank God René had given her several.

"Use this burner and call the number programmed in it to reach me."

Madame Olivera shuffled through a drawer and handed Aimée a much-thumbed photo of her daughter and a young Senegalese man smiling.

"That's him, the *salopard.*"

"Madame, keep a packed bag by the door. If you see him, call me, then you take a taxi and board the next flight to Portugal."

AS AIMÉE WALKED out, she heard the roar of a motorcycle, reverberations echoing off the walls. Isabelle's crew? A gang? She looked around. The red taillight blinked at the end of the street and then disappeared.

Her nerves fizzed.

She couldn't be too careful. They could be checking up on her. Or worse.

She took out the burner phone Isabelle had given her and hit the speed dial.

"Aimée?"

"We need to talk."

"*Bon*, I'm at the squat."

"Not there."

Pause. "Trouble?"

As if she weren't in trouble already?

"I don't know yet. Are you off to work?"

"Soon," Isabelle said. "I'll leave early. Where?"

Aimée thought of a location. Told her.

THE BLAND BRICK façade of the prestigious architecture school on avenue de Flandre revealed nothing. Yet the interior was entrancing, as the entry opened up to the complex of courtyards, higgledy-piggledy buildings from different eras and displays with human-size maquettes of student architectural projects.

Avant-garde. Creative.

Cold, Aimée thought, shivering and buttoning her coat.

Aimée tramped over the jagged cobbles winding between buildings. Next door had been the Erard piano manufacturer, and it made her think how waves of history passed through the quartier, of the heritage and legacies of those gone.

Her grandfather used to come to Au Boeuf Couronné, the nineteenth-century brasserie celebrated for its beef and bone marrow dishes made from five bones. Nearby was the kitchen shop where he'd taken her once for a deal on a copper skillet, which still hung on her kitchen wall.

The abattoir at la Villette, the sugar refineries and biscuit factories had once reigned here, employing two-thirds of the residents. Those had closed, the jobs disappearing. Urban renewal pulled the manufacturing warehouses, printing presses and small ateliers down and put in the *périphérique*, the ring road, which her father had called an abomination. He'd liked old Paris.

Aimée found the small student cafeteria on the second floor

of a back building. Strains of violins and cellos drifted from somewhere below. *Peaceful.*

On the café's wall were blueprints stamped with space invaders. After purchasing two espressos, she sat on a bench under hanging vines and a robust rubber tree.

"I didn't recognize you, Aimée."

Aimée scratched under her wig and tightened the ponytail clips.

Isabelle sat down with a quizzical look, and Aimée handed her one of the cups.

"I think a motorcycle's following me."

She knew she sounded paranoid. And the bikers were her safety net.

Isabelle shifted on the bench.

"Explain."

And she did, wishing her chest didn't heave.

"First off, we don't police that part of la Villette unless asked," said Isabelle, pouring in extra sugar. "Still, if you had a description or license number, I could send out an alert. Get people checking."

Aimée downed her espresso. The hardness of the bench and angular lines of the postmodernist cafeteria were giving her a headache. "Look, Melac was in this area shortly before he got murdered. Maybe someone from a past case recognized and followed him. Exacted vengeance."

Isabelle sipped. Aimée caught the hooded look behind her eyes.

"What aren't you telling me, Isabelle?"

"I was waiting for confirmation," she said. "But word's out your former *flic* who died, Melac, witnessed a deal going down. By this I mean a large transaction."

"And you weren't going to tell me?"

"Did I say that, Aimée?" Isabelle took her hand. "I'm trying to help. It was an important deal."

Don't burn bridges, she could hear her father say.

"Important to you?"

"To the gangs involved. One of the Angels' cousin is a runner for them. Grunt work, but he passes on what he hears so we stay on top of what's going on."

"What gangs?"

"No one's saying it's a hit."

"Even if Melac saw it, he's not—"

"A *flic*," Isabelle interrupted. "I know, but he could testify. Once a *flic*, always a *flic*. That's how they think."

"Does this involve drugs, *les Modous* down near rue Bellot?"

Madame Olivera had intimated Melac had inadvertently seen a "client."

"I'll get back to you. There's a gang in Buttes-Chaumont who act like it's their private dealing ground." Isabelle squeezed Aimée's hand. "Trust me. If my Angels did it, you'd know."

"They resent me."

"You're an outsider. They'll resent you until they trust you. Until you're tested."

"So I need to show them?"

Isabelle slipped a key into her palm. Gave her a door code.

"They'll fall in love with you, don't worry," she said.

Before Aimée could ask how, her phone trilled. The burner phone from René.

"Leduc, I'm waiting," said Morbier.

The weasel René had given this number to Morbier. He'd known she'd have thrown the other phone away.

Isabelle stood up, waved and left. Aimée covered the phone with her hand.

"I'm not giving myself up, Morbier."

"Good. That would be more than stupid, given what I found out."

"You know who the killer is?"

"Did I say that?"

She heard a little voice in the background. Familiar. Was it Chloé?

Was he taking her daughter hostage? "Let me talk to her, Morbier."

"Meet me at your office."

Like she'd fall for that? Get trapped?

Aimée thought fast. "Café by the church at Metro Jourdain."

She hung up.

EN ROUTE SHE ducked back into Zia's café, nodded to her and then returned to the old pay phone downstairs.

Rustling up some coins from her coat pocket, she found enough to make a call. Thank God.

"Urbanisme Éclectique, bonjour," answered the receptionist at Sébastien's studio. "How may I direct your call?"

"May I speak with Sébastien? It's about my order."

Pause. "Ah, Sébastien left a message for you. He's sourced the timber. The project order's at the current site."

Code. He'd leave a key for her to stay at his ongoing renovation site.

"The decorators are handling the rest."

Code again. Regula was taking care of Chloé. For now.

How long could she depend on them, imposing on their work time and childcare?

But how long ago had Sébastien left this message? Had Morbier discovered Chloé's location to use her as leverage? Pretty low, even for him.

"When did he leave that message?"

"Just now, madame."

"*Merci.*"

HER UNEASE MOUNTED as she took the Metro. Every face, every passenger's movement heightened her fear.

Stop. Breathe.

She had to remember this disguise gave her a different look. And she had another one in her bag. She needed to think ahead. To plan an escape route. But she already knew one of her options.

Her grandfather had taken her to the quartier a long time ago when he'd come to buy anoraks for the two of them from the Breton shop that sold fishermen's jackets and raincoats. They were heavy duty, ready to battle gales and waves in the Atlantic.

She'd loved her fisherman's raincoat, and playing hide-and-seek with him in the places he'd shown her around the quartier.

"Shhh, it's our secret," he'd said. "Only the people who live here know about it. But there're lots of secret funny places here. Old walls, remnants of buildings, sink holes to the quarries, all from when this was a farming village."

He'd woven a spell, and they were off on an adventure, and despite missing school for an afternoon, she'd learned history. At least that was the excuse he'd given her father.

Morbier knew how to reel her in. He could have a posse waiting to arrest her. But for all Morbier's faults, she doubted he'd do that. He'd have to have something so convincing or damning that she'd give herself up if she wanted to ever see her daughter again. He'd strike a deal. Like always with him, nothing came free.

Anything Morbier offered, she'd pay for.

THE CAFÉ AT Metro Jourdain opposite the church looked as if it were sliding down the hill. Or like those villages in Provence

perched on a steep crag, clenching onto the rock by fingertips—
a wonder of human resilience. During the war, Jourdain was
one of the steep Metro stations used as an air raid shelter until
the Germans took the whole line to turn it into an armaments
factory. Luckily, they never finished it before Libération. This
hilly northeastern part of Paris was once home to the anarchists,
thieves who escaped into the lawless heights and lived tax-free
until the waste ground and outlying villages were incorporated
in 1860.

Full of *habitués*, too. Bearded old men reading *L'Humanité*,
the Communist newspaper, children scooting up and down
between the outdoor tables and their parents. And the flower
shop, the *fromagerie*, the small bookstore and bistros were filled
with locals. A bit down at the heel in spots, tarnished, but well
worn and vibrant.

Could she spot surveillance? Outside on the terrace, the
young woman pushing a stroller and picking a table opposite? The waiter who greeted her with a more booming than
usual bonjour as he handed her a menu—was he flagging a
watcher?

About to leave, she saw Morbier beckoning her from inside
the café, where the awning had hidden him.

At least the tall doors were open to the terrace and she knew
there was an exit out the back by the WCs.

"Leduc," he said, puffing on a cigarette. "The usual?"

She nodded.

He summoned the waitress. "Two cafés double, *s'il vous plaît*."

After she left, Aimée looked around.

"Make this quick, Morbier," Aimée said, her voice lowered.
"I'm here only because of Chloé and you know that."

"You left the hospital treatment, absconded from police custody while a suspect and dropped me in the *merde*."

He cleared his throat and nudged her ankle with his foot under the table.

His go-to signal for her to be quiet. Listeners nearby.

The waitress set down two steaming demitasses of espresso.

"*Merci,*" he said, palming her a twenty-euro note.

She got the message and closed off the area with several chairs and a sign reading RESERVÉ.

"But apart from that . . . I won't mention the boomerang effect it had on me, Leduc."

He took several sips. Always one for the dramatic pause.

"I'm waiting," she said.

"You know Chloé's safe, I imagine. You know I would never use her. I don't know where she is, and no one is looking for her on our end."

She wanted to believe him.

"Is that golden, Morbier?"

"Gold."

It made her think.

"Why?"

"First of all, you're family."

Of course, because the police connections made Chloé part of the "family": Claude, her great-grandfather; Jean-Claude, her grandfather; and Melac, her father, were all in the force once.

Untouchable. Or among his contacts they were.

"What's so important that you need to show me?"

Aimée watched Morbier. He looked tired. And too old to be doing whatever he was doing. But his mind was sharp as a razor.

"Tell me," she said. "Or I leave in thirty seconds."

She downed the double espresso.

"Two anonymous letters arrived at the *commissariat*. Denunciations. Pointing the finger."

"Let me guess. At me."

He stared at her. "One. And the other saying Melac's murder points to *le Balafré*."

He handed her the photocopied letters.

Le Balafré. Eager, she read the one on top.

Printed in Arial, size thirteen font, double spaced and chilling.

> *I heard this couple shouting as I walked on the quai up from Stalingrad. Louder and louder. The woman accused the man of something, and it turned into a big fight. She had a knife, and I got nervous. The lights were out but the blade flashed in the moonlight. I didn't want to go closer and then the bridge was going down. I could see it from the reflection on the water. The man was screaming and she kept knifing him.*
>
> *I ran to find a public phone. None around anymore. I should have called and maybe saved his life from the woman. She wore black leather pants and has short spiky hair.*
>
> *Sophie, concerned citoyenne.*

"*Et alors*," she said. "There's a public phone near the bridge by the old brick pump house."

"And you happen to know this how?"

"I passed it en route," said Aimée. "The homeless *mecs* use it. It's in clear view. Go check."

"I did."

"There're a lot of details he got wrong in this."

"*He?*"

"It's got to be the killer who identified me. Yet where Melac was killed wasn't by the drawbridge. The bridge by the murder scene is narrow and arched and for pedestrians only. This writer's confusing it with the Crimée bridge farther up the canal, the only drawbridge left in Paris."

He'd made a mistake. Gotten it confused. Of course, she reasoned, he'd been following Melac, who'd been up by the bakery—and the baker had witnessed someone fiddling with the Crimée bridge. Maybe he'd been planning to attack Melac there but Melac had changed direction and gone to meet her.

"Get this analyzed."

"We did. They're eighty percent sure it's not a woman."

"Add my twenty percent."

She read the handwritten note next—a photocopy, torn from a grid-lined sheet and labeled with a police stamp: GRIDDED NOTEBOOK SHEET WITH BALLPOINT PEN.

Le Balafré's back. I saw him near the canal. His old haunts. He killed my friend's sister. I told anyone who'd listen that I'd seen him and he didn't look like the police drawing. Anyone who'd listen but they ignored me. Her brother didn't see him well in the elevator since he didn't have his glasses on. But he felt guilty and nervous because he should have watched out for his sister while his maman worked at night. Not let her go to the birthday party. He was afraid to tell his maman, he told me later. He was trying to help and then no one cared if he changed his mind. They wanted a face to look for.

Chilling, Aimée thought.

"First impressions, Leduc?"

Surprised, she looked at him. He wanted her opinion. Or did he? A big red flag waved.

Quit the doubting and get to it.

"I'd say he's telling the truth. After all, it's been years, and no one's recognized the killer from the police drawing. But it doesn't refer to Melac's murder."

She figured the writer was a classmate of the brother or a neighbor in the building.

"You see how *Anyone who'd listen* is underlined? Clearly, the letter writer attempted to inform the *flics*. They must have thought him too young to be taken seriously. He felt hurt, shut down, disillusioned, maybe?"

Aimée thought. Tried to lay out her impressions, stream of consciousness.

"If this was the victim's brother's friend, how old could he be?"

From inside a worn Leclerc shopping bag, Morbier pulled out a thick khaki folder.

It had LE BALAFRÉ on the cover. He thumbed it open, consulted the colored tabs and opened it to a photo and report.

"You're stealing police files now?"

He pulled out a new pack of Gauloises, tore the cellophane from the wrapping, opened the silver foil and tapped out an unfiltered cigarette.

"Want one, Leduc?"

Tempted, she declined. "I quit."

"You're always quitting."

Damn him. "Let me have the first hit."

And just like that, it was like they'd never had an argument. She wasn't a fugitive and her eyesight was magically back to normal. And he wasn't going to arrest her.

Morbier scratched a match on the table's jagged corner. The flame lit the tip of the cigarette, and she sucked in the smoke, filled her lungs and somehow didn't cough. Light-headed for a moment, she enjoyed the nicotine tang and handed it back to Morbier.

No matter what people said, the rush cleared her mind.

"Haven't the *commissariat* and vice division noticed the file's missing?"

"Who said it's missing? Flonet, after your dad's time, got stuck on this case after being one of the first at the crime scene. He wasn't a supergenius, but plodding and methodical. Detail-oriented and like a dog with a bone, he never gave up. A good *flic*."

Aimée stared at the victims' photos, sickened.

"Eight victims. Four were sixteen years old, and the other four were grandmothers in their seventies. Same MO."

Just what Jacquot Devries said.

"Meaning?"

"Ritualistic. Wire cord tying the wrists and neck so any struggle would strangle them."

Again confirming what Devries had said.

"Several times Flonet thought he'd come close. One time he just missed him."

"How did he know?"

"He found the victim strangled and her neck butchered from the cord. The blood was fresh, hadn't even clotted in the old woman's wound. I've seen rage killings but nothing like this."

Saddened, Aimée shook her head.

"Were the others like this?"

"I'm not finished. Flonet photocopied each page of the file as it grew, duplicated the photos until he retired."

"Isn't there a word for doing that? *Illegal?*"

"Flonet removed nothing and did this on his own time. His reference bible, he called it. He worked it even after his retirement."

"Classic hobby for a retired *flic*, eh?"

All *flics* had one case that got away from them. The one they couldn't let go of. She remembered her father's—the counterfeiter.

"But this one isn't your obsession, Morbier."

"Flonet's widow gave it to me. He'd put so much effort into this. It shouldn't go to waste. She said he wanted me to have it. Knew I'd pass it on until someone got this psycho."

"And you're passing it on to me? Why?"

Morbier gave an enigmatic smile, taking a hit. He exhaled and the bluish smoke spiraled to the ceiling.

Entranced by the way the smoke kept its form, its mission to rise, yet slowly evaporated, she thought about how this killer had evaded capture for all these years and remembered how Melac's killer had handcuffed her. Had spoken like a *flic*.

She'd said that all along.

"Wait a minute. What if the serial killer has remained uncaught all these years because he's one of you?"

It took one to know one.

Morbier inhaled and blew out a ring of smoke. "Why would he stop after 1994? Not that I'm agreeing with your theory."

But knowing Morbier, he probably did.

She ran her fingers over the granules of sugar spilled on the round marble table. "If *le Balafré's* military or in law enforcement—one of your own—it could make sense that some testimony and evidence got thrown out or ignored. Or misfiled." She thought back to her conversation with Devries. "Say *le Balafré* got interrupted after 1994. Things got hot, the investigation was coming close to him. Now he was afraid of being exposed or caught, his activity was at risk. So he moved. Or had a car accident. Died."

Morbier stubbed out his Gauloise in the chipped Formica ashtray with a blue faded Ricard logo.

"All the police work, evidence collection, witness statements and nuts and bolts were on point. Scrupulous and as detailed as we were in the eighties, there was no DNA testing like now."

"Isn't there crime scene evidence? Didn't you conserve the victim's clothing and the wire cord?"

"Everything." Morbier took a long draw. "The DNA found on Carine's clothing and the seven other victims matched. It took a while, until we got the technology for this. But as of two years ago, no found DNA matched anyone in the criminal database."

"So he wasn't in the criminal database . . ."

Her gaze caught on a short witness statement. Little follow-up. She pointed.

"But what about this kid's statement? He knew the family."

"If you mean this person, he's one Roget Dubois. You'll find him, but he's . . . emotionally unstable. Has cried wolf too many times."

Or was traumatized by what he'd witnessed?

"Sounds judgmental," she said. "But what does Melac have to do with this? This was never his case, or his era. He was a teenager in Brittany." She heard herself echoing René's thoughts.

"You're a detective, aren't you?"

She sat back, getting frustrated. "You've already accused me of murdering Melac and advised me to confess and plead self-defense."

"It's complicated, Leduc."

Never a good response.

"*Alors*, I'm covering for you but can't do it for much longer," he added.

Covering for her?

The young woman with the stroller on the terrace was watching them. She put on a black wool cap. A signal?

The waiter leaned over her with his tray.

Unease traveled up her spine.

"Read between the lines, Leduc."

A crazy thought hit her. Morbier was setting her up and using her to mask his real intel and investigation. He gave her the file so she'd investigate his theory about *le Balafré*. If she got caught, he'd be clean and she'd take the fall.

"You mean I'm your beard, your cover? And you'll keep the dogs off me?"

Twisted logic but so like him.

He shrugged.

"That's crazy."

"Keep in touch."

Code for *oui*. He played both sides of the field. For now it suited him to share info and let her go.

No surprise there.

She swore under her breath and took the thick file. She stood, then slid around the chair, blocking the space and edging back.

"Leduc, wait . . ." A half-hearted shout.

But she'd jumped past crates of beer and cartons of paper supplies, a laundry delivery of towels, napkins and aprons—white and pristine, hanging from a rail in the hallway—and ran.

Not a smart move. She'd sent the dull throb in her temple into high gear.

Merde. Double *merde*.

This smelled. Smelled like Morbier was using her to test a theory that the serial killer rapist was in the force—which in his capacity, he couldn't do.

This wasn't her job. Or was it?

If this related to Melac, it was.

She realized she wasn't going to find the killer only to save her skin—she needed to find justice for Melac, the father of her child. She owed him this.

But only the files would give her a heads-up on that.

Morbier was using her. Nothing new. Nothing came free from Morbier.

He always demanded repayment.

Wednesday Afternoon • Near Metro Jourdain

SHE'D COME UP with several leads to explore: a possible case involving Melac's old job in counterterrorism with Suzanne Lessage, his former colleague; the *brigade criminelle* case with Madame Olivera's daughter, and the implications that a neighborhood thug had seen Melac and enacted revenge; his uncle in Brittany and whatever he might know; and the job Melac had worked on in surveillance. Oh, and a serial murderer and rapist *flic* whom Morbier had tried to connect to Melac.

She hurried on. Thoughts raced through her head.

Who was the ghost?

She ducked into rue Fessart, removing her dark glasses and her wig as she walked. She stuffed them into the new bag she'd resupplied at Sébastien's worksite. Then she tied a wool scarf around her head, removed her coat, put a jean jacket over her shoulders and tied the sleeves sweater-like in front. Now she sported a different look. Head down, she turned the corner, then another, keeping pace with passersby. Not easy on the narrow streets behind the church.

On rue des Solitaires, she caught a piece of luck as a delivery man was passing through the gate at Cité du Palais Royal de Belleville, a long private cobbled passage full of small houses with front gardens leading through several courtyards to the next street.

She entered behind him and turned into the first doorway—a charming trellis with wilting roses framing it—and almost tripped over a bicycle.

Should she?

She hated stealing.

Her decision was made for her by a couple walking past the gates on rue des Solitaires. One of them spoke into a phone. "No sign. Target must have turned."

A Chihuahua had started barking from the house, its teeth bared at the window, yapping and jumping and gaining the couple's attention. Aimée ducked down and hoped she blended into the stiff hedge manicured to within an inch of its life.

Why wouldn't the dog stop yapping?

The woman turned around, stood in the middle of the narrow rue and ran her gaze over the grill gate. Her movements and reaction spoke to training and skills way beyond Aimée's ability to subvert. But Aimée didn't have to be better or smarter or quicker—she just had to get away. Aimée considered tossing dirt clods to distract the duo and point them in the other direction. *Weak.* But it was all she could think of with the yapping dog going into high gear and clawing the window. Its nails scraped the glass.

What if the couple came to investigate? She made herself breathe.

The next moment, the woman and the man had turned and headed back toward where they'd come from. They were running now.

Aimée didn't know what that was about. Or care. She had to use it.

Act like you belong, her father had taught her. Don't hesitate and never look unsure. Exude confidence or entitlement as the situation warrants.

Birds twittered from an orange tree with sparse-leaved branches. The sounds of someone practicing piano scales and the splash of water from a faucet drifted over the passage. *Peaceful.*

Aimée dusted the twigs off her jacket and walked over the cobblestones. She nodded to a young woman watering red geraniums at a window framed by pale blue shutters. From inside this postcard-perfect maisonette came a child's laugh. Like Chloé's. Her gut wrenched.

How she missed her daughter.

The young woman nodded back. Aimée kept her feet moving one in front of the other over the cobbles and didn't run.

Look like you belong.

She could do this.

Couldn't she?

If the duo, who she figured were secret agents from domestic intelligence or the *flics*, returned, the young woman would say she'd seen only residents pass *comme d'habitude*. If pressed, she'd remember someone in a jean jacket and turban.

Impatient, Aimée couldn't wait to read the info Morbier had given her. It had to be important since he'd gone through all this to meet up.

With *flics* canvassing the quartier for her and the clock ticking, she needed safety. Yet Morbier had made a point of showing her Flonet's file and the letters and emphasizing Roget Dubois. She had to find him.

She ducked into a musty cellar stairwell off one of the courtyards and thumbed through the thick file, looking for Dubois's address. An address on rue Petit had been crossed out. The other address listed was on passage du Plateau.

Close by.

She exited the tall, heavy double doors from this oasis of tranquility to the bustling rue de Belleville and its blaring horns and thronged pavements. A pâtisserie, café, florist and phone store were all jammed with late-afternoon shopping and life.

She tried to blend in with the shoppers and parents toting children after school. Tried to look busy and occupied like everyone else. To not stand out.

At rue de la Villette she turned the corner and kept pace with a couple as if she were with them.

Along the way, she recognized the round chimney, from what was once a laundry, peering over the rooftops, and a passage branching off the narrow street, which was an artery to northern Paris. She could imagine a panoramic view from the top floors on this side—a sweeping view all the way to the Left Bank.

When she reached a school, she stopped and got her bearings. From in front of Cité Florentine, a crack of a passage, she could see the street going downhill and the green of Parc des Buttes-Chaumont ahead.

Too far. Why hadn't she noticed?

On the opposite side of the street, she backtracked and passed a limestone mansion, set back from the street, fenced and with a gatehouse and gravel entryway. Like the landed gentry in the countryside. How in the world did this remain? It looked like it had been divided into apartments.

Passage du Plateau—as the crow flew—lay behind this mansion. Maybe once it had connected. A service entrance?

But it was so narrow that her shoulders almost scraped the walls. It was much older than the mansion. Medieval, from when this had been outside the city. She pulled out a cap and ditched the turban.

She knocked on the door of 23. No answer. Knocked again. "Delivery," she shouted. "I need a signature."

Still no answer.

"He's at the bar."

The voice had come from an overhanging window above.

"Bar?" Aimée looked up to see an older woman with a dust cloth.

"Just *en bas*, down there and around the corner."

THE NEEDLELIKE PASSAGE du Plateau gave way to another narrow street that slanted then veered right to the bar. A few patrons sat outside at tables over cloudy apéros. Kind of early, but then it was always apéro time for some. An original painted glass panel advertised AMOURETTE, depicting a woman of the belle epoque, faded and half worn off.

"Monsieur Dubois? Delivery." She raised her voice, waved an envelope she'd found in her bag.

One of the drinkers gestured inside.

The bar, an old bistro with a cracked tile floor and red-and-white checkered tablecloths, served simple bistro fare, evidenced by the chalkboard with the specials and by the lingering tomato aroma. The menu du jour was *fait à maison*, made in house. Her stomach growled.

Too bad lunch was over.

On the zinc counter, *très traditionnel*, were unwashed glasses, coins stacked by the beer pulls and an old-fashioned cash register. Little had changed from the last century by the look of it.

"*Allô?*"

A head popped out from behind the frosted glass-paneled door at the back. "*Un moment.*" The speaker disappeared.

Like she had time for this?

"Monsieur Dubois?"

The only answer—a clang of a pot.

Too bad if he was busy. So was she.

She marched across the tiled floor, a cracked mélange of

brown-and-blue design, reminiscent of her grandmother's farmhouse. It needed a scrub.

Local place, homemade fare, last remodeled in 1900, if that. At the window to the kitchen she heard metallic sounds and peeked inside.

"*Excusez-moi*, but if you're Roget Dubois, we need to talk."

"Impossible." He had on a hairnet over his dirty-blond hair, wore a long apron and was mashing garlic in a press. He looked about Aimée's height. Early thirties. The muscle in his cheek twitched.

"As in you're Roget but can't or don't want to talk? Or you're not Roget? Either way . . ."

The small kitchen was jammed with spices, pots, cans of olive oil and the pervading smell of caramelized onions and tomatoes. The cooktop took up most of the space. She felt claustrophobic.

"Who are you?"

"*Détective privé.*" Too bad she'd given her last card to Jacquot Devries, the journo. "It's about the letter you sent the *flics.*"

"I don't know what you're talking about."

"The anonymous letter indicating *le Balafré's* back."

"If you're not a *flic*, what's it to you?"

She kept going. "You wrote that no one listened to you about the victim on rue Petit, that the police drawing was wrong and the victim's brother told you so."

The dense, hot air had a layer of grease. She couldn't breathe.

"Why don't you answer my question," he said.

"Let's get out of the kitchen and go somewhere quiet."

"*Zut alors*, my *grand-mère's* sick so it's on me to stock and to prepare sauces for tonight."

She heard a flush and the spray of a water faucet. The lace-curtained old-fashioned glass door opened, and a woman with gray hair entered, then took an apron from the hook.

"Don't lie, Roget. Go clean up the bar."

It seems *grand-mère* was back in charge. She shooed them out.

Roget's eyes crinkled in fear, and the muscle in his cheek twitched into high gear. For a moment she thought he'd sprint out of the bar, get away.

"You're not in trouble. Look, we can talk while you work, okay?"

He hesitated.

"You wash and I'll dry."

At the bar, he plunged the glasses in the sink full of suds. While he was looking away, Aimée found the mini recorder in her go bag, stuck it in her pocket and powered it on.

"Why do you say *le Balafré's* back? Did you see him?"

"You're not a *flic*. Why should I talk to you?"

Back to zero. She just didn't have time to finesse an interrogation with him.

The suds splashed. After a quick rinse, she grabbed a towel. She'd have to tell it to him straight.

"*Vraiment?* I'll give you the ugly truth."

He looked at her expectantly, worried. If he was in his thirties like the victim's brother, he had a childlike attitude.

Time to stretch the truth. "Roget, they think it's a *flic*. That's why I've been pulled in."

His mouth gaped open. The towel squeaked on the glass.

"They? An inside job?"

"I'm privy to the investigation but not 'on' it, so it allows me to investigate my way. *Le Balafré* doesn't know. *Comprenez?*"

Roget scrubbed the glasses harder.

"Talk to me, Roget. Where did you see him?"

Roget looked around. Rinsed.

She waited him out, impatient. No one liked uncomfortable silences. She picked up a wet wine glass and dried.

On the terrace, the apéro drinkers were playing cards. the wind picked up, and small whirlwinds of leaves swirled in the gutter.

"I didn't make it up," he said.

Despite her impatience, she had to take this slow.

"I understand, Roget. If I thought you'd made it up, I wouldn't be here." She hoped that reassured him, and dried another wine glass.

She'd love an espresso and felt inclined to turn around and work the machine herself. Roget seemed jumpy. Aimée didn't want to lose him. He sent out panic vibes, but she couldn't let up.

"From all accounts, this investigation went wrong from the start," she said. "Can you fill me in on what happened from the beginning?"

He turned to the espresso machine. "Coffee?"

She thought he'd never ask and nodded.

"Tell it as you remember it, Roget."

He did. Once he got started, it all tumbled out while she dried and listened. He'd been a classmate of the first victim's brother. Roget detailed how it had unfolded from his then-sixteen-year-old's perspective. How no one had seen the girl, Carine, after she left for her friend's birthday party wearing a miniskirt and eye makeup, which her mother forbade. How Hugues, her brother, remembered seeing a man with acne scars in the elevator. How Roget had seen a pockmarked man at the back of the building before he and Hugues went to the movies that night. How later all of them had mentioned this man to the police.

How Carine's friends said she'd never shown up at the party. How Carine's mother called home as usual that night and she hadn't answered. Hugues's shock when next day his sister's body was found in the cellar below the building's laundry. The horror and pain.

How Hugues showed him the police sketch and said no, it was not like the man he remembered seeing. How Roget then remembered the man with pockmarks on his face, who looked nothing like this portrayal.

Aimée found another towel and kept drying.

He spoke of this in vivid, sharp details, as if it were yesterday.

"Are you in contact with her brother? The family?"

"Why?"

"You say in this note you saw *le Balafré* again. Wouldn't you share that with them?"

Roget shook his head. "They moved a long time ago. I'm not good at writing. Or using the computer."

But he'd written to the police.

She took a guess. "Dyslexic?"

His lip went out in a pout.

"I hate that word. It's a label."

"My cousin, too," she said. "School was always so hard for him. But he's found his niche, what he loves doing. He even owns his business."

He still hadn't answered her question.

"I believe you," she said. "I do, but let's talk about the present-day sighting. That's vital now. Please give me the details."

There was silence, apart from the splash of soapy water and the low conversation and slap of cards from the outside tables.

She tried another tactic. "Do you know Jacquot Devries, the journo who wrote for *Le Parisien*?"

"Him? He's still a nosy reporter. He didn't listen, like all the rest."

"You mean you told him what you've told me?"

A nod. "Ages ago."

"I think he's changed his thinking and wouldn't doubt you now."

"Like I care? *Pwahh* . . . He's a waste of space."

Aimée wouldn't argue with him. Or get sidetracked. She needed to keep her goal front and center. A patron beckoned from the terrace to settle the bill.

A few minutes later, Roget returned and stacked coins in a pile by the beer pulls.

"Where did you see him, Roget?"

"In the park."

She thought of the nearest: Parc des Buttes-Chaumont.

"You mean Buttes-Chaumont? By the playground?"

Why had she asked that? Was it because she took Chloé there often?

He nodded.

"But there're three playgrounds, a donkey ride and . . ."

"It's on my way to my other job. Something about him made me look twice. It was as if he was watching me."

Paranoid?

"What do you mean? How can you be sure?"

"I felt stuck to a wall with a pin. Inspected like a specimen."

Was he delusional? Crying wolf as Morbier had said?

"How could he recognize you after all these years? You looked different then. So did he."

The phone rang in her pocket. René.

"I've got to take this," she said. "Hold on."

Out on the street, René's voice competed with the noise of a siren.

"I need to give you something. It's important."

"In person?"

The grinding of the garbage trucks, metal on metal, grated in her ear.

"Where can you get to in thirty minutes?"

She thought quick. Remembered la Vache Bleue, the alternative art space under the old railway arches on the canal at quai de l'Oise.

She gave him the address.

"*D'accord*," said René. "See you in thirty."

"This better be worth it, René."

But he'd hung up.

Great.

Interrupted right when she was getting through to this young man who acted like a sulky teenager.

But Roget seemed like he'd closed off while she was gone. Maybe she'd missed her chance to get some real answers out of him.

"Please, talk to me," she said. "I need more than what you've told me to find this man."

If he even exists. She was ready to give up on this Roget. He was unreliable.

No attacks had been attributed to *le Balafré* for years. Was he in prison or dead, like Devries had posited?

Wait, what had Isabelle said about rumors?

Now she remembered. She'd almost forgotten.

That's right—Isabelle said on Sunday a young woman had been attacked near the canal. The attacker had been interrupted and fled, but he'd left a wire.

Le Balafré's signature.

She filed this away to think about later.

Could this Roget have been traumatized and permanently affected by what had happened to his friend?

Still no response. A waste of time. He offered nothing new.

"*Désolée*," she said, setting down the towel and grabbing her bag.

"The man did this jerky, kind-of-nervous thing with his fingers. Like crazed spiders. I heard his ring, a metallic sound, tapping on the play structure. That's what caught my attention."

She turned around.

"Just like that, in the park?"

Her skin tingled. A buzz went up her spine. Was that in the file she'd only glanced at? Not general knowledge?

"Can you show me?"

He tented his soapy fingers, made them crawl and twisted them like Aimée did with Chloé when they played "Itsy Bitsy Spider."

"You're sure?"

"I don't know. I just kept walking. He looked older, too. He had a light beard, you know, like people do to cover up bad skin."

"You're sure?"

"How could I forget that weird man?"

"Did he recognize you?"

"I'm not sure."

A hunted look filled his eyes.

"What happened?"

"I just saw him get on a motorcycle."

The Angels or someone else?

She looked at her Tintin watch. *Merde*, she'd be late for René. A lump settled in her stomach.

"Meet me later at the park, show me where, okay?"

"Only when the park's closed."

"I need proof, *comprenez*? Proof that he's here. To stop him before he attacks again."

Roget scribbled something on a beer-stained coaster.

A diagram with *X*'s and *10* P.M.

"Follow that. It's how everyone gets into the park."

AIMÉE STOPPED AT the fix-it shop she'd passed down the street. To beat several Metro changes, she forked over a wad of euros and bought the used kick scooter she'd seen in the window—it was a dull silver with pink handlebars. Going down the hills, she'd reach her destination quickly. The brisk air, the lights twinkling in the dusk—they gave her an exhilarating sense of freedom, as if she were flying past the park, cars and buses.

Her cheeks reddened in the chill. She felt alive.

Let the killer try and catch her.

By la Vache Bleue, the canal split left and north into Canal Saint-Denis. Here, hidden ateliers and cultural spaces nestled off the quai; art lessons, tarot readings, tango and salsa classes, along with Afro-Caribbean and Portuguese fado music at night. Everything happened in the coved trestles under the old *petite ceinture* railway—*très alternatif.* The fence was blue, the greenery decorated with colorful lanterns and Tibetan prayer flags. Wind chimes tinkled and leaves rustled on the plane tree branches.

She'd made good time, had beat René. So she sat down on a log bench, folded the *trotinette* and set it against her knee. She then opened the file on *le Balafré* and gave it her full attention.

On October 12, 1986, a few days after the homicide of sixteen-year-old Carine Joffre in the cellar of her apartment building, a police investigation had accounted for all the building's tenants and visitors within the eighteen-hour period of her murder. This resulted in a police sketch of a suspect, widely disseminated in the media, depicting a man around age thirty, with chestnut hair and pock-marked skin on his face. This composite sketch was created based on the testimonies of several people who had seen a man, unknown to any tenants, of this description in the building the evening of the murder. Witnesses included the victim's half brother.

That much she knew.

Why hadn't Roget's conflicting testimony gotten logged? It made her wonder what else hadn't made it into this report. She continued reading.

Sometime after the departure of her mother for her evening job, Carine would have taken the elevator to go to her friend's party. Her attacker had then probably overpowered her, dragging her into the cellars to rape and kill her. She was found with her hands bound together as if in prayer, strangled by common electric wire and tied in a kneeling position.

Le Balafré, as the suspect was nicknamed due to the sketch of his pockmarked face, was then suspected of a second murder exhibiting the same signature. Anne Roussel, sixteen, disappeared in April 1987. Her body was discovered underground in a blockhaus, now a site of techno parties, in a kneeling position with the same type of ligature wire tying her wrists. This old German bunker at the edge of the nineteenth arrondissement was near her parents' apartment. A list of six more rapes and murders committed between 1986 and 1994 with the same wire ligatures and disturbing staged scene of prayer were attributed to him, per the Paris prosecutor's office.

Hideous, Aimée thought.

According to this report, in 1994, after the eighth murder was linked to *le Balafré*, the case evidence samples from each crime scene were compiled, compared and tested for DNA. The resulting DNA on each of the victims' clothing and on the wire used to bind and strangle them corresponded to the DNA of one person. However, none of the DNA had been matched to anyone in the existing criminal database.

Aimée looked up and saw René by a hewed chunk of wood shaped and painted red like a billiard ball. Near him was a hanging installation of old tobacco pipes and Italian olive tins with faded labels strung together by mustard-yellow silk threads.

"Where's the blue cow?" he said.

"In back." She pointed to the life-size sculpture.

"Why's the cow upside down?"

Upside down—just how she felt.

"Art?"

"I'd never find this place on my own. You must know it exists to find it. Perfect for Saj," said René. He sniffed. "They even burn his kind of incense."

Aimée sneezed.

"What's so important, René?"

"You need help."

"I know that."

"Legal and physical," he said, ignoring her tone as he pulled out his phone.

"Both of those take time I don't have," she said.

A dull thud grew in her head.

"If we want to keep the business running—a business in which I'm also a partner and shareholder—I need to work with our clients, honor the contracts to avoid bankruptcy. Saj needs stability, too. Not to mention what will happen to Chloé if you go to prison."

The thudding amped up to a ringing in her ears. All the precursors to an attack of blindness. This couldn't be happening.

The other day, she'd gotten up, kissed her daughter goodbye, then gone to work—and now she was a fugitive. Was being hunted.

Her head throbbed. Tangles of what looked like black twigs webbed her vision, and she felt dizzy. She closed her eyes, put her head down.

"What's the matter? Are you all right?"

"Fine. Just give me a second."

If she waited, the nausea and dizziness would pass.

Wouldn't it? She took a deep breath. Then another.

"Too much stress, Amy. Like last time. Don't you ever learn?"

Amy? That's what her American mother called her.

But it couldn't be her. She was wanted herself—on the Interpol's watch list.

She blinked, and the bright light pierced her vision.

"Wait . . . René?"

Someone stuck a pair of glasses behind her ears.

"Keep these on, Amy."

There was no mistaking that American accent.

"Maman?"

Bile rose in her throat. Any minute she'd gag. She kept her eyes shut.

"You're going to stand up," her mother said. "I've got your arm. Follow my lead and take small steps. I'll guide you. We're getting in the car."

"What car?"

"Not the one that followed you," she said. "Don't worry."

"But what about my scooter?"

"Still a kid, eh?"

"Where's my bag, my things?"

"I've got you. Breathe, Amy. For once, listen to your mother."

THEN THEY WERE walking. Not toward the quai because she couldn't smell the water or boat oil, only odors of greenery and car exhaust. And the echo of their steps against stone. Or brick. She heard a car door open, then felt a hand on her head and a whisper in her ear.

"Bend down. You're climbing into the back seat of a rental car. Keep down and lie on the floor. No matter what happens."

Was René driving? Where were they going? Why was her mother here?

All she had were questions.

But the big one—what car had followed her?—raked like wire up her spine.

She didn't know how long she lay on the car's carpeted floor, which smelled like peppermint bonbons. In the background she heard the low hum of the news channel RFI on the radio. She must have closed her eyes.

The next thing she knew, she heard an automatic garage door closing. The back door of the car opened, and fresh air blew in and over her bare ankles. By the time she struggled out of the car and to her feet, the nausea and dizziness had faded. She was wearing Jackie O dark wraparound glasses. She could see.

She stood staring at her mother, Sydney Leduc, at her large dark eyes and high cheekbones—the look they shared. Her mother looked healthier than when she'd last seen her in Bel-Air . . . what, a year ago? Two, more? Had it been that long? She wore a deep blue embroidered caftan, pointed citrus-green Moroccan-leather slippers and a thin silk scarf studded with mirrors and tassels.

A hippie boho look of a woman who could afford it. She looked like one of those women of a certain age who chased down the latest trends. Would Aimée resemble her mother when she got that old?

Yet on her mother, it looked *parfait*. She looked vibrant, and her skin glowed. Not bad for an old radical. Her hair was now dark blond, and she was tan and healthy.

Only two reasons for that—a miracle spa treatment or a lover. Both, maybe?

At her age?

"Where have you come from, *Maman*?"

She couldn't help wanting to know.

"Guess."

"Casablanca?"

"Close. Algiers. I was working."

In that outfit? Aimée almost choked.

"You wear something like that to work?"

"Undercover, Amy," Sydney said, taking her elbow again. "Take it from me, a professional. You need some pointers."

Her mother had that right.

"Why are you here?"

A latent maternal instinct?

"Morbier sent for me."

Shocked, Aimée didn't know what to think. Sydney Leduc couldn't be bothered to check in with her daughter for more than a year, but all Morbier had to do was send a signal and she would come jetting to his aid from a far-off country?

But then again, hadn't her mother always put Aimée as the lowest priority?

It still stung how all her classmates' mothers had picked them up from school and attended their piano recitals. Her mother had never come.

She wanted to strike out and kick something.

No. She had to grow up. Had to deal with this woman. She couldn't relapse into a little girl having a tantrum because her mother had abandoned her.

"Don't tell me you're jealous," said Sydney. "Mommy issues again?"

It was as if she could read her mind.

Or was it painted on her face?

"Not the time, Amy."

It's never the time with you, she almost spit.

"You come here like some winged hippie *warrioresse* to, what . . . impart wisdom? Tell me what I've done all wrong? My baby's father was murdered, and I've been set up for it."

"And you're going to find justice. That's also why I'm here," she said. "Feel better?"

Aimée nodded.

"Let's take the elevator," said her mother.

"You could have called me."

Why had that come out all pouty?

"It's better for me to show up on-site when there're problems to be solved. Plus your phone's tapped and your office and apartment are under surveillance."

Sydney treated this meeting like a job. Forget a warm family moment.

After all this time, why did her mother surprise her?

The elevator opened onto a panoramic view encompassing Paris. Under the clear indigo sky, cotton ball clouds floated and sun glinted over the Sacré-Coeur to the gold dome of the Opéra Garnier, the glass roof of the Grand Palais and the khaki ribbon of the Seine and even the Tour Eiffel. The small winding streets below led to Buttes Bergeyre. Aimée spotted a tiny strip of grape vines harkening back to when this had all been a vineyard.

René's eyes popped. "Who lives here?" he said, awe in his voice.

The house, built into the rock, was an engineering feat. She felt like she was in a plane's cockpit flying over the city.

"Let's say a well-known writer has contracted Sébastien for a remodel," Sydney replied. "It's vacant and safe for twenty-four hours."

And Sébastien hadn't tipped her off that her mother was back in town? *Zut!*

"What a place," said René. "If it's the author I think it is, I'm paying for some of this remodel. I love her books."

He reached on his tiptoes to the lowest shelf and ran his finger over the leather spines of the books. "Like a female Maigret. You'd like them, Aimée."

Aimée never had time to think, much less read. But at least her mind had started up again—her brain was functioning.

She saw several cases of bottled water—for the workers, she imagined—and took out three Evians, then passed them around. She took several gulps before turning to her mother.

"First, I need to make sure Chloé is safe," said Aimée.

"About that, here's the bad news," said René. His frown lines etched deep in his brow.

She fought a sense of panic as he set down a legal form. Aimée leaned in to read it. Melac's sister in Brittany had filed for custody of Chloé.

She made herself breathe.

"That woman's trouble—even Melac avoided her. She's bad news, all right, René."

"Does Chloé even know her?"

Aimée shook her head. "She has no right. Melac and I never married or really lived together. What am I supposed to do about this?"

Her mother checked her phone. "It's taken care of."

Aimée had a strange feeling. "Did you take my daughter without my permission?"

"Yes and no." Aimée's mother sat down on a rattan chair and

sipped the Evian. "They've crossed the border into Switzerland. Should be arriving at the chalet in ten minutes."

"Switzerland?"

"Outside Geneva, a little place I use. Your name's on the deed. Part of your inheritance, all legal. No chance of anyone accusing you of kidnapping charges, since it's your *maison secondaire*."

News to her. Again.

Was that legal?

"Does this involve an unnumbered Swiss bank account?"

"*Tsk*, Amy, that's so eighties."

Of course it was. Now it was about loading assets to offshore accounts. Shell companies.

"Babette had exams," said her mother. Babette, Aimée's jewel of a nanny, was in nursing school. "So I found a new Babette, her cousin, and she, Auntie Regula, and Cousin Gil will keep Chloé company."

Aimée wanted to be angry but felt a grudging admiration.

"Handled just like that?"

Her mother looked at her Rolex.

"That's what I do, Amy. I handle things," she said.

"You could have handled some of this by phone."

"But it's always better to take care of things in person."

Too bad she hadn't felt this way when Aimée was eight years old. Back when Sydney had chosen to disappear instead of staying with her family.

Aimée had so many questions.

"Why did Morbier reach out to you?"

"This isn't the first time, Amy. Morbier and I understand each other," Sydney said. "Can't say we're best friends, but he tries, in his own way."

Again, news to her. Well, maybe she'd always had a feeling,

growing up, that Morbier communicated with Sydney, since Aimée's father wouldn't. But still.

What else hadn't she known?

"He really wants your family to work. He confides in me, not that I encourage him. Morbier asked for my help, saying 'this Melac thing' had stumped him and he didn't know where to turn."

And he'd called Aimée's mother?

"Do you think whatever 'this' is got Melac killed?" René asked.

Again Aimée saw Melac's body caught in the grill of the canal bridge in the inky black night. She felt the freezing water, the stickiness of his blood dripping from her hands. It hit her in the gut, like a delayed reaction after going into shock.

Breathe. Breathe and focus.

She tuned back in just as Sydney asked her, "So Melac hadn't told you his uncle thought he knew who the serial killer was, but that the man was dead?"

Aimée fell into the chair. Her jaw dropped.

Where had that come from?

"*Non*, but the last thing Melac said to me was he thought he'd seen a ghost," she said. "Did Morbier say Melac was investigating this serial killer? Why? Tell me exactly what Morbier said."

Sydney looked disappointed that she had to explain it once again. "Melac's uncle thought a gendarme he worked with in the motorcycle unit was *le Balafré*. Melac had gone to the man's funeral several years ago. That's it."

"I don't understand how a serial killer connects to Melac's murder."

Her mother set down the empty Evian bottle. "I've got no idea."

"What if this gendarme never died? Say he was back on the prowl," Aimée said, talking almost faster than she was thinking. "Have the *flics* checked any unexplained murders to see if they match *le Balafré's* MO? Or maybe Melac happened to accidentally see him and recognized him? A coincidence?" She shot a look at her mother. "Papa said there were no coincidences in crime."

Sydney stood and looked out the window to rue Georges Lardennois. Her alert gaze swept the street below—like a pro. "He was right."

"As about so many things, *Maman*," Aimée said, watching for a reaction.

Nothing. Of course. She really was a pro.

"My taxi arrives in a minute," Sydney said. "Sorry, but I'm in the middle of an operation. Don't worry, Chloé's safe." She reached for a travel bag Aimée hadn't noticed. "This is for you."

Surprised, Aimée looked at her. "What about you?"

"I travel light. So should you. Inside you'll find new burner phones programmed with the Swiss number. Give one to René. If anything happens, destroy the SIM cards. Meanwhile, you might want to make sure you're not followed. Sébastien, either."

How could Sydney leave without actually giving Aimée anything she could work with?

"But even if he saw him again—in the flesh—Melac would have had to prove the man was a serial killer," Sydney said, "exhibit evidence of crimes he'd committed. Show proof that he'd faked his own death."

A long road.

"But Melac ran his own investigation business," said Aimée, "and his computer files don't contain any contract or case like this."

"I won't ask how you know that," said her mother.

"I should talk to Melac's uncle again and see what he knows."

"How well do you know the uncle?" asked René.

"I don't," said Aimée. "Met him twice."

"Were they estranged or on speaking terms?"

"They were close."

Weren't they? She thought back to the call she'd made to him, his curt response. "His phone was tapped."

"Tapped as in, he's under investigation? Or he's targeted like Melac?"

"Like I know?" Aimée said. "But he made it clear his line wasn't safe."

Talking to him on the phone again wouldn't work. She needed to talk to him face-to-face.

That would be difficult. She had never felt so close and yet so far from the truth. With a groan, she hung her head.

All of a sudden, her mother was hugging her. She was enveloped in soft arms, that cloud of muguet—lilies of the valley—her signature scent.

"Close your eyes, rest, breathe. And you'll be fine. Chloé's safe."

"If anything happens to me—"

"It won't," interrupted her mother.

"Don't say things you don't know are true. No more lies from you."

Her mother batted her eyelids. "I mean, I can't—couldn't bear to lose you after we've . . ." She stopped, her voice thick with emotion. "I love you. If anything happens, I will defend Chloé with my life. She'll be safe. Always."

Aimée nodded. What more could anyone ask? And with her mother, a trained assassin and agent, this counted.

Then, in a puff of perfumed air, Sydney was in the elevator. Gone.

Aimée watched through the window as the taxi drove away. Not a real taxi Parisien, with the red light and distinctive markings, but an unmarked car that resembled a taxi at a quick glance.

Dealing with her mother was like those Russian nesting dolls, brightly painted *matryoshkas*. You opened one doll and found another inside. And then another. A riddle wrapped in a mystery inside an enigma, as someone had said. She couldn't remember who.

"Road trip, René? I want to talk to the uncle in Brittany."

René wagged his finger.

"*Pas du tout.* I'm doing the road trip and you're getting a thermos of coffee ready for me."

Not his usual herbal tea?

"I'll call you when it's done."

She wanted to go. But what if her eyesight went south? Not to mention she still had a lot of loose ends to follow up on here.

René excelled at interrogations—no one expected a man of his stature to have a pit bull side. He never let go.

"Work remotely from here. You're good for twenty-four hours. It's ideal, clean from any surveillance."

Ideal, all right. She was supposed to meet Roget Dubois after dark. She was so close to Parc des Buttes-Chaumont she could practically spit on it.

Armed with a thermos, recharged phones and laptop, René took off from the garage in his rented Renault Clio. Not his first choice of car, but the model was easily adaptable to his pedal extenders and cushions for extra seat height. He calculated a drive of four and a half hours. He'd sleep on Melac's farmland— the Clio's seat fully reclined—and at dawn he'd be up to find Melac's uncle at the harbor before he set sail. He promised to check in when he got there.

Aimée boiled water, her only culinary skill, and made *une cafetière* of strong coffee.

The mesmerizing view of Paris gave her an excuse to drink her coffee, gaze at the city and plot out what she knew so far.

Go back to the beginning, her father had always said.

She popped a Doliprane. It was almost time to meet Roget. She debated whether it would be better to stay here—safe—and rest her eyes.

But if he'd actually recognized *le Balafré*, she had to know.

Wednesday Evening • Parc des Buttes-Chaumont

OUTSIDE ON RUE Manin, Aimée kept to the shadows. A half-moon hung in the night sky, and the wind rustled a stray newspaper on the pavement. The street bordered the western side of the park, and few people were out. Every gate she passed was locked, and only a few of the cafés were still open. Under the plaque commemorating the 1944 Resistance attack on *la petite ceinture*, Aimée followed Roget's instructions; she slid to the side three loose metal bars—marked by a small chalk smudge—and ducked through into the park's high shrubbery.

Good thing she'd changed into red high-tops, courtesy of her go bag. If only she'd remembered a dark balaclava to hide her face.

Crouched down, she hunched through the tunnel carved in the shrubbery, trying to hold her breath and not inhale any bugs. The chirr of insects, a croak of a frog and trill of night birds made it feel like the countryside in the middle of Paris. Once it had been.

Would she make it in time? Would he even come?

She walked past the wooden Guignol puppet theater. Chloé had watched transfixed when Aimée took her, then had squirmed off her lap to run to the playground. She felt a lump forming in her throat thinking that one day Chloé would run off forever. Someday Aimée would hold her in her lap and it would be the last time and she wouldn't know.

A path wound up the incline, through alders, beech and black pine trees, dim in the moonlight amid the pervading smell of damp grass. The evening chill made her glad she'd buttoned up the wool coat and looped the warm scarf around her neck.

Above, the Greek-style Temple of Sybil perched on Île du Belvédère, a rocky promontory connected by suspension bridges arched over the man-made lake. One of them, the "suicide" bridge, was where love affairs ended with spurned lovers jumping off into the lake below.

As she approached the path to the grotto, she let her senses take over. She paused, closed her eyes and tuned her ear to the birdsong and the lapping water in the lake. Right now she needed to be aware, alert to anything out of the usual. She didn't want to interrupt a drug deal or stumble on people making love, which often happened at night in the parks.

Focus. Concentrate. All she heard was the cascading water hitting stone in the grotto. Built in the old gypsum and limestone quarry on the south side of the park, the grotto was sculpted with artificial stalactites. Chloé loved them.

Her little one was in Switzerland. Across the border in another country without her.

Grow up. Time to quit the pity party. Focus.

But it was too late by the time she grew aware of pounding footsteps. Someone grabbed her arm.

"We can't stay here."

It was Roget. The glow of blue police lights spread over the bushes.

"What's going on, Roget?"

Roget took off. She broke into a run, following him. Ahead a searchlight beam roamed over the trees, illuminating the shrubbery.

Of all the times. Since when did the *flics* waste time on park raids? *Useless.* There was plenty of crime to go around on the street. Roget stopped and stood stock-still, and she almost ran into him.

The searchlight framed a figure. He was face down in the shallow water—his arms out.

He looked familiar.

A dog was barking.

The clouds drifted, and sparse moonlight illuminated the suspension bridge above the path. Silver glinted—metal crutches.

Good God.

"There's a body," Roget whispered. "Over there."

The dog continued barking, pawed at the water. The wet hair fanned out in the shallow water. She knew him.

Aimée pulled Roget back.

"It's Jacquot Devries, the crime reporter. And his dog, Bette." Roget had gone quiet. "But how could he get up there on that bridge with crutches?"

"What do you mean?" Roget shook his head.

"Were you meeting him? Did you arrange this?"

"*Moi?* No way. Nobody knew I was meeting you."

This seemed too coincidental.

"You detested him, *non?*"

Roget sputtered. "He didn't listen, said I'd made everything up."

She remembered him saying this as she'd dried the glasses at his grandmother's bistro.

The searchlight beam swept the bushes, almost brushing Aimée's feet. The smell of algae and ripe lake scum filled her nostrils. Any second the searchlight would catch her. *Had* Roget made all this up? Was he unhinged, as the report noted?

"Did you kill him?"

Roget backed away, hurt and confusion in his eyes. "You're just the same, blaming me."

She was accusing him like everyone else had.

"I'm sorry, Roget." *Idiot.* Now he'd never open up to her. "Forgive me. Seeing his body scared me. But I had no right to accuse you."

She hoped he'd buy it.

A pause.

"Why did you want to meet me tonight?" she tried. "Did you remember something?"

"I did. I meant to tell you."

"What's that?" Again he shook his head. His lip was trembling. "I'm being watched by the one who pushed the journo off the bridge."

"Who do you mean?"

"There might be marks on the journo's wrists, like Hugues said."

She froze.

"Hugues, Carine's brother?" Aimée asked.

A nod.

"What marks?"

"Hugues told me when they . . . when they found Carine, there was cord on her wrists."

"Did Hugues tell you anything else about *le Balafré*?"

But suddenly Roget was off and running back in the direction she'd come. The pea gravel spit from his footsteps on the path. *Merde!*

Ducking through the spruce branches, she tried to catch up with him. She didn't hear him anymore. Was he on the grass? What did she know about him except that he was paranoid and held a grudge? He might very well have thrown a reporter he detested off a bridge. But if he hadn't, Devries's murderer might be on to him. The path dead-ended. *Great.* She was lost, with no one to trust and a killer on the loose.

Focus.

She squatted, felt around in the shrubbery for a hole, a break in the bushes. Nothing. She lay flat and still on the dirt. She closed her eyes and listened to the sounds: a night bird's song, rustling in the bushes followed by the tramping of footsteps.

Right behind her. *Merde.* Perspiration dripped down her neck.

Finally her hands found a gap in the leaves. The tunnel. Head down, she pulled herself ahead by her palms, concentrating on using every protesting muscle to get all of her out of sight. If only she could find the loose metal rungs in the park's fence, find the way she'd come in.

On her hands and knees, Aimée backtracked through the bushes, gnats stinging her face and juniper branches scratching her hands. The cold earth dug under her already-chipped nails. Dense vegetal smells reigned until a whiff of burnt rubber almost made her sneeze.

At last—the end of the tunnel. Beyond the fence, the lights of the street glowed dim in the mist. *Thank God.* About to push herself forward, she saw two parked police cars and several blue uniforms piling out. Then came the whine of the siren echoing as the first responders—always the firemen—pulled up.

She had to find another way out. Her gut screamed to get going.

She followed a flicker of firelight shining through the branches on the right. Burning tires explained the smell. The fence was broken here, the only barrier a misshapen chicken wire easy to crawl over.

Now she faced a steep drop to the disused railroad track. The haunt of badgers, raccoons and the occasional fox, or partyers and homeless people, depending on the season.

A couple, arms entwined, stood by the fire, but Aimée saw no one else. For now.

No choice but to grab the well-used half-frayed rope tied around the base of an alder tree, say a prayer and lower herself, bit by bit.

Her fingers kept slipping as she rappelled down the steep embankment. She cursed inside, trying to wedge her high-top toe into the hard dirt, desperate to get a foothold.

Her grip loosened. She felt herself slipping.

Falling.

She flailed for branches or vines, but to no avail. She landed on her *derrière*.

What a racket. *Good God.* The couple by the burning tires turned and shot her a look.

Would they rat her out?

But they were more concerned with the bottle they passed back and forth.

She struggled to her feet and followed the metal train tracks glinting in the moonlight. With every step, she tried to land on the rail tie and avoid the crunching gravel.

She risked a glance up but didn't notice any blue lights from a police car, flashlight beams or shouts to stop.

Somehow despite all the noise she'd made, no one had appeared.

Yet.

A sharp, pointed fence topped with razor wire blocked the tracks to the zone closed off to the public. Cliff-like embankments narrowed and lined both sides.

Great. She was stuck. Like a panting pig in a cage, ready for slaughter.

She unbuttoned her coat and climbed the fence. Somehow she pushed through the pain, the exhaustion. Once at the top, she laid her coat over the razor wire and wrapped her scarf around her hand like an oven mitt. Her ears tuned to the night sounds of insects and the distant wheeze of trains from Gare du Nord's marshalling yards.

The razor wire and angle of the metal fence reminded her of photos from Ravensbrück, a Nazi concentration camp for women, which her old neighbor had shown her once. Her neighbor had been the only one in her family to return alive from the camp.

Adrenaline spurred her, and despite the scratches and the strain in her muscles, she climbed over the fence and landed on the other side.

Gasping. Trying to catch her breath. Where was she now?

She heard voices, a conversation, above on the steep bank.

She flattened herself and tried not to move, tried to slow her breath.

"We responded to an emergency call," said a male voice.

Had the murderer called it in?

"An object was clogging the lake's drain, causing it to overflow, sir. The gardener investigated and found the body."

Silence broken by the crackling of a walkie-talkie's static. She'd almost stumbled into a police conversation.

Quiet. She had to keep quiet and get info.

"The ID's wet but the victim's a Monsieur Jacquot Devries. He's got a press sticker on his license. A well-known muckraker."

Muckraker meant he'd ticked off the *flics* in his reportage.

"His crutches are on the suspension bridge. Seems like no one saw or heard him fall. The park's closed. An old dog's whining near his body."

Poor Bette.

A pause.

"No idea why, sir?"

Another pause.

"Maybe he forgot which one was the suicide bridge."

How cruel could they get? *Do your job*, she almost shouted.

The walkie-talkie clicked off.

Aimée didn't dare move.

"*Alors*, a man on crutches with a heavy cast would need a lot of time to get up there and jump," said another voice, presumably his partner.

They stood just above her in the trees on the embankment.

"You'd just have to haul yourself over the railing. If there's a will, there's a way."

"The *commissaire* doesn't buy suicide. He's having the park surrounded, roadblocks put up . . ."

Gravel spit and crackled as they walked away.

Aimée didn't hear the rest. She didn't need to.

Was it possible Roget had pushed the journo from the bridge before meeting her? Killers often used meetings as alibis. To set this up would have required planning, expertise and physical strength. Did Roget possess those qualities?

Was his mental instability a cover?

Layered on this was the blatant police prejudice against the journalist. Did he know too much about *le Balafré*?

She had a slim chance to get out before the roadblocks. Here, she was a fugitive. No way could she be found at another murder scene. The grinding headache had returned.

Her phone vibrated in her pocket.

René, checking in?

She let it go, would worry about it later.

Aimée spied metal rungs in the wall leading up to the graffitied, boarded-up station. Plastic bags whipped in the wind. Within seconds she'd scrambled through a beaten path to a hole in some siding. Beyond that was the park's metal fence. She put her last bit of energy into climbing over it—thank God for the alder tree branch next to it.

She landed on her feet and kept moving, staying in the shadow. So far, she hadn't run into any police activity. If only a taxi came by—where was her taxi karma when she needed it? She crossed the street and huddled in a doorway as a police van passed by.

Up at Botzaris Metro, she hopped the turnstile. Then heard a shout from the ticket booth. Not turning back, she ran to the platform and jumped on the 7bis, one of the shortest train lines in Paris. She kept her head down and changed at Place des Fétes, then rode three stops to Belleville, changed lines and got out at Colonel Fabien. It was such a roundabout way to get there, but she'd avoided roadblocks.

By the time she climbed the steep street and entered the house through the garage, her head's throbbing was nearly unbearable. She drank water, popped some Doliprane and watched the searchlights scanning the Parc des Buttes-Chaumont outside her window. She shivered and pulled the duvet close around her.

Thursday Morning • Brittany

RENÉ DOWNSHIFTED AND parked at the Breton village dock. Seagulls cried under a gunmetal sky. Dawn had broken. Second thoughts assailed him about this brilliant idea of driving to Brittany and questioning Melac's uncle.

He'd taken a wrong turn off the highway, run into a detour and lost valuable time.

His hip ached; dampness exacerbated his hip dysplasia. Driving and sleeping in the car hadn't helped, either.

The cobbled Breton fishing village, all white limestone façades, metal shutters and geraniums in window boxes, fronted the narrow harbor. Five or so fishing boats were moored, and fishing nets stretched over the concrete dock wall to dry. Picturesque as a postcard.

At the mouth of the harbor, he noted a white lighthouse capped by a red dome with a light blinking from the rocky point. Lens, lantern, catwalk . . . René remembered those lighthouse terms from the one sailing lesson his mother had insisted he take.

René got out of the Renault and wiped off macaron crumbs from his suit pants—an indulgence requiring a side trip to Ladurée en route. He'd bought a box of *fraise* macarons for Chloé, too.

He stretched his legs. Noticed a seagull's fluttering wings.

René needed more coffee—he turned his back on the postcard view and scanned the buildings around him for a café.

Just then, a loud splat. A seagull had bombed him with a stinking whitish, green-gray glob that landed on his shoulder.

Damn bird.

Nature was fine as long as it stayed on a postcard.

He hadn't even brought a change of clothes.

"You got baptized, eh?"

A grizzled man in yellow waders, a blue rain slicker and a wool cap grinned at him. He was tan, weather beaten and healthy in a Breton way. A poster for the hardy fisherman. He stood on a gangplank hauling plastic buckets from the deck of the ship. René wondered if he'd throw him an oyster. Or offer him "authentic" local crêpes on his beaten-up boat.

"Baptized?"

Ruining a designer jacket like that?

"Never stand where we gut the fish," said the fisherman. "The gulls like to take a dump after they eat."

Dégoûtant. René took off his jacket and scraped what he could off on the wooden pier. He'd chalk it up to experience and put it on Leduc Detective's expenses.

"You wouldn't be Alphonse Melac, monsieur?"

"Who's asking?"

René pulled out his business card.

"I think you know why I'm here."

"Do I?" The limber, ropy muscled hands took the card. "A fancy investigator from Paris, come all this way to cause trouble. Since when do they send a *petit* version? You the preview?"

René ignored the insult.

"Why do you think that, monsieur? Are you guilty of something?"

"Get on the boat."

"Why?"

The man lowered his voice. "You want to know about my nephew, then we talk out at sea. Leave your phone in the car." He gestured to satellite dishes and antennae sprouting from the tiled rooftops at the harbor café and the harbor master's cabin. "We could be overheard if we stay onshore."

Wiretapping was one thing, but this looked high-tech for a fishing village—was this to monitor smugglers trying to get contraband ashore? Cigarettes, liquor, drugs . . . Or something else?

But he didn't doubt the paranoid fisherman. Alphonse had been a gendarme, his nephew had been murdered and right now this was how he wanted to play it.

René threw his stained jacket and his phone in the Renault's back seat. Thank God it was a rental.

When he returned to the gangplank, the man handed him a rain slicker that fit his chest, although the hem hit his ankles. He looked like a cartoon character. As Alphonse unlatched the gangplank, pulled up the anchor and chugged through the harbor, a downpour started, pelting needles of rain. René felt glad for the slicker.

René joined Alphonse in the cabin as he piloted the small fishing boat. The moment the boat cleared the harbor, the choppy water and waves crashing on the rocky coastline made the bile rise in his stomach.

Another reason René disliked sailing: the damn sea.

"You don't look too good."

René willed down the bile, kept his gaze on the horizon and breathed.

Sometimes that worked.

"What I want to know is why your nephew said he saw a ghost before he was murdered."

Whitecaps crashed against the jutting rocks. The small boat

shuddered. René grabbed a rail bar, amazed how this beat-up thing crested a wave.

"You get to the point, eh?"

After driving half the night, why waste time?

René gritted his teeth. "Are you just paranoid or is it more than that?"

"We'll talk after I clear the lighthouse point."

René noticed the small worn statue of Saint Pierre, patron saint of fishermen, bolted to the dashboard. He imagined the small boat getting swept up by a current and pummeled against the rocks, then smashing into pieces.

Why had he agreed to this?

Alphonse Melac stared straight ahead, his hands gripping the captain's wheel. He steered toward a rocky outcrop that proved to be an inlet. Here the turquoise water calmed.

Nervous, René tried to keep some form of composure and stop his hands from shaking so much. Tried to keep on target, as Aimée would say.

"What are you afraid of, Alphonse?"

"I have a healthy respect for the sea. We don't call that fear."

What kind of answer was that? It sounded like a cop-out.

"Any idea of your nephew's killer? If so, why haven't you informed the authorities?"

"Don't insult me, *petit.*"

"That's not an insult, I'm asking you questions. My name's René."

"Shouldn't your partner in the detective agency be questioning me?"

"She's being framed."

"Convenient."

"She's injured and could lose her sight permanently. So I wouldn't say that's convenient."

Alphonse's lips pursed into a thin line.

Stubborn.

"Chloé, your nephew's daughter, is your blood."

Still no reaction.

"Chloé's father's dead, her mother's been blinded and framed and is wanted by the *flics*. Don't you want your nephew's daughter safe and taken care of by her mother?"

Alphonse's knuckles whitened as his right hand gripped the captain's wheel. His left hand adjusted a knob. The man's hand was shaking like René's own trembling one.

"Why don't you want your nephew's killer caught?"

"Who says I don't?"

Pause. Spray like spittle splattered the porthole.

"Talk to me, Alphonse."

Alphonse took off his wet wool hat glistening with droplets. He shook it, then jerked his thumb to the open deck, and René followed him to the bow.

René's cheeks glistened with the sea spray, and his lips tasted of salt. Waves crashed in earsplitting shatters on the rocks.

Above, clouds skittered as they wove inland. The fresh air and smell of the sea counteracted René's nausea. *Thank God.*

"Tell me her version."

"Her version? She was attacked, she could have died. She was there when her child's father was murdered."

"Go on," said Alphonse.

René explained Aimée's stumbling onto the scene under the bridge, hearing Melac's moans, dropping her keys, trying to reach Melac when a knife was put in her hands. How to her, the killer had sounded like a *flic*.

Was that a tear dripping from Alphonse's hooded lids? Or salt spray?

René couldn't tell.

"Your turn, Alphonse," said René. "I need your help. Who do you think murdered your nephew?"

"This makes me feel so old." His brow creased. "No one should ever outlive their child."

"Child?"

"After Jérome's mother got put away, I practically raised him and his sister. *Alors,* my gendarme job was the only source of income. I volunteered for overtime, anything to keep the kids clothed and fed. But I wasn't home much."

René gentled his voice. "I'm sure Jérome appreciated your care."

"I applied for a position in the motorcycle squad. There were few openings and they had a competitive entrance exam, yet it meant higher pay and more hours. Luckily—or so I thought— I made the cut, along with a young *flic* who'd transferred to Brittany. Jérome was still in school and impressed by this new motorcycle cop."

René knew there had to be a point to this story. He was telling this in his own way. And guilt layered his voice.

For all her impatience and tactlessness, Aimée knew the best thing was to listen. She'd taught René not to fill the silences.

So he waited.

Alphonse took a deep breath, then sighed.

"He was a teenager," he said, regret in his tone. "We argued when I was home. But he looked up to this *mec.* Thought him a hero. I never saw or caught this *mec* doing anything, but something about him felt off. At the station, things were left unsaid, and no one wanted to point the finger without any proof. I couldn't disillusion Melac. He'd decided to become a *flic,* saying this guy inspired him. The guy quit after two years. Left."

"How does that relate to seeing a ghost?"

"Melac and I attended this *flic's* funeral. He died in a motor-cycle accident some years later."

Dead was dead. "So you're implying what, exactly?"

"Figure it out."

"I'm not here to play games. What do you mean?"

Alphonse jerked his head to the boat deck and toward the bow. Beyond, the deep, dark-green open sea roiled like a bubbling pot of cassoulet.

A wave jolted René. Terrified, he grabbed the railing. Tired and battling nausea, and his brain had fogged to boot.

Was Alphonse a suspect? Had he killed his nephew for reasons unknown and thrown the blame on Aimée? And René had walked right into it. Made himself easy prey. Alphonse would throw René overboard.

René grabbed a yellow life jacket from the rack, slid his arms into it and readied his feet in a jujitsu stance as best he could with waterlogged shoes on the slippery deck of a boat churning at sea.

He needed to get him talking.

"Spell it out," said René. "You're giving me pieces. Nothing fits together."

"It's bigger than me. There's been a cover-up. Jérome's house was searched. Done by a pro. Subtle, but I could tell. I've done it myself."

"What did they take?"

"His computer wasn't there. I suppose he could have taken it to Paris."

René almost said *no problem*, since he'd planted a bug on the server. He could track Melac's computer, if it hadn't been trashed.

"Anything else?"

"Jérome asked me about that dead *flic* on Monday."

The day of his murder. Significant? If so, how?

Sea-foam beaded René's clenched fist on the railing. "You said there'd never been proof, but could this man have been rumored to have committed a crime while on the force—or, say, involved in corruption?"

"Pick a reason. He was protected. I don't know why."

René still didn't get the connection.

The crashing waves and damn cries of the seagulls made it hard to hear.

"So you're implying . . . "

"Sounds far-fetched, but I wouldn't put it past him to be alive and under the radar. In hiding."

René's grip was slipping. He felt numb with cold. His gaze was blurred by the mist, and droplets clung to his eyelashes.

"If you mean he faked his death," said René, "why? What was he hiding from, and why kill Melac now?"

"You're the detective."

Thursday Morning • House at Buttes-Chaumont

AIMÉE GREW AWARE of weak sunlight warming her ankles. Strong fingers massaged her calf, and her headache was gone. The fresh tang of squeezed oranges floated through the air.

Heaven.

Her eyes opened to a filmy haze. Slowly it cleared—she could see the pine trees in the park, the pale sunlight. And that smell of him—deep musk—as his fingers ran over her knee, her thigh . . . She moaned, about to grab and pull him on her. More heaven.

She sat bolt upright.

"What in hell are you doing here, Bellan?"

"Whatever you want," he said, unbuttoning his shirt.

Was she dreaming? Their last conversation had ended with his hanging up on her; he couldn't be in contact with a fugitive or he'd lose his custody case.

"I'm a murder suspect, and . . ."

He laid his finger over her lips and nuzzled her ear.

"I'll believe someone set you up big-time until the DNA samples arrive and prove otherwise."

Had this all been a game?

"But on the phone you said . . ."

"Big ears were listening, Aimée."

Big ears meant the intelligence branch he worked for in the Ministry.

Great. Unnerved, she wondered how he'd sussed out her location. If *he* could, sooner or later so could the killer.

"How did you find me?"

"Seems you forget I'm an *agent secret*."

"Then I need to leave. It's not safe here now."

Even though his warm arms enfolded her. The arms she'd missed.

He sighed. Whispered, "Your mother told me."

"Quoi?"

"Reciprocal info, you know. Give and take."

Did it never end? Her mother, the old radical, still worked with the CIA. Now her tentacles reached Bellan.

Spies and double agents were everywhere in her life.

"Tell me you didn't kill him, Aimée?"

"Is that a serious question?"

She sat up, the duvet falling around her. The puffy down hiccuped a flying feather.

She shivered. The nightmare was back—the darkness, the glinting knife, Melac's blood on her hands. Horrific.

"*Non*, Bellan," she said. "I can't believe you would ask." She closed her eyes, trying to get a grip on her emotions. "How will Chloé ever understand her father's gone?"

Bellan shook his head, wrapped her in his arms. His chin stubble grazed her neck, his smooth hands . . . Everything she'd missed.

"She has you, Aimée."

If she didn't screw up and get caught.

"Did you still have feelings for Melac, Aimée? I mean, we . . ."

Of course she had. She'd loathed him, but they had been through so much. She owed Melac. The fleeting feelings were there. Always would be.

No time for that now.

She rolled over and straddled Bellan. "Quit talking."

TRILLING NOISES CAME from somewhere near her. The duvet got in the way. Where was that cheap burner?

Her fingers came back with it, the plastic brittle in her palm. Her other arm reached out for Loïc Bellan—but found only cold sheets. She was alone in the twisted duvet.

She sat up slowly. The world righted itself, and her gaze took in the trees, the mist shrouding the Tour Eiffel in the distance, the pearly dome of Sacré-Coeur.

Her body purred, refreshed and warm. It was amazing what sleep and . . .

René's burner number popped up.

"*Allô?*"

"Aimée," said René, "can you hear me?"

"Go ahead, René. Did you learn anything from Melac's uncle?"

A sucking in of air came over the phone.

"Disturbing stuff, Aimée," he said.

"You mean the Celtic spells, witchcraft and Breton crêpes got to you?"

"I'll be pulling into the garage in fifteen. I'm driving around the park twice to spot if I've got any tail. Put the coffee on."

She jumped out of bed and felt the world tilt for a moment. She breathed, tried to *destrésser* and take it more slowly. She showered and opened the windows. By the time René arrived from the garage, she'd gotten rid of Bellan's scent and poured water into the *cafetière*.

René looked worn. Exhaustion showed in his green eyes and the fine wrinkles around his mouth—expression lines, the Dior cosmetologist at Printemps called them. What had she gotten him into? How could she be so selfish?

It had been his idea. He'd insisted. But she'd let him.

"You didn't sleep, did you?"

"Enough," he said.

She glanced at the clock on the wall. He must have gotten the information and then turned around and driven right back.

"If you call curling up in the Renault's back seat *sleep*."

She pushed the *cafetière*'s plunger down and poured him a cup of steaming strong coffee. He accepted this instead of his herbal tea. And it alarmed her.

"What's with all the traffic and roadblocks?"

Of course he didn't know, since he'd gone to Brittany.

She recounted meeting Roget in the park last night, Jacquot Devries's body floating in the shallow lake.

"You escaped?"

"By my teeth."

Aimée gestured to the Parc des Buttes-Chaumont outside the panoramic window, the low mist evaporating and revealing the bare-branched trees and scurrying crime scene technicians wearing disposable white jumpsuits in the section still cordoned off.

René's eyelids drooped. He'd nod out in a minute. She hated pushing him but needed information.

"So spill what you found out. Update me and Saj, and I will take it from there."

René nodded. For once he didn't protest. This worried her even more.

He sank in the leather chair, sipped and told her what he'd gleaned from Melac's uncle. She listened, sitting cross-legged on the polished wood floor in a pool of weak sunlight, one eye on the crime scene several floors below and across the street in the park.

Her mind ratcheted back and forth between what René was

telling her and the two murders. She tried to make sense of what René said.

"*Attends*, René, so Alphonse Melac believes François Vérgove, a hero to young Melac and former motorcycle *flic*, faked his own death, probably to avoid arrest. It was rumored that this Vérgove was corrupt and committed crimes while he was on the force, but nothing was ever proven. He went into hiding and somehow is still protected by the system, or a local bigwig."

She reached for her old Moleskine and pencil from her go bag.

"That it?"

"More or less."

"And he thinks this might have something to do with Melac's murder—why?"

"According to Uncle Alphonse, Melac idolized this man when he was a teenager. François Vérgove inspired him to become a *flic*."

"And now Uncle Alphonse thinks François Vérgove, back from the dead, might be the ghost Melac saw the night he died?" Had the disgraced cop killed Melac for seeing him alive? But that didn't explain the elaborate preplanned setup of his murder. "Didn't he mention thinking Vérgove was the serial killer?"

"Not to me."

Where had Morbier gotten this info he shared with her mother?

"*Zut alors*, Alphonse Melac's completely paranoid." René sipped. Steam spiraled into the air. "He thinks his boat's wiretapped. His house and phone, too."

Aimée jotted notes and thought.

"What about Melac's farm?"

"Burgled," René said. "His computer's missing."

"And you believe Uncle Alphonse about all this?"

"If he's lying, he should be acting in the Comédie Française. He might be paranoid, but for good reason. I wanted to see him as a conspiracy theorist, but he's scared and cautious."

That was her impression, too.

"Aimée, for theory's sake, say this former gendarme, François Vérgove, heard Melac call you and leave you that message? And then he murdered him?"

Her heart skidded.

"Two for one," she said, remembering. "The man who attacked me—he said that."

"Say he considered you collateral because he suspected you know more than you do."

"Uncle Alphonse suggested this?"

"Implied." René shrugged. "Factor in how you've been set up."

"We still don't know why this *mec* would kill—if it even is him—what he's hiding or what this secret he's been protecting is."

"Melac recognized him? Knew too much about an old case?"

Yet another case of a *flic* rumored to have unsavory dealings covered up by the force. She smiled, no humor in it.

"Or he's *le Balafré*?" said René.

Somehow this always circled back to the serial killer.

"Like Morbier told Sydney," he said. "The *flic* Melac idolized is the serial killer."

"René, it's all conjecture. What we need is proof. Evidence. Something to link this theory." For the first time, she noticed René's shoes were water stained. She knelt to remove them. "You need to sleep. Saj will find out who François Vérgove is. Was. When you wake up, we'll know where to look next."

She plumped the couch pillow for him. Without ceremony, he fell asleep under her oversize cashmere scarf. She kissed him on the cheek and drew the damask curtains. He smiled in his slumber.

First, she had to find out about Vérgove, about his history and time on the force.

She pulled René's work laptop from his leather bag, then booted it up and encoded an email to Saj with brief instructions. Saj would decipher the code—they changed it every month—and know how to proceed.

She had a name and a possible suspect and could get a photo of him to show around for identification.

The only snag was that he was dead.

If she was chasing a ghost, it wouldn't be the first time.

She had to keep other lines of inquiries open and hedge her bets; Vérgove could be a dead end. Like her father had said, never close a door—open new ones and always keep them open, or one will slam shut on your fingers.

A pang of longing hit her. How was Chloé?

She checked the phone her mother had given her. One missed call from last night, which she'd totally forgotten to follow up on. What kind of mother was she?

Merde!

Chloé could be sick, hurt, in an accident or—

She hit call back. No answer. What had Sydney said—don't call, I'll call you? But why hadn't she called again?

"What's this jabbing into my back?" René had woken with a snort. He clutched a palm-size antique cloisonné box with an intricate gold inlaid art nouveau design. "There's a note sticking out of it."

Aimée snatched the box and lifted the lid.

A tinny, scratchy tune bleated from inside. An old lullaby. Inside lay a pair of hoop earrings, thin gold loops, with what looked like a button.

She knew that writing. Bellan had written *might come in handy.*

Loïc Bellan. So this morning hadn't been a dream. He was on her side.

"Let me see that, Aimée."

René turned the items over in his palm, lifted the peach satin lining up and grinned.

"Someone's left you a lock-picking tool and the most cutting-edge microphone I've ever seen. Any idea why?"

"Guess I'll go and find out."

A damn shame she'd lost her *passe-partout*, the master key Morbier had loaned her, which she'd never returned. But Bellan's *petit cadeau* looked useful. She underlined her eyes with kohl, swiped Chanel Red over her lips and dotted her cheeks with it for color. Even on the run, some things stayed *de rigueur.*

A pigeon haloed in the vanilla light strutted on a windowsill, purple-green throat glistening. How amazing to see all this detail with her returning eyesight. Last night's rain had left a fresh vegetal smell riding the air.

Her phone bleeped.

"*Oui?*" She kept her voice low.

"You told me to call you," said Madame Olivera. "I saw him."

Him? Then she remembered. *Le Modou*, the Senegalese drug dealer who'd hooked her daughter, Maria. The dealer who might have the scoop on the murder.

"Where?"

"He's dealing across the street. I don't know for how long. Can you come?"

"I'm on my way."

AIMÉE HURRIED OVER the rain-polished cobbles. Everything shone, smelled fresh and awake. Almost like an overdue spring day.

For her outfit this morning she'd abandoned the arty bobo for black on black. The uniform in Paris. Simple, à la mode and anonymous, with thick-soled combat boots, leggings and a long black coat. The coat could be turned inside out and made shorter by removing snaps. She'd stuck ballerina flats in her pocket.

Aimée paused in the doorway of a crumbling eighteenth-century laundry with faded signs reading TEINTURERIE, NETTOYAGE.

Her eyes scanned the street. She saw a man smoking on the sidewalk, watched him approach a parked car. Something about him struck her—the drug dealer?

It was too late, he was leaving.

Mais non. As he turned his head, she realized it wasn't the man in the photo Madame Olivera had shown her.

She entered the courtyard, mounted the stairs and knocked on the Portuguese woman's door.

It opened after a brief rustling.

"Come in," Madame Olivera said, her body half-hidden behind the door.

Aimée noted the high pitch of her voice. Unlike before.

"That wasn't him, Madame Olivera."

"My mistake. *Entrez.*"

Why? Aimée's gut clenched. Something was wrong.

"I'm running late."

Madame Olivera blinked twice. Her eyes radiated terror.

"It's n-not private in the hallway, please come in."

Among the apartment's colorful hangings, Aimée spotted a wall mirror reflecting the man concealed behind the door. He wore a seagrass-green shirt and was clutching Madame Olivera's shoulder.

"Of course," Aimée said, keeping her voice calm.

At the same moment she pivoted, grabbed Madame Olivera, shoved her aside and kicked the door wide open, slamming the man in the face.

"Ahh . . . *merde*," he yelled.

Her pivot and kick weren't up to René's black belt standards, but the element of surprise made up for that, she hoped. She rued the fact she hadn't let René drag her to more of his jujitsu classes.

The man's nose was bleeding and he was on the floor, grabbing for a gun that had fallen on the carpet. She kicked the gun away, then followed up with a kick to his kidney, and as he doubled up, to his ribs.

She'd seen this in a movie. Her thick-soled boots more than made up for lack of skill.

Madame Olivera looked on in surprise. "How—"

Aimée didn't have long before the man reacted. "Quick, go get dish towels and scarves. Now."

Mobilized, Madame Olivera sprang into action.

The man grabbed her ankle hard in a pincerlike hold. She lost her balance and caught herself on a chair, tumbling to sit on his thrashing legs. Madame Olivera was back, roping his wrists with a wet dish towel while Aimée tied his ankles with a winter wool scarf.

All the while he was shouting and cursing at them.

Aimée stuck another dishrag in his mouth, then picked up the gun and opened the barrel, dislodging the bullets one by one.

She checked his pockets for more bullets. A knife. But there were no other weapons.

She wiped her fingerprints off the bullets, handle and barrel and inside of the gun. Then stuck it in his hand.

Madame Olivera sucked in her breath. "*Désolée.* He just appeared and then forced me to call you."

Aimée believed her.

"How did he know?"

The woman worried her work-worn fingers over her pocket. "These gangs have spies everywhere. Lookouts. He'd heard you were looking around. Thought you'd be useful."

"Useful?"

Aimée was thinking it was the other way around—she wanted info from him.

"That's what it's all about here. Learn something, use it against another . . . slither up the ladder. Snakes, all of them. He's skinnier than before."

So he'd fallen on hard times. That made two of them.

Aimée led Madame Olivera away from the struggling drug dealer, then whispered, "Didn't you pack your bag? You should be going to the airport."

"I'm not leaving. I'm seeing this through."

"Let me talk to him. I need to find out who killed the officer who was going to speak at your daughter's parole hearing. Then we call the *flics*. We both get what we want."

Madame Olivera's lip trembled as she shook her head. She'd picked up a kitchen knife. Alarm fizzed up Aimée's neck.

"I don't care if I die now. I'll take him with me."

"*Mais non*, he needs to go behind bars, where he put your daughter."

The stale scent of fear drifted from the man tied up on the floor.

"Killing's too good for him," Aimée said. "He needs to suffer."

"He could get off," Madame Olivera said. "Go free."

"Not if I'm around. Listen, you don't want to get stuck with his murder, go to jail, appear in court. Don't end up where your daughter died. It's him—you need to send *him* to prison, and I'll help you."

After a long moment, she nodded and said, voice like steel, "People die in prison."

"Okay, follow my lead."

"But his other gang members will come looking for him."

"Give me your phone."

She did, making sure the *mec* saw her. Aimée turned and rang Eli Rochas. He was her only contact in *les stups*, slang for *narcotiques*, the drug squad. He owed her big-time. Voice mail. She whispered him a message and prayed he'd get it in time and keep it on the down-low.

She took a deep breath. Then another. This would work.

Wouldn't it?

She knelt on the floor by the hog-tied prisoner and consulted her Tintin watch. She affected what she hoped was a this-is-just-business tone.

"There's enough time for you to get away. *Comprends?* You're small fry. Not important to my boss." Aimée pincered her thumb and forefinger and pulled out the gag. "No screaming or this goes back in."

He spit and snarled. "Who's your boss?"

"*Pas important.* And we can keep it that way. I need you to tell me everything you know about the murdered *mec* on the canal. Otherwise I call my boss."

"The man who had his throat slit in the canal, *c'est ça?*"

Aimée tried not to cringe. "I'm listening."

"Why?"

"You want to leave here in one piece, *non?*"

He laughed. "*Mes camarades* are waiting for you."

His gang. True or not, she could bluff, too.

"Au contraire, the Angels from rue de l'Ourcq are waiting for you. And they don't like you."

That registered.

"I just want to know about the murder."

"What's it to you?"

"You're wasting time," she said, glancing at her watch. "The Angels are en route."

A sparkle of fear lit his eyes.

"You're crazy. I didn't kill him. We don't do murder."

So killing a young girl by getting her addicted didn't count?

"I'm a merchant, *c'est tout.*"

A dealer of death.

She stuffed down her feelings and shot a glance at Madame Olivera, who looked like she was about to grab her knife again. Aimée shook her head.

"This lady's upset, so it's in your best interest to help me out. Then you can go."

He spit at her. A green frothy blob landed on her boot. Seething inside, she smiled.

"Fine. I'll find someone more cooperative. You're obviously not the kingpin anymore."

Aimée stuffed the scarf back in his mouth, grabbed under his arms and hauled him to the apartment's standing oak beam, then tied him to it.

"Let's go," she said to Madame Olivera. "They'll take care of him."

He was twisting and struggling, trying to talk through the scarf damp with his saliva, kicking his feet and straining to get free. Panic flecked his eyes.

"Give me the killer's name, what he looked like, how he talked, where you saw him—anything."

She took out the wet scarf filled with his drool. His eyes skittered. His body shook.

"I'm waiting," said Aimée.

"He's got facial hair, a scruffy beard, talks like a *flic.*"

Terror shot up her spine.

"Where was he seen?"

"On the quai by the bridge."

"How do you know?"

"I don't know exactly. He goes to a clinic."

"What clinic?"

"I've been away. Could be a hospital. That's all I heard."

"Heard?"

"Word on the street," he said.

She believed him.

Aimée took Madame Olivera's hand, then said, "It's time to go."

His bound hands scrabbled. "You can't leave me like this."

"Bonne chance."

Aimée handed Madame Olivera her packed bag by the door, then pulled her out, down the stairs and into rue Bellot. A dark car with blacked-out windows cruised down the street, behind it a van, which stopped.

"Keep moving," Aimée said.

Eli Rochas stepped out of the car. Dark hair and matching dark, intense eyes scanning the street. If he saw Aimée, he ignored her. He made a slight motion with his left hand and the van door slid open. *Les stups* had arrived just in time.

"They'll let him go," said Madame Olivera.

"Au contraire. My contact at *les stups* will take care of that."

At least she hoped he would—he owed her. With a price on her head, she couldn't be sure. Yet the *mecs* in *narcotiques* were cowboys and rode their horses the way they wanted.

Aimée dropped Madame Olivera's phone, stomped on it.

She looked around. "Time to go. Now. Run."

Thursday Afternoon • Rue de l'Ourcq
The Biker Tattoo Bar

ISABELLE CHECKED HER log sheet for the supplies and loading schedule to the assigned vans. She looked around for the rest of the crew. No one.

Idiots. If she didn't hurry, she'd punch in late for her cleaning job at the start-up, and she couldn't afford to miss work. Yesterday, Luca had had two doctor appointments, so she'd called in sick. She couldn't keep using that excuse much longer or she'd lose the job, lose the chance to get her brother into adaptive housing with therapy. This program was the only one of its kind in France.

She left via the back bay near the ramps and slipped out into the gravel parking lot. All this to double-check that the proper cigarette cartons were loaded into the designated van. Fuming, she didn't hear the swish of fabric behind her until she felt a gust of warm breath on her neck.

She whirled around. No one. Nothing.

And then she was lifted off her feet, pulled backward into the storage unit. A damp cloth was pulled over her mouth and nose as she felt her wrists being tied.

She didn't know how much later she came to. All she could do was pick and scrape at the binding on her wrist. Her ragged, bloodied fingernails felt raw. She was in the squat's back room, overheated for once. Stifling.

An overhead light blinked on.

She was tied to a chair. Blondie the biker loomed over her. She wanted to kick him.

"Let's make a deal. Tip me off when the cigarette shipments are about to come in, the distribution routes, the timetable, and I'll let you go." He flashed a police badge, which he then stuck in his shoe. "And leave you alone to take care of your disabled brother."

An undercover *flic*. She should have picked up on him before. And he was corrupt. He'd let her go, eh? Taking advantage to line his pockets.

"Answer me."

She pretended to think.

This glass-roofed atrium had been a winter garden once. Where were those pruning shears she'd left in here to trim the plants? Why hadn't whatever was binding her come loose?

"Sounds easy. But it's complicated. I'm a cog in the wheel."

"Don't give me that. You're the acting boss, from what I see."

"*Moi?* I answer to higher-ups."

"So you say."

"You think they'd leave someone like me in charge? It's temporary, the boss got appendicitis. I just help here with the warehouse," she lied. "Better deal with big guys and let me go."

She ran this network. But he didn't know that for sure.

"I can't wait around," he said.

"Do you know how many are involved in distribution and sales?" She side-eyed him. "I don't know the details of the business. No one knows. No one talks or they're out."

Blondie took her chin in his hand. Raised her face.

"But you will, *non?* If it's to save your brother."

Salopard. The gang mistrusted Blondie, and he wouldn't get far. But that didn't help her right now.

"*Alors,* all I know is this: a buyer goes to a wholesale

dealer—incognito, word of mouth—whose name no one knows. This business means being ready to jump at a moment's notice. No advance warning. You've witnessed this. All of a sudden we're told a time, place and shipment amount."

"That's it? Why should I believe you?"

"Have you seen any evidence here to the contrary? What kind of *flic* are you?"

He raised his arm, about to hit her.

But his phone trilled. He turned and answered.

Flics were offered a cut, and no one—consumer or seller—minded. This way no one got hurt or killed. Turfs were respected, and the only angry people were in the ministry tax office.

Everyone hated them.

He hung up.

"Had time to think about it?"

"My boss will offer you a cut," she said. "Every month, no matter what happens."

That should keep him happy.

"Tell me where Aimée Leduc's hiding."

A *flic* knew Aimée had been hiding with her. *Merde.* Her fingers felt for the ties, anything.

"How do I know? She came and went."

Blondie slammed his fist down on a water-damaged table. Her body twitched.

"Like I'd believe that?" he said, sneering. "Tell me or I rat her out."

"Why's she important?"

"I need her help."

Liar.

She knew his type. Blondie had something to prove. She figured he'd probably screwed up a drugs raid, been demoted to cigarette smuggling and wanted a way back up the ladder.

He'd gain points by nabbing Aimée. After he turned her in, he'd attempt to rig a contact with Isabelle's supplier and bungle it up. She'd been around *flics* long enough to know this Blondie wasn't the sharpest knife on the rack.

Maybe she could use that. Outsmart him.

"I don't know where she went," she said. "She's gone."

"Don't give me that."

Thursday • Metro Stalingrad

AIMÉE STOOD AT the Metro entrance with Madame Olivera. The budding plane tree branches fretted overhead, and the pale cream sun cast patterns on the pavement. Above, behind a wrought iron balcony, daffodils nodded in the breeze.

They'd peeked from a doorway down the street as *les stups* left with a cuffed *Modou* in tow.

Awe shone in Madame Olivera's eyes. "I've got no idea how you do this. You're a female Steven Seagal."

Aimée grinned. *Nice comparison.*

"Buy a new phone. At Gare du Nord take the RER B to the airport," said Aimée. "Go."

Madame Olivera turned. She stopped on the Metro steps and came back up. She'd taken something from her ragged shopping bag, and she was holding it out to Aimée.

A photo of a young woman in a chef's outfit with a large smile.

"My Maria. Please remember her like this."

And then Madame Olivera joined the crowd going down the Metro steps and was swallowed in the crowd.

At least Aimée had done what she'd promised—gotten her some justice.

Something Melac had wanted, had tried to do.

Now, to find Melac's killer.

As she walked on the quai, theories swirled in her mind.

Again she wondered if Melac had witnessed what he shouldn't have. It felt like she was clutching at cotton wisps floating away—out of reach, elusive.

Her phone trilled.

"Aimée," said Saj, his voice hurried and low. "You're being tracked. Your contact, too. They're near."

"Who?"

But the line cut.

By contact he meant Isabelle. Good God.

Think.

She took the soft pink Repetto ballet flats from her coat pocket, put them on and reversed her coat. She tied a scarf bandanna-style around her head, donned blue-framed glasses and smiled at the women at the street market.

A line of older women trailed from the pop-up shop for Italian scarves. Aimée browsed as one woman was slapping shut her flip phone. She slid it in her pocket as she conversed with her friend. Aimée leaned forward, her coat hiding her hand, as she slipped the flip phone out of the pocket.

No code to open it. Perfect. And GPS had limited tracking with the few cell towers in the nineteenth. She couldn't have planned it better.

She hit René's number.

"Special delivery."

She hung up.

Then did the same for Saj's number.

Aimée put the woman's phone back in her pocket and strolled away.

Thank God she practiced pick-pocketing on a regular basis.

Saj and René knew the code.

Now it was up to them to come through.

PASSAGE WATTIEAUX BACKED a series of two-story houses, taller apartment buildings and what was once a school, judging from the faded sign reading ÉCOLE DES GARÇONS. Aimée kept her eyes peeled for cameras, watchers.

She registered no suspicious people or vehicles. So far.

She used the key Isabelle had given her. It didn't fit in the back gate. *Merde.*

She took off one of the small hoop earrings Bellan had left, twisted the metal and used it to pick the lock.

Handy, all right.

With this tiny rod to use as a lever, she jiggled the other hoop's rounded tip flat, inserting it until on her second try the tumbler yielded. She pushed the well-oiled gate open and hurried over the patchwork of fallen plum blossoms in the back yard.

Finally it felt like spring.

Deep tire tracks were grooved in the mud. The wet ridges made it hard to walk, and her thin ballet flats got encrusted in mud.

A young woman was tied to a chair in the glass atrium. Voices were raised. She was yelling.

It was Isabelle.

Aimée gasped. Blondie paced around Isabelle. Aimée edged closer to hear what was being said.

What could she do?

She had an idea.

But before she could act on it—footsteps crunched on the gravel walkway.

Someone else had joined this party.

Thursday, Earlier • Two Blocks from
Leduc Detective on rue du Louvre

SAJ, ALL SIX feet of him, replete with an Indian muslin tunic over his flowing dhoti and Nepali wool socks in Birkenstocks, folded himself into the passenger seat of René's rental. His knees hit his chest, disturbing the cowrie shell and turquoise beaded prayer necklace.

"You couldn't get a larger vehicle, René?"

René fumed. He'd almost gotten two speeding tickets in his hurry, and right now they couldn't afford getting pulled over.

"And you couldn't dress down, Saj?"

Saj grinned. "I know you don't mean that. I'm wearing my electrician's jumpsuit underneath—the one Aimée gave me. To avoid suspicion."

René hoped so.

Saj pulled out a dark knitted cap and stuffed his blond dread-locks inside.

"But what about the equipment, Saj?"

"Such a worrywart, René." He patted his back. "All the gear we need is in my cross-body bag. I'm beta testing new mini-size prototypes."

"Ahh . . ." Finally good news. "Our *bons amis en Zeelakon Vallée.*" René turned into the dark impasse. He pulled over. "Go around the front. You know what to do."

"But I thought Aimée said we should—"

René interrupted. "I'll meet you inside, Saj."

Saj waded off in his hastily donned work boots, and René felt the lock on the back gate. It was open. In the small yard, he heard shouting and mounted the old wine carton beside the glass atrium's half-open windows. René was craning to listen when a hand gripped his shoulders. He gasped and lost his balance. It was Aimée.

But it was too late.

Glass broke and he was tumbling inside.

He landed on the worn tile in a carpet of broken glass. In front of him was Aimée's friend Isabelle, tied to a chair. A sliver in his thumb emitted tiny drops of blood.

Great.

A burly blond man looked at him in surprise. "Who the hell are you?"

Quick. He had to move quick. He sucked his thumb, spit out the glass and pulled himself to his feet.

And then Aimée was right behind him, whispering in his ear, "Can you keep him busy?"

Thursday • Squat Behind the rue de l'Ourcq Biker Bar

RENÉ'S JUJITSU KICK knocked Blondie sideways. Aimée heard a hard crack as his head hit the tiles and his eyes rolled into his head.

Impressive. René hadn't lost his touch.

Aimée undid the ties around Isabelle's wrists and helped her up from the old rattan café chair with its seat unraveling.

"What happened?" asked Aimée. "Are you all right?"

"Fine." Isabelle rubbed her chafed red wrists. "He claims he's an undercover *flic* and asked a lot of questions about you."

Great.

"Quick, René, tie him up before he comes to."

Aimée went through his pockets, front and back. She found a pack of Menthol cigarettes—jazz musicians smoked those in the sixties.

No ID. But if he really was undercover, he wouldn't carry ID on him.

Except for in the places her father had taught her to look: the seams, socks or shoes.

She found his police ID under the removable orthotic in his right boot. It was faded and worn.

"What if he's dead, Aimée?"

"Don't get my hopes up," she said.

She felt for his pulse.

"Unfortunately alive and soon to be kicking," she said. "How long has he kept you here? What did he want?"

"You name it." Isabelle shook her head. "He wanted me to rat on you, tell him our supply network chain. He threatened to screw up my brother's housing place."

Merde.

"He'd never do that that, Isabelle. I wouldn't let him."

"He knows too much about me, about us here. Most *flics* we just bribe. They look away. Like Latour did." Isabelle slid the broken glass shards on the wooden floor with her foot and shook out her freed arms. "They're happy, get free cigarettes," she said. "And everyone benefits, more *fric* in their pockets."

Money, the great equalizer.

"But this felt different, Aimée," Isabelle said. "Why didn't he arrest me? It's against the law to hold me like this."

"He might have gone rogue. Who knows if he's still active in the force."

"Rogue?"

"Acting alone."

At least she hoped so.

Isabelle rubbed her reddened wrists and winced.

Again that feeling washed over Aimée—someone was protecting faux *flics*.

"Who's this Latour? Is he on the force? Have you had dealings with him?"

Isabelle nodded. "I know of him. My father dealt with him."

"Do you mean he bribed him?"

That came out wrong.

"Sorry, Isabelle, I meant . . ."

Isabelle gave a little grin and shrugged.

"We call it the price of doing business here, Aimée. But I

think he's retired. Owns a *péniche*, it's a *resto* and club after hours. He got into boating commercially up on the coast."

Why did this niggle in her brain?

"So he was the local *flic* during the *le Balafré* era?"

"I'm not sure," she said. Her voice choked. "*Zut*, Aimée, I've got to shut down. Move."

"Relax, Isabelle. Do nothing yet," she said. She cupped Isabelle's chin, raised it so her gaze met Aimée's. "We'll deal with Blondie."

Somehow.

At that moment, René returned with Saj.

"Good job, partner," she said.

"Once I saw this young mademoiselle, I had to jump into action."

René winked at Isabelle and smiled. Flirting. He was flirting.

"Saj found some old bugs. That's what we came to tell you. He's disconnected them and wonders if the mademoiselle would like new ones installed courtesy of Leduc Detective?"

Aimée's jaw dropped.

"*Bien sûr*," said Isabelle. She returned René's smile.

"I don't know you," he said. "But I hope you smile like that often."

Isabelle laughed. "Only with special people."

Then he was following her into the tattoo bar's warehouse.

Saj caught Aimée's gaze. Put his palms together in greeting. "Namaste, Aimée. I've already installed a few bugs for our own surveillance as requested."

So they could keep an eye on this place. René's request was a formality.

Stray blond dreadlocks fell from Saj's red wool cap. Instead of a smile, his brows knit in worry.

"What's wrong, Saj?"

"Disturbed auras crown you. It's time to align your chakras."

Not this again.

A beeping came from her coat.

"You're the one who's been emitting. The tracker's on you."

She took off her coat and followed the beeping until she discovered the covering on the coat's top button.

Saj removed it.

"Want me to throw it in the canal?"

"Let's attach it to Blondie's jacket and throw him in the canal. See who picks him up."

As Saj prepared the button, she memorized Blondie's info from his ID: Georges Bouvier, from Saint-Brieuc in northern Brittany. Not far from Melac's place.

A coincidence? Her father always said there were no coincidences. A connection—but how?

She needed to lay out what she knew and use Saj and René as sounding boards. And she needed to do it before the tattoo bar was raided and the *flics* caught her.

"WHY DIDN'T YOU throw him in the canal?" asked Saj.

Aimée shrugged. "Good as."

René had chained him inside one of the Angels' delivery vans; the Angels would be on guard duty until she figured out what to do with him. Instead of leaving the tracker in Blondie's coat, Saj had stuck it to the wall near a tattoo machine.

She and Saj had walked to the drawbridge at the rue de Crimée and paused at the bridge railing.

"Is this where . . ."

"Melac was killed? *Non*, farther down, where the canal narrows by Jaurès."

Saj bent his head in prayer. Aimée did the same. For a minute, she let herself grieve.

The gel-like surface reflected filtered light spilling through the trees. A whiff of a floral perfume came from a woman hurrying by. Across the bridge a child's laughter echoed off old stone arches.

"Melac's spirit's here."

"How do you mean, Saj?"

"He's trying to say something."

She remembered how he'd tried to say something—his cry of pain as he'd gurgled for her help.

She had to dam up this emotion that was flooding her. She hadn't let it knock her down. But she had to remember what he'd been saying . . . Could she replay the horrible moments in her mind?

Bile rose in her stomach.

Flashing lights from police cars bounced off the quai.

Danger was so close she could smell it.

"We have to go, Saj."

She needed a new hiding place. The locations where they— whoever *they* were—had tracked her would be the first places they'd look.

Think.

"Saj, didn't you tell me once you went to a meditation center here somewhere?"

Saj nodded just as René pulled up in the Renault Clio. "I'll show René the way and then we can all meditate, cleanse the aura and release the bottled-up chakras."

THE MEDITATION CENTER, a small storefront with a nine-teenth-century façade and faded green sign reading PHARMACIE had closed. Aimée realized she was back in Little Jerusalem, the Orthodox enclave. A thought hit her.

"Let's try the synagogue down the street."

"You think they'll let us meditate?" asked Saj.

"No idea. But I know the rabbi."

The former rabbi of Temple E'manuel in le Marais—she'd consulted him in the past. He met her at the synagogue's door, which was through a nondescript building lobby with no signage. Thank God she'd remained in contact with him.

"Glad you remember my new posting." The rabbi nodded a welcome to Saj and René. But was he glad?

"Can I ask your help, Rabbi?"

He'd aged. He had graying forelocks yet a lively step to his walk. "How?"

"We need someplace quiet. A refuge."

"Here? We're overscheduled with a bat then a bar mitzvah and the upcoming High Holy Days. *Désolé.*"

Why had she thought he would help her? It was the last thing a man in his position could do.

"*Bien sûr,*" she said with a resigned sigh, trying to mask her desperation.

Hunted and nowhere to go.

"But you, mademoiselle, I owe," said the rabbi. "I'll talk to my friend. *Un moment.*"

He left.

René looked around the lobby filling with young Orthodox Jewish men wearing black coats and hats. "You trust him?"

"He's a rabbi, René."

"I mean to keep our visit quiet. No doubt he's heard the radio."

Merde. That was a good point.

The rabbi gestured to them from the opposite end of the lobby. He led them through a polished walnut door, down a stairway, through another door and into a deafening wall of noise. They were on a metal walkway crossing over blasting furnaces and water-heating units. The yellowed floor-height ceramic canisters reminded her of mustard pots.

Did he mean for them to hide under here?

The noise was enough to send her headache into a migraine.

Her father's words came back to her: moaning over opportunities gets you nowhere.

The rabbi opened a metal fire door leading to another walkway open to the gray sky. Low mist and drizzle fell. She pulled the collar of her coat up and shivered.

They went down another metal stairway to an asphalt playground with a seagull perched on the white spattered wall. By the gate they passed the plaque commemorating the 390 Jewish children who were rounded up in the arrondissement by French police and deported to Auschwitz. Along the other side was another plaque remembering *résistants* in the quartier.

The rabbi noticed Aimée's gaze.

"This happens when people look away and don't help. So I will always help. People need to remember the *résistant* groups here and the German deserters who joined them."

"German soldiers?" René asked.

A quick nod. "Not everyone liked the Führer. Nothing's black and white."

The rabbi fished a slip of paper from his pocket and passed it to René.

"My friend's expecting you."

René accepted the paper, read it and shook the rabbi's hand.

"Isn't this the address of the Russian Orthodox church, Saint-Serge de Radonège?"

The things René knew.

A nod from the rabbi. "In this business we all stick together." He winked.

THEY COULDN'T GO back to the Renault so Aimée hailed a taxi. Their destination, 93 rue de Crimée, was fronted by an iron gate. Aimée nudged Saj to overtip the driver.

"Business expense, Saj," she said.

They pushed the gate open and climbed a narrow path, passing tables and chairs that seemed to have been abandoned and an old yellow building with a LIBRAIRIE sign barely visible. At the summit was a hidden treasure of Paris: a brightly colored wooden church—a cross between a Russian dacha, a Tibetan temple and a doll-size Swiss chalet.

Parfait.

The hand-painted sign read that it had been built originally as a German Lutheran church and was confiscated after World War I, then abandoned until 1924 when Russian émigrés fleeing the Bolshevik Revolution had bought it.

Inside, scents of incense and candle wax pervaded the church. The arched ceiling supports were covered in painted icons with dull gold halos over the saints and had muted blue, ocher and turquoise designs on the dark wood.

The priest, consulting what looked like a medieval bound manuscript at the lectern, wore a wispy white beard and a white smock over a black cassock. A woman, her head wrapped by a shawl, scraped wax off a row of white candles. In the corner under an orange persimmon fresco, a young boy opened a violin case and began to tighten a bow. The priest looked up, put a finger to his lips and pointed to the side door embellished with gilded designs.

Aimée followed the others down a hallway. They were greeted by a young man with an outgrown mohawk, black jeans and a pink sweatshirt emblazoned with *I'm with la femme Nikita.* Didn't he know the eighties were gone?

At least he has good taste in films.

He led them to a wooden bunker-like room with bunk beds, pine walls and thick wool floor rugs, then left them to their business.

"This feels like camping."

"You love the outdoors, René." She smiled and sat cross-legged on the floor. "*Non?*"

"First off, Aimée," said René, apprehensive, "did you notice those antennae and big dishes on the roof outside?"

She nodded. Someone was listening. "Will the Russian Big Ears bother us?"

"Shouldn't," said Saj.

"Pretty *sophistiquée* for a church," said Aimée. "Russian or not."

Saj pulled out his equipment, two laptops and tracking devices. Meanwhile, René took out tape and colored markers from his briefcase. While they set up, she took out her notebook, then ripped some back pages and stuck them on the wall. Just like at Leduc Detective.

She missed the inherited family office with her father's worn wood desk, the photo of him fishing on the Seine, her grandfather Claude's old *sûreté* commendation on the wall. A wave of sadness engulfed her—as if she were drowning in a sea of loss. All she held dear—Chloé and their world—wasn't here. She'd never been separated from her daughter this long. It was her fault. If she'd arrived earlier, taken his calls, Melac wouldn't have been given a Kabyle smile, as *flics* still called a slit throat—slang from the Algerian War.

Quit the pity party. She could lose everything if she didn't find Melac's killer. She had to fight.

While Saj hooked up his equipment and René booted up his laptop, she taped up her crude diagram of the arrondissement mapped out with Melac's last-known locations. Lots of unknowns.

Did *le Balafré* connect to the gendarme François Vérgove? Two phantoms, both suddenly back from the dead?

Had Melac trailed a lead—a wisp of the past—and died for what he'd discovered?

"Melac's uncle Alphonse left a message at the office," said René. "Shall I play it from the answering machine?"

She looked up and nodded. René hit play.

Alphonse cleared his voice. "As I am next of kin, the police are asking if I want to proceed with funeral arrangements. I'm letting you know because you might have certain wishes."

This wasn't what she'd expected to hear, nor something she wanted to think about dealing with. He sounded formal and stiff. This conversation would have been uncomfortable enough, even if he didn't know his line was tapped.

"I'll respect whatever you wish when you let me know."

Click. "What do you think, René?"

"You can worry about it later."

"I agree," she said. Then it was back to her analysis of the facts of the case. She began to write down the names and players in Melac's life in his last few days:

Suzanne Lessage, his former counterterrorism team member, and Paul, her husband, who was Melac's best pal and sailing buddy.

Why was Suzanne, who'd come once to her for help, now blaming her and refusing to talk? Why, as Melac's good friends, didn't they know more of his state of mind, or about his last job?

Melac's contract for a surveillance job in Brittany.

A routine job or not?

The old brigade criminelle *case: Madame Olivera's daughter and* le Modou, *the Senegalese drug dealer.*

Had *le Modou* followed Melac to get retribution for losing him business? That was supposition at this point.

The Angels bikers.

Possible paranoia that Melac might have witnessed their cigarette dealing and taken revenge? That was a long shot.

Blondie, who'd worked an angle with les flics.

Upset that Melac had stepped in their turf? That was another long shot.

Uncle Alphonse in Brittany.

Alphonse Melac was convinced he was being surveilled. Why?

Melac's teenage hero, François Vérgove, a gendarme in Brittany.

Alphonse thought the man might have faked his own death. Could he be the ghost?

The serial killer/rapist le Balafré, whose case Melac had been studying at the archives the night he was murdered.

But Melac wasn't a match for his target victim nor his signature MO.

She needed answers.

Under "sightings," she noted down what the Russian baker had told her:

The man, medium height, in a dark windbreaker, seen in the vicinity.

That could describe anyone.

She also jotted down the bartender's comment:

The fight he saw at the bar on rue Tandou minutes before Melac's murder.

His timing was approximate. And what had Isabelle's bikers found out about the fight or other sightings? Nothing.

"Here're the players so far," she said. "Help me concentrate on who looks promising. Let's corroborate them with his last activities, routes and jobs on my diagram. If they don't fit, we cross them out."

"Wait," said Saj. "Who's that *mec* Isabelle mentioned? The retired *flic* with a boat cruise business."

Her mind skipped back. "Latour."

Saj's fingers clicked over the keys. "Latour was involved in Melac's last job. Hired him for surveillance."

Why hadn't Latour's name come up earlier? He could have the answer.

There's no such thing as a coincidence, Jean-Claude Leduc would have said.

She added his name to the list.

"I'm going to talk to him."

"He's a former *flic*. How's that wise, Aimée?"

"I'll go incognito. Say I'm from Melac's insurance."

She'd make something up on the fly, like usual.

Saj popped up from his seat. "A quick search reveals Franck Latour, retired gendarmerie *nationale*, married, grown son. Not many other details."

"Keep searching, Saj." Aimée rifled in her bag to change her outfit.

"The info is sparse." Saj paused. "He could have changed his name by deed poll."

A tingling shot up her arm.

"Changed his name?"

"A hunch, but I've seen this before."

What could this mean?

"*Vraiment?*" she asked, doubtful.

"I'll double-check. I found his address, though," he said. His dreadlocks, piled on his head, were held with a chopstick. Something her mother did with her hair when Aimée was small.

"Find what you can," Aimée said. "I can go in cold because I'm insurance, right?" She put on unflattering brown-framed glasses and a shapeless coat. "Call me when you know more."

Saj handed her a tiny portable mic that fed into a mini recorder. She slid it into the coat's inside pocket, grabbed some paper and looked at her Tintin watch, which had miraculously survived everything she'd put it through in the last four days. Then she sucked in her breath and headed for the quai.

Thursday Afternoon • Latour's Péniche
Anchored at the Quai

SHE FOUND THE low-lying *péniche* anchored at quai de la Marne, a wide cobbled bank under budding plane trees. Near it were nineteenth-century brick buildings of the city's *service des canaux*, who supervised the canals, and a haute couture fashion-design academy.

Who knew?

The black-and-white *péniche*, ringed by portholes and topped by a wood-framed captain's cabin with a French flag, held a gangplank to the quai with a chain across it. Once a working barge, it now catered to the dinner-cruise crowd.

She slipped under the chain, mounted the gangplank and found her footing on the wood slats. Under her feet she felt the sway as a barge chugged by. Her stomach clenched, and she felt the first tinge of nausea.

"*Excusez-moi?* Monsieur Latour?"

A bearded man wearing a cap and blue Breton jacket peered out from the captain's cabin door. This man looked too young to be Latour. He pointed to the CLOSED sign.

"Where's Franck Latour, owner of this *péniche*?"

He shrugged and turned, about to go inside.

"Sorry, but it's important. I need to reach him."

The man shrugged again. On the deck's notice board were sailing times and a note about complimentary presail apéros at le Canard, the café on the quai run by former boxing champion Houdon.

She mounted the last step to the deck and grabbed the skimpy rope that passed for the boat's railing, determined to find Latour. Again she felt the deck shifting in the wake of another barge and battled the rising nausea.

The man waved her away, coughing. His voice came out low and muffled. "Ill. Terrible cold."

But there were a lot of colds going around. Was he trying to get rid of her?

"Then please give me his number so I can reach him."

A shrug.

"I'm from Eole Insurance," she said. "It's concerning Monsieur Latour's surveillance contract."

The man coughed several times. "Is there a problem?" he asked, his voice muffled.

Like she'd tell him? But she wouldn't get fobbed off that easy. She wouldn't leave without getting something from this *mec*.

"Would someone at this café know how to reach him?" She pointed to the apéro flyer.

He coughed, shrugged again and closed the cabin door.

Helpful, this *mec*.

She saw the café on the other side of the canal.

Great. Another bridge to cross.

THE KHAKI-COLORED CANAL swirling under the bridge reminded her of lentil soup. Back on land, hunger pangs hit her. *Merde.* She hadn't eaten since last night.

The sixties-era café had been the victim of the Scandi-minimalist-style vibe. Instead of natural and *au courant*, the interior felt forced, pretentious; green plant tendrils trailed down the white walls, tables resembled tree trunks, sheepskin throws covered rough-hewed wood benches. The organic drinks advertised on the slate board bore matching gentrified prices.

In the rear, the ceiling had been turned yellow by years of smokers. There were no plants or rustic Scandi furniture but a dented zinc bar, seventies posters for prizefights and a table that would have wobbled unless you propped folded sugar wrappers under its feet.

An older man stood behind the bar counter. He had stubble on his chin, a gold front tooth, jowls reaching his neck and wavy gray combed-back hair. He'd put on the pounds and aged, but she still recognized Jules Houdon, the top prizefighter in her grandfather's time.

"*Cherìe*, you're lost. We're old school here. Your crowd's up front."

"Ah, Monsieur Houdon. My grandfather was a big fan," she said, smiling. "But I'm looking for Franck Latour."

"Who's asking?"

Several older men played cards at a table in back, reminding her of her father's Friday-night poker games at their kitchen table.

Why hadn't she updated her assortment of alias business cards in her go bag?

"Sylvie with Eole Insurance. Sorry, I've run out of business cards," she said. "Can you help me contact him?"

Houdon took out his phone, turned his back to her, made a call and, a minute later, turned back to her.

"He'll be with you in a minute," he said.

So she was being checked out. Maybe he was at the table playing poker.

"A drink, mademoiselle, before Monsieur Latour arrives?"

She shrugged. "*Une tartine jambon beurre* and an espresso would be *parfait*."

"Coming up."

He went behind the counter, grabbed a baguette, hacked it in half, sliced the half longways, slathered on butter, loaded slices of Bayonne ham on it, twisted a napkin around the end and handed it to her.

Just how she loved it. Just how her *grand-père* had made it.

"*Merci.*"

As he whacked out the coffee grinds from the machine, he carried on a conversation.

"I can tell you don't go for this bobo minimal stuff, eh. Am I right?"

Her mouth was full. Ravenous, she nodded.

"It's all changed here," he said. "Used to be different. We had constant barge traffic. Everyone knew everyone. We were a village. Now *pouf . . .* gone."

Houdon slid her steaming demitasse of espresso across the counter and added a thin wrapped square of chocolate on the saucer.

"Happened in the seventies when they built the *périphérique* on the old ramparts," he said.

Her father and grandfather had complained about the *périphérique*, too.

She'd inhaled the *tartine*—hit the spot—and wiped her mouth, then sipped the perfect espresso. She pulled out her lipstick stub of Chanel Red and dotted her lips. She felt human again.

"*Merci,*" she said, glancing at the wall clock. No Latour in sight.

He grinned, showing his gold tooth. "We're a hodgepodge. Know what I mean?"

She was almost afraid to ask.

"Hodgepodge?"

"More diversity here than Belleville," he said. "Here is the Bronx of Paris."

What else is new? she almost said. The local color felt like a distraction.

"You can live on a . . ." A pause. "On a man's salary. Raise a family."

A whiff of whiskey floated from him. He was stalling. Was this a trap? Had he called someone to collect her?

But it made her wonder if he'd meant to say *live on a policeman's salary* and caught himself.

She slid euros onto the counter with a little extra. "I'd appreciate Monsieur Latour's number."

"Quit talking her ear off, Jules." A man from the poker table had risen, strode over and set his empty glass on the zinc before tapping his fingers for a refill. He looked anywhere from mid-sixties to seventies. Fit and trim.

"I'm Franck Latour, mademoiselle," he said.

So he'd been there all along. A crafty *ex-flic*. Had her disguise held up?

She had no leverage, knew nothing about him. Only that he'd employed Melac.

Perspiration dampened her collar. Suddenly, the tartine she'd wolfed down threatened to come up.

"What's this about?"

At that moment, her burner rang. Saj's number appeared. Finally.

"Monsieur, I need to take this, *un moment*," she said.

Outside on the quai she whispered into the phone.

"About time, Saj. I'm talking to Franck Latour right now."

"Franck Latour's buried in Cimetière de Bagneux."

"What?"

"He'd be seventy-five if he hadn't died in 1944," said Saj.

She froze, her feet rooted to the quai.

"I don't understand."

"But there's also a Franck Latour in Paris who was a *flic* and now owns a *péniche*."

"How can that be?"

"The real Franck Latour's family perished in a bombing in late 1943. He joined the Resistance. Those facts are known," said Saj. "Delving into the archives, I discovered Latour was killed in a street fight during the German retreat in 1944. Several of his group were buried together in a common grave. No death certificates, or if there were, they're missing. The cemetery's outside Paris, and no one put the dots together."

But Saj had.

"If this Franck took another man's identity at war's end, who is he?"

"Couldn't find any proof, but there was a Hans Reiter, German Wehrmacht soldier, who went missing in action in 1944, during the same incident in which Franck Latour was killed. When a man going by the name Franck Latour registered for the police academy after the war, he used the same Avenue Secrétan address Hans Reiter's uncle Franz Reiter had been living at in 1938. Best guess? The German Hans Reiter deserted and took on deceased Resistance hero Franck Latour's identity to avoid execution or a prisoner of war camp."

She almost choked.

"He wouldn't be the first. The nineteenth had a community of Germans who'd worshipped here at this church. Wasn't so unusual at the end of the war to change sides and burn uniforms."

Typing sounds came on the other end of the line. "Watch out, Aimée," said Saj, "Franck Latour's regarded as a Resistance hero. He served in the police and the community for years."

She remembered what the rabbi had said.

Her thoughts swirled. If true, he'd invested a lot in his life and wouldn't want his past raked up. But more than fifty years after the war, did it matter?

Her goal was to find out his dealings with Melac. She took a breath and felt the breeze off the water, then hatched a plan. She switched on Saj's tiny microphone.

Back inside the café, she joined Latour, the possible ex-Nazi, at the counter.

His pinkie finger held a chunky ring bearing gendarmerie insignia, and his thumb had a blackened nail. For a man his age, he looked in shape, with muscular arms showing under his blue-and-white striped *marinière* shirt. He wore jeans and had high cheekbones under a shock of thick white hair. A well-preserved Aryan.

"*Désolée*, monsieur," Aimée said. "I'm here to ask you about Monsieur Jérome Melac's contract with your firm."

"Why?"

"As you heard, I'm with his insurance carrier, and a claim's been filed."

"Filed by whom?"

Typical deflection. Ask questions, don't answer.

"Routine insurance questions need to be answered, monsieur." She angled against the counter, facing him so her mic would get better reception. "Our policy holder's a homicide victim whose records show you employed him for surveillance."

"Terrible. He was murdered on the canal, *c'est ça?*" Latour shook his head. "I'm sorry this happened."

She believed him.

She tried to banish the last view of Melac with his bloody throat in dark gel-like water. She needed to get with it or she'd fall apart. "How long did his contract run?"

Houdon had retreated to the poker table. Now she and Latour stood alone. She hoped Saj was getting a good recording.

"Talk to my office."

"My boss needs information, monsieur."

The man's sharp blue eyes watered. Had he drunk an apéro? Or three? No doubt he could hold his liquor.

"I'll get back to you," he said.

She strained to hear a trace of a German accent.

"What was the nature of the surveillance work Monsieur Melac was doing for you? Were you satisfied with his work?"

"I'd need to consult our files."

"What about your interactions with him? Our record shows that he spoke with you."

"Records from where?"

There. A faint trace of a rolling *R*. Slight, like a whiff of smoke.

"I'm working from an insurance claim, monsieur." She pretended to consult her notebook, which was turned open to a shopping list—*training pants, wipes*—and tapped it with a pen. "I need detailed information concerning the surveillance he performed while employed by you at the time of his death."

A slight jitter in his veined weathered hands.

"I've got nothing to say until my office confirms your inquiry."

A wily fox. But wouldn't he be after hiding all these years?

"You're a retired policeman, monsieur. We would think you'd be more than willing to help the inquiry since the victim's firm has filed a claim."

She hoped that sounded good.

Latour drained his glass, then set it back on the coaster in the precise wet ring he'd picked it up from.

Aimée downed her espresso and offered him the chocolate

square with a little smile. "Wouldn't you like for me to go away so you can get back to your game?"

Would he go for a blatant flirt? He seemed too smart for that.

His palm opened, and she pressed the chocolate in it. His hand enclosed hers.

Men.

His warm, weathered hands reminded her of her grandfather.

"Sometimes we do things we regret later, mademoiselle," he said, giving a half smile.

Latour turned to his poker cronies.

With her free hand, she unclipped the mic and the mini recorder from her jacket and placed them behind the round aluminum sugar container, the kind with a roll lid. Hopefully this would capture the conversation after she left.

Latour turned back to her expectantly. He was still pressing her hand.

"Understood," she said. But she didn't.

Like a real *millefeuille*, this man. Many-layered. And for an old *mec*, not hard on the eyes.

A long pause.

Only the low murmur from the card game in back.

"I'll have the file ready." He squeezed her hand. "Say, tonight at six P.M. on my *péniche*."

She nodded, winked and took her bag off the counter. Then she called to the back, "*Merci*, monsieur Houdon."

He looked up from the table, cards in his hand.

AIMÉE LEFT WITH a full stomach, an espresso buzz and more questions. At the first bike repair shop she found, old fashioned and reeking of oil and rubber, she bought the only model available. A dented three-speed; the wicker basket on the handlebars had sold her.

She left out of the shop's back courtyard after changing her look to sunglasses, a jean jacket and neon leg warmers that covered her pants and the tops of her ballet flats. A new look on a new mode of transport.

She could ride the Metro only for so long before she'd get recognized by the Metro *flics*. An all-out search bulletin had hit the *télé* and radio. Just what she needed.

With her wardrobe in a brown shopping sack in the handbasket, she felt incognito riding through the nineteenth arrondissement. She rang Saj from her other burner.

"I hope you got all that," she said, catching her breath.

"And more on the recording. Are you smoking again? You sound like you're suffering from invading toxins."

She wished. A cigarette would help her think.

"I'm pedaling past Latour's *péniche*," she said. "No activity I can see. Anywhere else I should case out?"

"René's shaking his head," said Saj. "Come back to the church and help us identify the speakers. The mic hasn't been found yet but they've dispersed."

"Great. On my way."

She circled back to the bike shop. The owner was busy with clients while his young daughter stocked parts.

Aimée smiled at her. "Do me a favor?"

"Make it worth my while," said the owner's daughter, freckled and about twelve.

A girl after her own heart. Aimée slipped her a couple of euros and told her directions.

Three minutes later the girl returned with the mini recorder and mic from the café.

"No one saw you?"

"The old-man owner knows me. Too drunk or busy to see me take it, though."

Another pair of euros. "Keep this between us, eh?"

She nodded. Paused. "A man's been standing across from our shop across on the quai."

Great.

"Know him?" Aimée asked.

She shook her head.

"Can you describe him?"

The girl's brows crinkled.

"Beard, cap, blue jacket, nothing special. But he's been standing there a long time."

A nobody. But didn't predators hide in plain sight?

Smart kid.

"Tell your father about him after I leave. And keep out of sight until he goes."

She biked away from the canal, walked the bike down a pedestrian street and slipped through an *allée*.

Nine minutes later, huffing and puffing, she'd ridden up the gravel hilly drive, parked the bike behind a hedge and found René and Saj in the chapel annex. An odor of plywood and sawdust clung in the air. Motes of light danced in sunbeams. She sneezed.

"Sit down, Aimée. There's a call for you."

"Something's happened to Chloé?" Was it that call she always feared? Chloé had drowned in the lake in Geneva, or there'd been a car accident, or the chalet had been buried by an avalanche?

Her worst terrors confirmed—René handed her the phone.

"Goose bite, *Maman*," said Chloé.

"A goose?"

"*Oui, Maman.*" A sniffle as that sweet dulcet voice quivered.

"Does it hurt, *ma puce*?"

Her mind ran to infection, parasites in fowls.

"Bad goose."

Aimée took a breath. "I miss you, *ma puce*."

"Miss you," said a sleepy Chloé.

Nap time.

Aimée's mother's voice came on next. "No skin broken. But our guard goose nipped her and she got him back."

"Shouldn't the hospital check her?"

"For what? She's a big girl. She just wanted you to know."

Aimée's heart twisted.

"I miss her."

A sigh. "Nail the bastard. We're waiting."

The phone clicked off.

Flashes sparked in the corner of her vision—she had to sit down. Close her eyes. Empty her thoughts.

No chance of that.

"You okay, Aimée?" asked René.

She nodded, but wished she hadn't as it sent her vision swirling. She took several deep breaths, then opened her eyes.

No blurring or double vision, thank God.

"Saj, play the conversation after I left the café."

If only it could furnish a clue, a detail to find Melac's killer. Something. Saj connected a speaker.

"I'll play from where his phone rings and Latour says he's 'got to take this.' Listen." Saj adjusted the volume on a speaker.

A fuzzy crackling. Then voices.

"I separated the background noises as much as possible. Can you identify who else is speaking?"

Aimée listened, thinking back to the two men and Latour who'd been at the table. They hadn't spoken.

She heard glasses tinkle, then Latour's voice: "Not now. Don't make it more difficult."

"That's Latour."

Who was he talking to on the phone?

"Six P.M." he said through the speaker.

That meant someone else knew he was meeting her at six. Was he speaking with an assistant who would bring Melac's contract?

She recognized Houdon: "Time for another game?" A low laugh. "What'll you do now?" A slap of cards, the slosh of liquid.

"Stop this once and for all. He can't get around DNA testing."

The conversation got swallowed as the sports channel came on the TV. A boxing match.

Saj stopped the recording. "Nothing after that."

She stood and on the taped pages wrote down *DNA testing*.

"Thoughts on how these fit together?"

"Sounds like he's peeved with the caller, yet he relayed the time of your meeting," said René. "The DNA comment? I don't know."

"What's the link between Melac and Latour or . . . Reiter?"

"He employed Melac for surveillance, details unknown. Both were law enforcement."

No information there. Aimée stopped herself from sighing in frustration.

Outside the window, the wind swirled the leaves in gusts.

"Any more about his Nazi past?"

"I'm still working on that. After more than fifty years, I doubt we'd find enough proof. But if you could, it's leverage."

"How about personal life? Family?"

"I thought you'd never ask." Saj pointed to a buff-colored file. "Wait until you see this connection."

Inside, she read that Reiter had been married twice. His second wife had died five years ago, leaving him a widower, but his first wife, Marie Vérgove, had abandoned him and their son, François, who had nevertheless taken his mother's name as a teen. The son joined the gendarmerie instead of the police force.

Her heart thumped.

Hans Reiter, now Franck Latour, was the father of François Vérgove, Melac's idol from Brittany, whom his uncle had told René about. So Melac had been working for François's father. Nothing odd about that.

However, the file was missing something.

Her gut said it connected to *le Balafré*.

She had to try a hunch. Impulsively, she borrowed René's phone and called Morbier.

"Morbier, are you scheduled for a DNA test?"

Pause. "How did you know, Led—"

She shushed him. "No names. When and where?"

Another pause. Longer this time. "Where my partner and I met the first time. At the end of *l'heure bleue*."

The period between day and night when the sky goes darker blue. The best time in summer to smell flowers. This brief moment was when the birds burst into song.

He'd hung up.

She'd heard the story often enough. He and her father, Jean-Claude, had met at the police station in the *mairie* of the nineteenth. And at *l'heure bleue*, 6 P.M.

"What's that about, Aimée?"

She reached for the extra laptop René had brought and powered it on.

"I'm burrowing into a police employee site."

"How can you? It's intranet, not online."

"The police union's online, and I'll get in courtesy of Morbier's password, if he hasn't changed it."

"Why?"

"I'm in." Now she was clicking over the keys, scanning pages on the site. She had only half an hour to get to the boat.

So much to look at. It had to be here. Where?

Two minutes later, she sat up and pointed.

"Look, René, it's an alert from the Préfecture to the gendarmes employed in the Paris region, active or retired, not previously contacted to submit to force-wide DNA testing."

"How does that matter?"

"I'd say *Le Balafré* is suspected of being in the military or law enforcement," said Aimée. "He's an insider who's hid and sabotaged the investigation for years. He'd freak out if he had to submit his DNA, which would match the DNA found on the first victim in 1986."

Saj and René shared a look. "How does that connect back to Melac?" René asked.

"It's been staring me in the face all the time," Aimée said. "Melac knew the murderer. He'd idolized the man in Brittany who inspired him to be a *flic*. What if that man and *le Balafré* were one and the same?"

"Why do you think that?" René frowned. "I thought that man had died. How does a dead man give his DNA? If he wasn't dead, as the world was led to believe, but alive and killing again, *that* would be a secret worth killing Melac for. But where's the tie between Melac, this François Vérgove, and the serial killer?"

It was silent in the chapel annex as they considered the possibilities.

"I know it's a leap," Aimée said, "but that's what Morbier was implying, and there are now two suspicious *ex-flics* with secrets to hide. No coincidences, remember? It's all we've got. And who better to ask than his father?"

Saj took a break from online digging and lit incense in the chapel annex to "cleanse and invite healing."

Before she left, she made a call to Bellan. Voice mail. Why didn't he answer his phone? She left him a hurried message asking for info and to meet her.

"You can't go alone," said René. "I'm joining you."

She'd need backup. She couldn't rely on her unpredictable vision.

This time she unsnapped her coat's knee-length layer, pulled on black denims and her red high-tops.

But how to disguise René?

Out on rue de Crimée, she wedged her extra jacket on the bike's rear wheel frame, then helped René to throw his leg over and sit.

"Toe in and rest your heels on the wheel hub to balance yourself."

"You're serious?"

"Chloé loves it when I go fast."

His balance jiggled. "Where's my helmet?"

"Just hold on. It's all downhill from here."

René sighed wearily. "I hope not."

She rang the bicycle bell as she kicked off into oncoming traffic on rue de Crimée. Horns and René's shouts assailed her. Praying under her breath as she struggled to steer with René's weight, she pedaled like mad and somehow crossed to rue de Lorraine, then sped downhill to rue Petit and took a sharp left to rue de l'Ourcq. From there, it was a straight four-block shot to quai de la Marne.

A detoured bus lumbered along ahead of her; every time she tried to ride around the diesel-spewing exhaust, she risked riding into the oncoming cars. The sidewalk was jammed with schoolchildren and impossible to navigate.

René's hold on her shoulders was a death grip.

"One more block, René. Quit squeezing me."

Late. She was late. Ahead, she could see the bridge and dark-blue silver ribbon of the canal. The *péniche* lay anchored as before, the gangplank down. She rode onto quai de la Marne and was about to park, when a thundering shook the ground. Glass shattered.

As if in slow motion, she saw yellow sparks and boat parts shooting in the air. Black smoke billowed.

The explosion sent a shock wave. The blast knocked her and René off the bike and into the air. She landed hard on the cobbled quai.

"René? René!"

A blistering wave of heat sucked the air. René sprawled close to her, his eyes wide and blinking.

His mouth was moving. He was speaking. But she couldn't hear him.

And then realization dawned. This explosion had been meant for her. Her heart almost jumped out of her chest.

Wood and metal debris rained down. Flames erupted from the burning hulk with a gaping hole in the *péniche*. Papers and pieces of clothing, charred and torn, carried on gusts of hot wind.

Good God. Would body parts be flying next?

It brought her back to her father's death in the bomb explosion in Place Vendôme. But now wasn't the time. She fought tears as she grabbed René's arm and pulled at him to scramble away. On all fours, they made it under a bench.

Amazingly few people had been on the quai. But what about Latour? Only then she noticed the man lying on the quai.

He looked familiar.

Bellan, huddled with his leg cocked at an unnatural angle. Inert. Blood pooling in the cobble cracks. Her heart jumped.

He'd gotten her message. Had come to help her and gotten injured, or even—

Don't think the worst.

Don't.

Sounds were coming back, muffled and dense.

"Bellan's hurt," she said, although she couldn't hear her own voice. "Call SAMU, René."

Suddenly, the noise rushed at her—cries and shrieking and car alarms pierced the air. She jumped.

The red-and-white fire rescue boat, equipped with a three-man response team and a mobile pumping station for fire engines, was speeding up the canal.

Talk about quick. But they were stationed literally at the next bridge down.

Move. What was wrong with her? She ran to Bellan, sprawled on the quai, and felt for a pulse. Weak, but beating.

Triage. She remembered that from her first year of premed. She tore her scarf and used a balled-up piece to staunch the blood coming from the jagged wound on his thigh. The other she tied in a tourniquet near his leg's femoral artery, by his groin.

His soot-stained forehead was at odds with his pale face and shallow breathing. He was in shock. She wouldn't lose two men on the canal.

"Loïc Bellan, you better stay with me." Her throat caught.

His eyes flickered open.

"Where else would I go?" A pained grin on his face. "Pocket . . . what you asked for . . ." His voice faded.

A paper packet bulged in his leather jacket. She grabbed it.

"Loïc, don't leave me . . ."

Someone was pushing her to the side. "I'm a doctor, make room."

Aimée moved out of the way as rescue workers surged around Bellan and the blown-up *péniche*. She struggled to catch her breath but ran back to where René was still crouched.

"Is he all right . . . I mean will he . . . make it?" René stammered.

Oh God. She hoped so. "He's got a pulse. He's a fighter."

"What did he give you?"

Her heart skipped.

"A police file."

They watched together as Bellan was loaded into an ambulance, having lost consciousness again.

One of the response crew pointed to a bloody arm that had fallen on the cobbled quai. With gloved hands, he picked it up. Aimée recognized the hand with a pinkie ring and a blackened thumbnail. The stars hadn't shone for Franck Latour, or Hans Reiter.

A third murder.

Had the son, François, blown up his father before Aimée could get further details from him?

She stayed in the shadows, watching a rescue worker pick up a half-melted shoe that Aimée recognized.

"Look," the rescue worker was saying, "there's a *flic's* ID inside. Search for another body."

She gasped. She'd put Blondie's ID back in his shoe. How had he gotten away from the Angels?

But it made some kind of sense. He'd worked with Latour, according to Isabelle. What kind of web was this?

René was pulling at her arm. "We better leave, Aimée, or they'll ask us for witness statements."

Being an eyewitness to a murder wouldn't look good. Not to mention, she was on the lam.

But the swirling papers thrown up from Latour's *péniche* might tell her something. They were too good to leave behind.

"Let's go."

"Call a taxi, René. Now."

A minute later, she'd collected most of the swirling charred papers on the quai. She had to hurry before the arriving arson team and *les démineurs*, the bomb squad, swarmed the *péniche's* smoking hulk to examine the explosion's debris.

"Aimée, I grabbed a taxi," said René. One of the arriving arson crew was gesturing to her. A *flic* was walking her way.

She ran like hell.

IN THE TAXI, breathless, her head throbbing, she thrust fifty euros at the driver.

"Where to?"

"Just drive, monsieur."

Soot blackened her hands. The elbows of her jacket felt sticky with grime. She handed René half of the papers and got to reading the other half.

"What are we looking for?" René thumbed through the charred papers she'd given him.

"We'll know if we find it."

On the taxi radio the news blared. "Explosion, fatality . . ."

"That was quick." René shot her a look. Then whispered, "I think it was meant for you."

Her hands stank of smoke. She barely listened as she scanned the papers, a mélange of half-legible medical bills.

"Must have been a linear explosive, a bad DIY job. Otherwise the paper would have burned better."

"Not a pro, you're saying?" René stared intently at the half-burnt paper from the quai.

"With explosives, anyway. Suspect number one, François Vérgove."

"Aimée," said René slowly, "remember I said if Chloé ever needed tubes for her ears after all those infections . . ."

Where was this coming from?

"Infection, singular, René," she interrupted. "Chloé got *one* ear infection when she started preschool."

She wouldn't have this argument again with René, who obsessed over possible maladies awaiting Chloé even more than she did. Not now, of all times.

"Robert Debré's hospital for children," said René. "Best in France."

Of course she knew it. Her retort of "*et alors?*" died on her lips. René was pointing to a charred medical memo from Hôspital Robert Debré. Her gaze locked on the contents: Giselle Vérgove, eight years old, hospitalized with complications from bronchitis. The guardian listed was François Vérgove, her father. The date was two days ago. Maybe Vérgove's funeral was a sham and he'd faked his death to Melac and his uncle, then moved and had a family but kept his name because, after all, why couldn't he? He'd keep his police employment benefits. And there was no reason Melac would be searching for him if he'd thought Vérgove was dead.

"Let's go see if anyone there knows anything. Maybe she's still there."

She pulled out another bill and handed it to the taxi driver. "Get us to Hôspital Robert Debré in ten minutes and you'll get another one like this."

She felt guilty going to chase down a clue when she should be with Bellan at his hospital bedside instead.

Her bones told her this was where she'd find François Vérgove—ideally before he killed again. Bellan would understand. Wouldn't he?

After all, Bellan had gotten her Vérgove's police file, proof of who he was. Inside she read that Vérgove was presently collecting disability, that he lived near Bordeaux. So he hadn't been declared dead. Here was Hans Reiter's son, very much alive. But it worked only if she confronted François Vérgove, né Latour, and got his DNA to prove he was *le Balafré*.

As the taxi chugged along the cobbled streets, she saw the huge children's hospital mushrooming white and modern, downhill from Butte du Chapeau Rouge. She'd looked over it from the journo's window. Beyond it wound the *périphérique*.

"Do we have a plan, Aimée?"

"Find this child, Giselle Vérgove, who will lead us to her father."

"What does her father look like?"

That figure on the boat haunted her. Even though she'd seen and spoken to him for only a minute, she knew she'd recognize him—if he was at the hospital. He'd been wiring the boat with explosives to kill her. He'd faced away, worn a hoodie and pretended to have a cold as an excuse not to speak because she'd recognize his voice.

The low throb in her temple returned. She borrowed René's phone and dialed the number on the hospital record. After several transfers between departments, she spoke to a nurse.

"Giselle Vérgove's just been discharged."

Great. The taxi was pulling up at the crowded hospital entrance. Traffic wardens blew whistles and directed taxis to the jammed taxi rank.

Merde. The place was more crowded than the taxi rank at CDG airport.

"When did this happen?"

"I'm not allowed to give out this information."

"*Mon Dieu*, I'm her aunt," she said, thinking quick. "Why didn't her father inform me where to meet them? Can't you tell me?"

"I'm not supposed to . . ."

"François is my brother. I'm supposed to help care for Giselle. Wasn't she supposed to be discharged later?"

A pause.

"He's bringing her home early. The doctor agreed."

"*Vraiment?* But why didn't he let me know? She's supposed to come to my apartment."

"She was discharged this morning."

Great. Her hopes sank. She heard a muted conversation in the background.

"*Mais non, desolée.* She left ten, fifteen minutes ago. A nurse heard him mentioning Gare Montparnasse. That's all. I'm sorry."

"*Merci.*" She clicked off. "Change of plans. Gare Montparnasse. Now."

The taxi driver turned around, shaking his head.

"I've got to take my turn to leave the drop-off zone or I'll get fined. *Désolé.*" The driver maneuvered over to the pick-up location where the taxi rank ahead crawled. Nurses attended people in wheelchairs waiting in line for a taxi. Another *flic* was directing traffic and wouldn't let them through.

This was taking too long.

"We'll never make it in time to Gare Montparnasse," Aimée said.

"In time for what?" René said. "We don't know their destination." Bordeaux?

Aimée's temple now throbbed in high gear. Her vision gauzed over. Everything fuzzed into a spiderwebs.

Frustrated, she wanted to kick something. So close. She'd come so close, and . . .

It all faded into charcoal. Then deep black.

Blind. She'd let the stress win and gone blind.

"Taxi . . . taxi?" A raised voice outside the window.

Did she recognize it?

"Drive closer," she said to the driver.

"No way," said the driver. "I'll get a ticket."

"Forget it, Aimée," said René. "Give up. This was a crazy idea. What were the odds we'd catch this guy Vérgove? We don't even know what he looks like. Let's go."

She knew it was desperate, a last-ditch effort.

"We need this taxi," a man was shouting. "I've got a little girl here who's just been discharged."

Aimée did know that voice. The last time she'd heard it had been on the canal, the cold wet night as Melac was dying and just before he'd whacked her and left her for dead.

Her father had always said there was no such thing as coincidence.

Her father had been right 99 percent of the time.

"René, that's him. Vérgove."

"What?"

"The man with the little girl—he's trying to hail a taxi. Describe him."

"Why?"

"I can't see." Her voice rose. She wanted to jump out and nab him.

"A fortyish man pushing a kid in a wheelchair, he's, uh . . . medium height, brown hair . . . nondescript. A sparse beard."

"Clear complexion or pockmarked skin?"

"Hard to tell. He's getting into the taxi two ahead of us."

Her nausea rose. "Stop him. Drive in front of it."

René rolled down the window and yelled, "Block that taxi. Alert the *flics*."

Too late. Aimée heard a *vroom* as the other taxi sped ahead, blasting past the shouting traffic *flic*.

"Follow him."

"What's the taxi's number?"

The taxi driver read the license plate out and Aimée memorized it as René dialed Morbier.

She listened as René sketched their situation for her god-father, the explosion of Vérgove's father's *péniche* and Aimée's recognizing his voice at the hospital. "We're two taxis behind him and his daughter."

"Let me talk to Morbier," she said. She felt René put the phone to her ear. "Taxi number 21256," she said. "We think he's en route to Gare Montparnasse."

"We'll take over, Leduc."

"*Zut alors*, he's right here. I found him."

"Takedown's our game. Not yours."

He was right. She couldn't see a damn thing. Knifelike pain lanced her head.

"But then how do I get myself off the hook?"

A pause.

"Oh, that?" Morbier cleared his throat. "Didn't I tell you? You're in the clear. CCTV found footage exonerating you."

CCTV footage proving she was innocent? They'd had it all along?

Morbier had used her again. Why couldn't she ever learn?

"And now you tell me?"

But Morbier had clicked off.

Not only was she a patsy but the *flics* had had François Vérgove in their sights the whole time. Disgusted, she understood why her father had left the force.

*Friday Early Evening • Leduc Detective on
rue du Louvre*

A HAZY GLOW had returned to her eyesight. She could
make out shapes and outlines. Maybe, just maybe, if she
rested, breathed and didn't use her eyes, she'd gain more
vision back.

Bellan's surgery had removed the metal debris from his thigh,
and with rehab his leg would be 110 percent. On the phone
from the recovery room, he'd told her, "I'll be out of here in no
time. Wait for me. *Je t'aime.*"

He'd never said it. This simple and heart-staggering *I love you*
before hanging up.

"Aimée? Earth to Aimée?" René was saying.

Brought back to the moment, she tapped her fingers on her
desk.

What had he been saying?

"Go on, René."

"So Latour was going to cave in and give up his son, François?" asked René. "After all this time, finally stop sheltering his
serial killer child, *n'est-ce pas?* So the son killed his own father
and Blondie, his henchman. All before he'd have to give his
DNA and be found out, *non?*"

Aimée nodded. *Dumb.* She felt a throb in her temple.

"Poor Melac, wrong time, wrong place. Wrong hero."

Meanwhile, Morbier had booked her and René flights to

Geneva. He'd known she'd take him up on it so she'd see Chloé. As if that would make up for the way he'd treated her.

In the armoire, she'd found a change of clothes: black leather pants, nubby YSL sweater and her go-to leather jacket. She'd packed her Longchamp carryall.

She had one more person to contact and then she'd go and catch the evening flight to Geneva.

After several tries, Isabelle answered.

"They caught *le Balafré*, Isabelle. It's over."

Silence.

"Isabelle, I'm . . ."

Rustling. A whisper. "He's here, Aimée."

A throttled sob.

Alarmed, Aimée bolted upright. "Who, Isabelle?" She changed gears and tried to think. "Pépe from the start-up?"

Echoing sounds of metallic banging. The buzz from a machine. Familiar. A choked sound from Isabelle. "*Non . . .*"

"Where are you?"

"Give me that," came a man's muffled voice.

Mon Dieu, he *was* there.

Pretend. She had to pretend, so she could save Isabelle. "Pizza l'Espresse, may I take your order?" said Aimée.

She heard scuffling, and then a loud slap. Then Isabelle's sharp cry.

The phone went dead.

"We got the wrong one, René."

"What do you mean?"

"*Le Balafré* has Isabelle."

"*Non*, we caught him."

"We caught Melac's murderer, René," she said, feeling around for her Beretta in her desk drawer and the small box of ammo. "But not the one who put him up to it."

"What?"

"You coming with me?"

A pause. "I'm a black belt, aren't I?"

RENÉ'S MERCEDES WITH diplomatic plates—booty from the ex-president's son on one of their last cases—hummed along rue du Louvre. A light patter of rain freshened the air. The sounds of traffic muted on the wet street.

En route Aimée had alerted Eli, her contact at *les stups*, again. No matter the *flics* protection ringing *le Balafré*, Eli's drug squad cowboys were more outlaw than cowboy. If anyone could bring him down, they could.

"You sure?" Eli had asked her.

"Don't you want the jewel in the crown before you retire?"

"More like the last feather in my nest."

She took a breath. "He's smart, Eli. Evaded detection for years."

"So have I."

René gunned the engine. His wipers swept fat raindrops across the windshield in double time.

"How do we play this, Aimée?"

"You mean me half-blind, waving my pistol won't work?"

"I remember the warehouse and biker bar layout," said René. *A jewel, that René.*

She got Saj on the phone. He was still at the Russian church, since he claimed the aura was conducive to meditation.

"Saj, you're monitoring conversation on the bugs we left at the biker bar," she said. "Right?"

"It's all static."

Merde.

René drove into the parking lot sans headlights. All of a sudden, the rain stopped. Aimée opened the car windows to a damp evening chill that sent goosebumps up her arms. René parked by a cargo bay and switched off the ignition.

A crashing noise followed by a scream came from behind the half-shut accordion door of the warehouse.

"What if he knows we're here?"

"I'd say that's a given."

René took her hand in the dark, guiding her inside the warehouse and into the damp hallway. She heard him gasp. After a second, his terse whisper sounded in her ear.

"Isabelle's tied up with wire. Like she's praying."

Aimée's hands trembled in horror as she remembered these details from Flonet's file.

"It's the killer's ritual."

She heard sounds of a fist hitting skin, a body tumbling against something in the warehouse, then an *ouff.*

"René . . . René?" No answer. Long seconds passed. Her heart wrenched.

And then her arms were grabbed before she could react. She felt a wet jacket and long, thick arms encasing her—hairy, damp arms below rolled-up sleeves. She caught a faint whiff of sea salt.

She was shoved forward, stumbling, through the warehouse to find herself in what felt like a barber's chair. A quickly tied rope around her wrists extended into a noose around her neck. If she moved her hands, the noose choked her.

Stupid. She'd walked right into this. And had gotten René hurt. Or worse.

Please, God, no.

Terror-stricken, she tried to think. On her left was the loud humming of a generator. A faint haze rimmed her vision.

If only her vision would clear. The concussion and stress amped up her ocular damage. What if she could never see again?

Her leather jacket's zipper flap rubbed her finger. It must be obscuring the knot. Right? If she could untie the knot, free herself . . .

"We meet again, eh?" said Melac's uncle, Alphonse.

His voice came from near her ear. Why hadn't she figured it out before? *Le Balafré* had been Melac's uncle all along. *Stupid, stupid.*

Disgusted, she thought of the years he'd attacked his victims under the cover of the gendarmerie based in Brittany. Now she remembered how Melac had rarely mentioned him—why had she thought them close?

She recalled the tattoo parlor layout. This had to be in the rear near the bar. Moaning came from somewhere on her right. *Isabelle.*

"Did you blackmail Latour?" she asked, her throat tight. The rope cut into her wrists. Stung.

"Which one?"

"The one who killed your nephew after Melac discovered you were *le Balafré.*"

A pause. "I drew the line at killing him," he said, matter-of-factly. "I couldn't do it myself, so the weakest link in the chain got the job."

The man was more than sick; he was a psychopath.

She had to push her feelings aside and get out of here.

"What did you hold over him?"

A snort. "François was a good *flic*, sharp. Better than his father. He'd have made commissioner. Melac idolized him."

"I don't understand," she said. She had to get his confession so Saj could hear this on the bugs he'd installed.

In her dreams. The damn loud generator was gumming the sound up.

She had to do this.

She tried picturing Alphonse from the two times they'd met in Brittany. She couldn't remember pockmarks on his face, but he'd always worn a beard. Wavy salt-and-pepper hair, short but muscular build, tanned weather-beaten face. Little resemblance to Melac.

A hearty Breton fisherman—one you'd never suspect. Hadn't her father said those were always the ones?

Faint red pinpricks of light pierced her cloudy vision. She realized the thrum was coming from the tattoo needle machine—it was still on and hooked to the generator.

She pictured the generator near the tattooing machine. Given the ancient building's wiring and faulty fuses, they kept prepared. She recalled the copper wires attaching to the old generator, the CAUTION label on it.

Her brain raced. Her fingers picked at the rope, each move slicing the skin on her wrist.

"But why? I don't get it," she said.

A sigh. "You want me to tell you my whole evil plan? Reveal it?"

Sound as cocky as him and maybe it will work.

"Yes, let's be an old cliché."

A deep laugh.

She needed to buy time and undo her ties. To soften him. Play to his pride.

"You fooled everyone. *Moi*, completely. I'd assumed Melac's killer was *le Balafré*. But my father always said to never assume. Now, look where it's gotten me." Would he see through her self-pitying tone? "So clever, using Vérgove as a front. What was your connection to him?"

A long sigh. "*Et alors*, back in the eighties, when I first met him in Brittany, François was embezzling police union pensions," said Alphonse. "He had all kinds of bad-boy habits, girlfriends with expensive tastes . . . He was juggling all that on a policeman's salary, and he got smart at tampering with pension paperwork to cover the gap. He'd have served twenty years if he'd gotten caught. Then his live-in girlfriend found out about some of the other girlfriends and all hell broke loose. His father begged me to help, so I made the problem go away. Hid the paperwork, covered his tracks. Made him disappear."

"By staging his death?"

"Closed casket, and the all ladies mourned. Became friends, if you can believe it. Young Melac bought it, like everyone else. Vérgove moved to Bordeaux, worked admin part-time at the *commissariat* on disability."

"How could it be that easy? He even kept his own name?"

"If you can convince people someone's dead, they never go looking for him. François kept his head down. Got married, had kids. The scandal died away, and he and his father owed me."

Big-time. He'd collected and kept them in his debt.

"But why did Melac have to die?"

A sigh. "François's youngest daughter was always sickly. That's why he came out of hiding, to bring her to Paris for her surgery. Melac saw him." A pause, then a condescending chuckle. "I know you're stalling."

Aimée shuddered. "It's too late," she said, improvising. "You've been found out. The police database has the serial killer's DNA, and since you didn't go in for screening, you're the culprit. *Le Balafré*."

"Very good. Melac always said you were smart. Still, not smart enough."

"How do you mean?"

"*Alors*, I've watched your daughter grow. She's a sweet one. I'll be waiting, and when I find her . . ."

And to think Melac had wanted Aimée to move Chloé to

Brittany, to this monster's playground. A convulsive spasm shook her.

She pushed her wrist restraints so hard they gnawed her skin. "You'll never touch my daughter." White fury filled her. She ached to kill him with her bare hands. "And you'll never get away with this."

"Another cliché." He laughed.

"You sealed your own fate with the DNA. Give up. The *flics* are en route."

"Even if they were, and they're not, I'm not worried. You know, every few years a new *police commissaire* jumps on DNA to solve the case—this time, *alors*, it's a close call."

So cocky. He was gloating.

"My boat's anchored nearby on the canal. High speed, twin diesel engines, brand new. Steps away and ready to sail to the Canary Islands. No extradition."

She smelled tattoo ink and burning rubber, felt warmth from a bright light. Was the generator overheating?

"Ingenious," she said, hiding her disgust. "So you planned this all out. Minute by minute and every detail?"

"That's what you do, you know, in good police work," said Alphonse, matter-of-factly. "Plan, find the vulnerable spot and apply pressure. People always break. François owed me."

The rope was cutting into her neck. The thick braid scratched her skin. She fought back her rising terror. Whirring from the tattoo needle machine revved louder. Would the damn generator overheat? Maybe she could use that.

She had to get loose. She was blind, her neck was in a noose, René was hurt on the floor somewhere and Isabelle was wired up. She needed a miracle.

No fairy tale and no one to the rescue. Eli hadn't made it. Nor anyone else.

She had to make the miracle herself. Keep him talking.

"And his Nazi father assisted you." Her voice rasped.

"Nazi?" A snort of laughter. "Nice one. You're not so dumb. But Franck deserted the Wehrmacht and 'joined' the Resistance just before the Libération. His uncle lived in the quartier and he grew up spending summers here before the war. *Et alors*, he took a dead patriot's identity because at the end, why not? He was twenty and among the many German émigrés in the quartier. Blended in. Simple."

"So you blackmailed him?"

"*Pas du tout.* Who cares anymore? Let him be a hero," he said, his voice now low and confidential. "It suits the Resistance myth, eh?"

He sounded proud. She could tell he was enjoying this. He'd eluded detection for years and thought himself some criminal mastermind.

"Franck and I had an understanding, *flic* to *flic*, you know. I covered for his son and he repaid the favor. So easy for him, nothing overt. It's about losing a file, forgetting a follow-up, ignoring a line of investigation."

No wonder the *Balafré* case files were incomplete. Statements were missing.

"You savaged these victims. You took teenage girls' lives."

"They would've turned into prostitutes. I prevented it. Saved their families the heartache, the sickening moral collapse, saved all the young boys they would have corrupted."

"What about the grandmothers? Why do you hate women?"

A low moaning came from her right. A sharp slap stung her face. She reeled, the buzzing in her head amplifying even louder than the buzzing of the machine.

"It's not my fault."

She tried to ignore the throbbing in her head. "Why not?"

"I had a condition."

Here it came—his excuse. His type always blamed someone else.

Softening her voice, she asked, "A condition?" She hoped she sounded sympathetic. All the while she kept creeping her fingers along the knot under her jacket. "Not sure what you mean by that."

Another pause. "When I was sixteen, my grandmother got me a job in a fish cannery. The first summer I worked there, there was an accident. People lost their lives and I lost my . . ." His voice trailed off.

"Manhood?"

"Partly." Pause. "My grandmother never let me forget it. Neither did the girls on the line."

Horrible. But no excuse. Still, one thing didn't make sense.

"I don't understand why you stage your victims in prayer. What does it mean to you?"

The heat was getting to her but her fingers worked the knot. Drops of perspiration slid down her neck.

A snort. "Don't play psychologist with me."

An acrid smell. Then a brush of air. He must have made an abrupt turn. More and more of him came into focus, his blurred blue shape defining into a figure. His twitchy fingers. Now she remembered that Roget Dubois had recognized him in the park—crazy, spidery hands. The pungent mildew and mold from the damp carpet's corners filled her nose, as did burnt rubber.

"But I want to know," she said.

"They needed to pray for God's forgiveness."

"Why?"

"After the accident, my grandmother made me go to confession." His voice had gone childish, sounded like a young boy.

"She said God was punishing me for my dirty thoughts and that I needed to pray and repent. But she was the one without God's love. She was the one who needed to pray. The girls all laughed if they found out about me. They were the ones who needed to confess their pride and sin."

Warped. The man was warped.

The stronger the smells were, the more her vision aligned, as if it was trying to keep up. Sensory overload as her fingers paced the thick rope tied in a bowline knot.

Melac had taught this knot to her. Clearly Alphonse thought she, a landlubber, couldn't untie it.

"It's time for Isabelle now."

Panic surged in her. But the tang of sea salt from his fisherman's jacket gave her an idea.

"Isabelle . . . Isabelle, remember what happened to Blondie?"

A low murmur.

"Isabelle, if you can hear me, let's—"

Isabelle's roar of pain spurred Aimée to act. Good God, was he . . . ?

"Stop it, *salope.*" His voice came from her left. Close. So close she could smell him—the dried salt and sweat.

A bloodcurdling scream echoed off the walls.

As Aimée's hands came free of the knot, she kicked at Alphonse. She could make him out now and kicked again as hard as she could. His arms windmilled as he fought to keep his balance. She kicked once more, connecting with hard muscle.

He tripped, landing on the tattooing machine. The live wires connected to the generator caught his forearms. Sparks flew. He struggled, pitching back and forth, trying to untangle himself. Aimée grabbed the electrified tattoo gun and swung it at him. She heard a whack, sizzle, crackling, then smelled singed hair, burning flesh. She swung it again. A flash and blur as more sparks erupted—but it wasn't from her faulty vision. Amid his yells, his skin fried on the exposed live wires.

The lights went on and Aimée reeled from the sudden brightness; once she adjusted, she could see Alphonse's jerking body collapsing on the floor, twitching and knocking the generator.

Morbier and Eli had rushed in, guns drawn and aimed.

"Aimée, are you all right?" said Morbier.

"Took your time," said Aimée, loosening the rope around her neck.

She made out a shaking, bruised Isabelle being untied by Eli.

"You okay, Isabelle?" Aimée asked.

"I am now," Isabelle said.

Alphonse's eyes rolled back. Froth dribbled from his mouth. His body went rigid.

"Shall we leave him like that?" asked Eli.

"Much as I'd like to, it's Isabelle's call."

Eli helped Isabelle up.

"Keep him alive so the victims' families can spit on him," said Isabelle, "then make sure he's put away for life."

Friday Night • Leduc Detective on rue du Louvre

AIMÉE CALLED HER mother.

"Sort everything out, Amy?"

"You could say that."

"Good girl."

What kind of compliment was that?

Stop. She hated reacting like a pouty ten-year-old.

"So let me speak to Chloé while you charter a jet to Paris," she said. "I'm tired and want to sleep for a week."

"Okay," said her mother. A pause. "You sure, Amy? Think about living here. It's a sweet life."

Sweet life among the 1 percent tax exiles and Swiss chocolate?

She'd avoided living in Brittany and felt certain now, more than ever, that she and Chloé would stay in Paris.

"Maybe later."

A little voice came on the phone. "*Maman . . . Maman?*"

"*Oui*, Chloé," she said. "Grab your fluffy bunny and get on the plane with Grandma, okay?"

Her phone clicked with call waiting.

"See you soon, *ma puce*. Big *bisous*."

She clicked over to the other call. It was an unknown number. Hesitant, she hit answer.

"*Oui?*"

"Your work's not finished," said the Ministry contact. The voice she'd dreaded. "The target's on the loose."

Her undercover sting assignment, the one she'd been so caught up in before Melac was murdered. How had he found her on this burner phone?

"But . . ."

"Remember our deal? It's still April in Paris and time to get back in the saddle."

Acknowledgments

SO, SO MANY helped with this story! Huge thanks in Paris go to Meghann Cassidy; the incredibly helpful and totally amazing Julie McDonald; wise Jean Abou; Pascal Varejka; Brigitte Chemouni for the walks; generous Patrick Bourbotte, Commandant, *chef de section brigade criminelle*; Laurence Allegret, Georges Ghio and Gerard Zimmer who shared stories of their quartier; Anne-Sophie, *une flic extraordinaire*, Louis from the bookstore La Lucarne des Ecrivains at 115 rue de l'Ourcq; François Goddard; the always knowledgeable and wonderful Dr. Christian de Brier; les *infirmières* du 104—the public health nurses at Centquatre in the nineteenth arrondissement; Mylène Mosengo and her sister Mireille Bafounda; Aliss Terrell; Gilles Thomas; Etienne Mazeaud; service des canaux; Anne Françoise and Cathy Etile toujours, dear Elke Moeller; Clement Neuve for *les secrets*; Gilles Fouqué; Adrian Leeds; the above and beyond helpful Françoise Poisson; Benoît Pastisson; Jean-Baptiste Ordas; ever curious Carla Bach; Inga Häckl. In the US, in my corner Katherine Fausset, wonderful Taz Urnov and inspiring Juliet Grames who helped this book in myriad ways, *merci* to everyone at Soho, who after so many books together, I'm honored to call family; cat maman Jean Satzer, Dr. Terri Haddix, Susanna Soloman; JT Morrow; James N. Frey who keeps me honest; Hannah; my son, Tate; and Jun.